The Runaway Breeder

Alana Dyer

Published by Alana Dyer, 2023.

Table of Contents

This novel is dedicated to all those that supported me. To the ones who kept on motivating me to keep writing and finish my first book even when I felt like I failed.

Even now, 3 years after my first release, these people still support and motivate me every day. Thank you for the love and kindness you all have shown me.

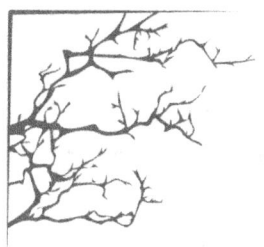

Chapter 1

Sitting in front of my mirror, my reflection staring back at me, I double check my appearance to make sure that I will leave a good impression today. My straight chestnut-coloured hair is piled on top of my head into a perfect bun and the off-the-shoulder blush coloured top and high-waisted black lace skirt that adorn my body hopefully portrays me as a confident young she-wolf that is ready to take on her role in this pack.

Last month, I had just turned sixteen, the age a wolf finds their role in their pack and—possibly—their mate. It is the time when all wolves are deemed "adults" in our community. An age when a she-wolf can choose to give up school and start a family with her mate if she so desires or choose a career path to help provide necessary jobs for their packs. In the eyes of the werewolf nation, any wolf aged sixteen that has shifted to their wolf form is able to take on responsibility and help with furthering the success of their pack. How we are granted these chances and opportunities is at the monthly pack meeting on the first of the month. Since I had missed out on last month's meeting due to my birthday being three days after the pack meeting, I was unable to obtain my pack position. But today, I will be taking my place as a functioning adult in Pine Paw. I couldn't help but smile at my reflection in excitement at the prospect of working and gaining respect from all, of no longer being deemed a pup and too young to participate in pack business. As of today, I will be able to become something more.

My eyes shot over to the picture of my cousin Chris and I in our wolves taped to the mirror. I take a deep breath and remind myself that my cousin will be there to support me no matter what role I received from the Alpha. Just after my birthday, when I first shifted into wolf form, Chris and I had gone for a run in the forest surrounding our territory. His idea was to get me accustomed to being on four legs instead of two. I remember Chris' black wolf form towering over my blue-white fur with black-tipped paws in the warm early-spring sunlight that the month of May had to offer that day, and the annoyance I felt knowing that I still have a few more years to continue growing into my wolf form while he could easily take me down. I looked like a pup compared to my cousin but being able to run around the territory and enjoy the early morning sun in wolf form felt incredible. There's no better feeling for a werewolf than your four paws pounding on the forest floor with the smell of the new leaves on the trees, the crisp pine, and the scattered scents of prey all around you. As a werewolf in wolf form, you feel complete in the forest.

On that day, with Chris chasing me around like we were a pair of pups, I finally felt that sense of being whole.

"Laina, let's go before we're late." Chris yells impatiently, snapping me out of my thoughts. Chris's voice carries from the foyer where I know he waits, most likely with a look of annoyance directed at me all the way up the stairs and down the hall to my room. Taking one last look at myself in the mirror and adjusting my shirt, I sigh, stand from my seat to look around for some shoes, and slip on a pair of knee-high black boots. I grab my cell phone from the desk beside the door while rushing out the room and scurry down the hallway.

"I'm coming!" I reply back to my cousin, hurrying down the stairs to where he waits for me. One thing that is annoying about Chris is his need to always be on time. Chris is what I like to call "time O.C.D." when it comes to being punctual. He would forget where he put his phone down and forget where the keys to his car were, but he will never fail to be early to a function or event. One example of Chris' habit of being early would be just a couple of years ago when we went to the movie theatre to see the live-action remake of "Beauty and the Beast." You can just imagine Jack and I waiting for an hour on Chris to find his wallet and car keys. He was running around the house like a chicken with its head chopped off only for the three of us to be miraculously two hours early to the movie because Chris had planned ahead that day for a late-night viewing. Needless to say, by the time the movie started to play, the bag of popcorn in my hands was a soggy, inedible mess for my pre-teen self to enjoy. I spent the entire movie with buttery hands and a bag of gross popcorn that I had since discarded on the floor.

"You look amazing." Chris gushes as I descend the final steps of the staircase and come to stand before him, doing a slight spin for my cousin to approve of my outfit. He has a look of pride in his amber eyes, ones that nearly cause tears to spill from mine. I did everything with my cousin Chris, who acted as a brother, a parent, and a best friend. His approval meant the world to me, especially with today being the next step in my adult life as a functioning member of this pack. His mate, Jack, saunters over, giving me a once-over and a wink before snuggling into Chris's side with a contented smile on his face.

"Thank you. You two look amazing as well." I reply with a blush as I take in the two complimenting each other with black slacks and button-down shirts of similar shades of blue. Jack and Chris are the first openly gay mates in the pack that had come out about ten years ago. This pairing had started a bit of a rift amongst the pack when the two had found each other while on a run in the forest. I remember the excitement Chris had when he came home that night. He whisked my sleeping form out of my princess bed at ten o'clock at night to make me a plate full of chocolate chip pancakes just to talk about coming across a grey wolf during his run through the forest. He couldn't tell who this wolf was, only that he knew just by scent that the two of them were meant to be mates.

At six years old, I remember sitting at the kitchen island, trying to stay awake with the knowledge of my cousin finding his prince charming and the scent of chocolate in the air. My parents were furious with my cousin, stating that a pup needed to sleep when they caught me red-handed with half a plate full of pancakes and a chattery Chris. But there was also a look of pride and excitement for him before they promptly ushered me into bed, while Chris promised to tell me more the next day after a pack meeting.

It was at that very pack meeting where Chris and Jack bumped into each other and, as if it were a scene out of a movie, Chris and Jack both exclaimed the word, "Mate!" Apparently, there was a huge uproar afterwards, with the pack in disbelief that two strong male wolves who could produce strong pups were mated to each other. For the next few days, I remembered the pack being tense and Chris explaining that he had to sneak out at night to see his mate because our pack was trying to keep Chris and Jack apart. I was heartbroken for my cousin, the man who told me stories about mates and how they are our other halves that we cannot live without. I remembered in kindergarten when this boy in class said his mother called Chris a freak and how I got in trouble for punching that kid in the face.

It wasn't until the previous Alpha had stepped in and stopped any and all complaints before any other incidents occurred that could harm the pack. He admitted to everyone that same-sex mates are legal in the werewolf community and gave the chance for others to flourish in their love life. It was the Moon Goddess' blessing and intent to pair mates of the same-sex together, so who were they, the pack, to judge. With the Alpha giving Chris and Jack his blessing, more and more wolves who had admitted they had yet to find their mates soon came out as pairs. It soon became normal to see openly gay and lesbian couples around the pack, and I couldn't help but beam with pride at how accepting my pack is to change. Chris and Jack's relationship is quite sweet in a Romeo-and-Juliet kind of way in the beginning, with most of their families and pack members being against their mating. But the two persevered and kept strong. The only difference from Shakespeare's Romeo and Juliet is that no one died in our pack for my cousin to be happy with his mate.

"Now, let's hurry up before we are late. That is not a way to start off as a working member of this pack." Jack states a little too cheerily and grabs both Chris's and my wrist, dragging us out the door and into the car. The pack house is about a half an hour drive from where we live, used for meetings, special occasions and for warriors and wolves without mates to live with. If it weren't for Chris and Jack being my family and guardians, I would have been living at the pack house long ago since my parents' deaths. Slowly, the big mansion comes into view and the drive comes to an end with the car coming to a stop in the parking lot and the three of us getting out in front of the old Victorian building. The nerves that have been missing this entire morning decide to make themselves present now while I climb out of the car, taking in the large number of pack members hanging around.

"Remember, you are to mingle with the other wolves while the Alpha assigns you to your position. Who knows, maybe you are his soul mate," Chris encourages me, kissing my forehead before he and Jack walk away to join the other parents and guardians. I smile sadly as I watch wolves my age talk to their parents one last time, wishing for once that my own had survived the rogue attack ten years ago so they could stand here and give me the advice to calm the nerves that send my heart into an unsteady rhythm. Shaking my head, I take a deep breath, sighing wistfully one last time before turning towards the building and heading inside with a brave smile on my face. Mom always told me to never show my true emotions when in a crowd of wolves. The strong prey on the weak, and I refuse to show any weakness.

As I enter the building, I am taken aback by the sheer amount of wolves my age, each ready to take on their responsibilities in this pack. Everyone is dressed in their best attire, hoping to leave a good impression as we all aim for the highest position possible. Many of the females have put a lot of consideration into their attire, switching their short shorts in the summer here for conservative dresses, blouses and slacks. Only the few females who aim to climb the pack hierarchy are dressed in revealing clothing, most likely trying to catch the attention of a Warrior, a Theta, or even the Alpha. But we all have one position we do not want to obtain: the Breeder.

Breeders are the she-wolves assigned to become the pup producers in the pack. Their job is to allow the mateless warriors of Pine Paw to breed them, with no say in who their partner is during the current breeding period. Its intended purpose is to add more wolves to the pack population and bring about stronger wolves for the next generation. Many wolves believe it to be an honourable position a she-wolf can obtain, but we all know the truth. Once you become a Breeder, you are nothing more than a slave, a tool for men to use your body for their own pleasure while they rape you into producing the next lot of pups for the pack. If you ask me, it is a barbaric way to increase the pack's population, but the chosen she-wolves have no say in their position of a Breeder and no say in ending this barbaric job. To say that the slim chance of being chosen for this position scares me is an understatement. I am terrified for any she-wolf, myself included, that might receive this position. Knowing that for the next part of their life, the she-wolf will be a slave until she produces the specified amount of twenty pups for the pack. It is a life of isolation and even torture and I send a silent prayer to the Goddess that I do not receive this role.

While everyone else mingles about the pack house, chatting about what positions they wish to receive and the lucky ones exclaiming when finding their soulmate, I stick to myself and make my way to a corner of the room where I can be left alone. Most people my age tend to enjoy mingling and talking to one another, but I always felt like an outcast. No one wanted to be friends with the she-wolf that lost her parents and was raised by two male wolve. No one wants to talk to a she-wolf who fights back when homophobic slurs are said. And so I sit and watch the room, waiting for when I can greet the Alpha.

The scent of perfume and cologne is strong with everyone together in such a closed-off space but it makes it easier to discern who belongs to which faction. The wolves standing by the punch bowl -most likely spiked with some form of alcohol – that smell like a grade eight locker room where boys use Axe as a shower-in-a-can are the ones built for power. Each male wolf built with muscle-on-muscle will become a Warrior and climb the ranks as they train and defend our pack. For now, these six-teen year olds fangirl about some sports game that was on last night and who won.

The group of small wolves that do their best to blend into the background with little to no scent on them will be Omegas. They will do the regular work around the pack from cooking and cleaning to taking care of the daycare and little pups. These Omegas are what we refer to as the working class since some of them will also help run the companies owned by the pack by doing a nine-to-five job like regular humans.

Then there is a group of wolves that fit between the Omegas and Warriors: I call them the Acolytes. They're standing by the bookshelves and seem to be in a heated debate about some type of medical theory. These Acolytes will fill in positions such as Pack Doctors, Nurses, Architects, builders and any task that requires in-depth schooling and specialized research and planning. We can't rely on humans to help build our community and risk exposing the werewolf race, so these wolves take the place of any jobs that require any university or college degree. If it weren't for my Alpha and Beta bloodline where I may become a mate to either an Alpha or Beta, I would be considered an Acolyte and part of that debate.

Taking a seat on an armchair once I reach my destination to the corner with a window I can stare out of, I spot the Alpha talking to a few girls who try their best at looking coy and sexy before him. I always wondered how pushing your body against a male would benefit a she-wolf other than being used and taken advantage of, but I made no comment of their behaviour. I preferred working hard for the things I wanted and being independent. The idea of needing a strong male to take care of and protect me like a precious doll seemed a little old-fashioned to me. It's not that I don't want whoever my mate is, but I crave being independent more. Christ jokes around saying that it's the Alpha blood in me wanting to be respected and not under someone else's control.

Two warriors are standing a respectful distance away from Alpha Sam but close enough to act on his command. These warriors are the ones that will step into action once Alpha Sam designates a she-wolf as the next pack Breeder. They are the wolves everyone fears since they have a higher status than the regular warriors. Not only do they protect the Alpha, but they are also given special privileges as wolves who forsake the mate bond, intending to stay mateless for the rest of their lives just to have their pick of the Breeder populace. At any moment, they can storm into a Breeder's home and fuck her as he pleases. Every mother warns her daughter to never go near the ten warriors dedicated to this position since some abuse their powers to take a she-wolf that catches his eye. There are many stories of she-wolves being raped to please these men when a Breeder is unavailable, and there is nothing the young girl can do other than accept her fate.

I keep an eye on Alpha, knowing that at any moment, he will make his rounds around the room and decide the fate of the newly-shifted. Disgust and annoyance are evident on Alpha's face as a she-wolf gets too close to him, pushing her "assets" into his face in hopes of seducing Alpha Sam. I blame her behaviour on the many reminders her parents must have given the poor blonde she-wolf before sending her inside the pack house. Most families hope to have their pup mated to the Alpha since this will bring honour and prestige to them. Unfortunately for her, Alpha Sam has never shown any interest in the pack whores let alone a newly-shifted she-wolf like her. Her greed will not get her the position she wants. My turn to speak to him will come soon. I know the two positions I wanted: Acolyte, as I have bypassed high school and am currently enrolled in college, and Warrior, as Chris and Jack have been training me to fight since I was seven years old, and intensified my training once I shifted, to include not only hand-to-hand combat in human form that has been drilled into me for years, but also combat in wolf form. Only Alpha Sam can designated these roles to me with my bloodline.

I turn my attention to the window, deciding to ignore everyone in the room and watch as small pups chase each other around in the yard, their laughter and squeals of delight floating in on the wind through the open window. They look so carefree, and I smile at their game of tag. The scent of summer wildflowers, the dew still clinging to the pack house gardens from this morning, and the fresh aroma of pine surrounding our pack house whisks away the nauseating stench of sweat, perfume and cologne permeating from the wolves in today's meeting. I know Chris and Jack want me to mingle with everyone, but I see no point. Many wolves do their best to stay away from me so I will stay away from them.

Movement from inside the room catches my attention out of the corner of my eye. I turn just in time to watch as Alpha excuses himself from the she-wolves, much to their protest and dismay, and makes his way in my direction, specifically to where I sit in my corner. I smile at our young Alpha Sam, who, at twenty-two, has yet to find his mate to rule beside him as his Luna of this pack. He is the most eligible bachelor that every she-wolf dreams to be mated to and is also why wolves my age steer clear of me.

"Laina, how ni-" He stops mid-greeting, standing before me and sniffing the air, and moves closer to where I sit while he focuses his attention solely on me. Excitement bubbles inside me with the possibility this brings. His scent wafts over me, and a feeling of calmness runs through every nerve ending in my body. Could I possibly be his mate?

Sam and I grew up together since my father was once his father's Beta. He used to babysit me during meetings where both of our parents would be busy with pack work. Even if Sam is six years older than me, as children, he would spend his free time with me, spoiling and treating me to anything my little heart desired. I remember one time he bought me a lacy dark red dress for my twelfth birthday. It was a little revealing for my taste at the time, but I still loved the attention Sam showered me with that day as we took a trip into the city. When each year passed without Sam finding his mate, it gave me some form of hope that maybe I could be his and he mine. Quietly, I wait for his following statement that will decide my fate and role.

"Breeder." His voice is filled with desire as his hands shift to grope my large breasts, a smirk playing at his lips. I gasp in surprise, fear spreading through me with this one word. This isn't possible, right?

The two Warriors' stoic faces soon morph into a smirk as their eyes scan me from head to toe. The dark skin wolf with dreadlocks winks at me as his eyes hold a trace of lust barely visible in his chocolate-coloured gaze. Deep down, I know he will want to take a go at me first. His partner, a redhead with tanned skin, reaches out to grab my left arm as the dreadlock guy takes my right, the grip tight enough to remind me that escape is futile as they will hunt me down. Whispers and sympathetic gazes are sent my way as the two Warriors lead me out of the building. Some she-wolves exclaim in the joy of not being chosen, while others wish me good luck even though I feel far from lucky. I can see some holding their phones, ready to capture a sobbing breakdown that follows each year when a new Breeder is chosen, but I refuse to give these wolves the satisfaction of a good show and instead keep my head held high. I keep my gaze forward and take each step towards the door with as much dignity as I can muster. Never show weakness when forced into an unfavourable situation is what my father used to tell me as a child.

Everyone knows what will happen after you are assigned as a Breeder. You will be whisked away from your family and forced to stay in a cottage guarded day and night, only able to garden in the medium-sized yard given to you. But the truth is, you are nothing but a slave to the warriors assigned to breed you. You will welcome an unknown male into your home, lead him to the bed you sleep in each night, and spread your legs whether you want to or not. You will spend the next six months carefully observed like a rat in a lab while you carry the pup inside you to a healthy delivery, and you will repeat the process a few months later, never given a say as to who will breed you. You are nothing to the pack even after gaining your freedom when the twentieth pup is born. And this is the life I will be living now.

The doors to the pack house close. The pack meeting will proceed as usual now that a new Breeder is chosen. This is when reality begins to sink in. I feel numb, my mind still wrapping around my new role as the men lead me to a black car. The doors are open, waiting to shut me inside and whisk me away from the life I know, but no one forces me into the vehicle. In moments, Chris and Jack will be informed of my position and rush over from whatever it is they are doing, with the prodding eyes of their friends questioning what is wrong, finding me where each Breeder waits for their final words with loved ones. Only a few minutes will be allotted to us, and then I'll be taken away where no one will be able to see me for the next twenty years or so.

Knowing Chris and his obsession with time, they will be here in:

Three.

Two.

One.

Cue a sobbing Chris.

"Laina, are you okay?" Chris's voice fills my ears the moment his arms hold me in a tight hug. I watch as the guards walk away to give us privacy, far enough to not hear a thing but close enough to chase after me if I decide to run. Since this is my last free moment as a regular pack member, the guards are not allowed to listen in, much like giving a prisoner on death row their final meal before taking them to the chair that will end their life. A few minutes of silence fall between us. Chris is sobbing into my shoulder as Jack sends me a grimace of a smile. We all know the situation is dire.

"I...I don't know what to do." I whisper, feeling Jack wipe away stray tears that had fallen from my eyes.

"What you do is behave, wait for a free moment, and run. Run towards the old treehouse, look for something pink, grab it, and keep running." I do not understand what Chris has said, my fuzzy mind unable to comprehend his words before I am ripped away from my best friend and pushed into the car, the door slamming in my face and the engine roaring to life.

I watch in the rearview mirror as my life fades into the distance away from me, the tears now flowing freely.

All I can think of: Is this how Katniss felt when she was whisked away from her family in District Twelve in The Hunger Games?

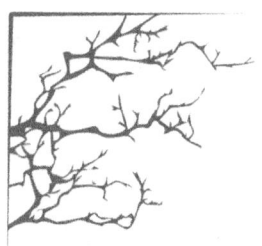

Chapter 2

As the pack territory slowly passes by, I decide to rest my eyes. Breeders are given an area on the far-west side of the territory where no one will be able to disturb them. That area is patrolled and guarded day and night. It will be a community I call home for however long my stay is, but deep down, I know I can never allow the cottage I will be living in to be my home. A prison, yes, but never my home.

Hope slowly slips away the further I get from the pack house and the closer I get to the cottage where I'll live for the next chapter of my life. At sixteen, I should be enjoying life as a carefree young adult, not being sentenced to life as a mother. I never wanted to raise pups just yet. I had a career in mind that I worked hard towards each and every day, had even managed to get into college for it early and was going to start classes in the fall. But now it's all gone.

Sighing, I decide to let the comfort of sleep take over. It would be too painful to keep looking out the window and only cause me to break down in front of the men who are probably fighting amongst each other over who will get to use me first after the Alpha does.

I feel the car come to a stop, waking me from the brief moments of slumber in my dreadful situation. The Warriors sitting in the front seats hold a soft conversation barely audible to my wolf hearing, but one thing for sure is that they still think I'm fast asleep and are fighting over who will carry me inside. Deciding that pretending to be asleep is a bad idea for my own safety, I open my tired eyes and take in my surroundings as best as I could within the confines of the vehicle. In front of me is a gorgeous grey brick cottage, with a small porch welcoming me to sit and read during the day. The building had a fairytale look with light blue window trim on the front door and roof and a whimsical aura surrounding it; this is definitely a place I would have loved to live in under any other circumstances. The garden surrounding the cottage clearly needs some TLC to bring out its full potential and beauty, but the white picket fence around the lot's perimeter gave the final touches that this place needs to welcome any newly mated pair. Unfortunately, it will be my new prison, with my own prison guards "protecting" me from now on.

The car door slowly opens, and the guards wait on either side for me to get out. I can't help but sigh in defeat as I climb out of the back seat and step onto the simple dirt driveway. The surrounding area around my new home is the forest I so love to run in. I can't see any other cottages, only the rise of smoke from many chimneys hidden between the tall trees, a clear sign that this area held a few Breeders. Maybe the guards will let me visit them and allow me out of the cottage for a bit every day if I behave well enough for their approval.

I know what is expected of me after I arrive at my new home. From the age of eight, every she-wolf has the Breeder rules drilled into their brains if they became one to prepare us for this position. Each new Breeder is given three days to explore the house and design it in a way the Breeder deems suitable for comfortable living, including painting any and all walls, decorating the interior to her preference and performing some landscaping in the front and back gardens. On the fourth day of being in the cottage, the Doctor assigned to take care of all Breeders will come to do a check-up and make sure the Breeder is healthy, with the Alpha in tow. If the Breeder is a virgin, it is the Alpha's duty to take matters into his own hands by fucking the Breeder as much as he wants on that day. Thank god the Alpha will be using a condom as per the rules since I've heard that once a Breeder is selected, the she-wolf's body will change to accommodate the new role and will be able to fall pregnant very easily. At least, that is what the rumours are. After that, the Breeder is given three days to be pampered and prescribed a dose of medication that they are expected to take to make sure her body is ready to start their new "job." On the eighth day after arriving, the top mateless Warrior is sent to the cottage and will come every day to fuck her like a cheap whore until she becomes pregnant. This is the new life I have been thrown into without concern for my own well-being. The Warrior who is chosen to breed me will continue this process as my designated partner and continue to make me produce his pups until he finds his mate. Then I will be given a new breeding partner, and the cycle repeats until I birth twenty pups.

Of course, there are exceptions. Warriors who choose to never find their mate are given the chance to pick any Breeder they want whenever they want and are allowed to fuck them as much as they want. They were the ones many she-wolves avoid on a regular day. But, as a Breeder, all I can do is spread my legs and allow them to do as they please without being able to fight against their advances, swallow with a smile and thank them for their time. The sad part about this is once the pups are weaned, they will be taken to wolves that can't have pups and be raised by these wolves as if they were born to that mated pair. I will never be able to be a mother to my own children.

After fighting back the emotions wanting to surface since being designated as the next Breeder, I fall to my knees finding the despair and anxiety that I kept at bay slamming into me at full force. This is real. I am a Breeder. And I will never know my babies once they are taken away from me. I am nothing but a baby-making machine now to this pack.

The guards must have felt some form of sympathy for me because they back away and leave me to myself, something I am thankful for even though just moments ago they were fighting about who will fuck me first. My dream of building my career, finding my mate, and raising a family is now lost in oblivion, scattered on the winds of pain that seem to course through my breaking heart. I will never have my freedom ever again.

Soon my cries morph into sobs, wailing until I am left gasping for breath. I want to run far away and escape my fate, but I can't. I would be caught in a heartbeat and punished. So instead, I remind myself that I need to be brave, to face this situation head on and dry my eyes as best as I can before I stand with determination pulsating in my veins. I march into the cottage, turn around and stop the guards from entering as they stare at me with confusion. I guess they aren't used to a she-wolf acting the way I have these last few hours.

"This is my house now! The only time I have no say in who comes in is when the Alpha or the Warrior who will breed with me comes in. Other than that, you two stay outside." They growl at my disrespectful behaviour, and I growl back just as loudly. I may have had a moment of weakness earlier, but I'll be damned if they disrespect me. I may be a Breeder now, but Alpha and Beta blood courses through my body thanks to my parents. No one will take my courage and the status of my bloodline away from me. Watching the warriors bend to my growl and back away, I give them a triumphant smirk before slamming the door shut. I will allow no one into this place unless it is the Alpha, the Doctor, my breeding partner or someone I trust.

Turning around and leaning against the blue door, I notice how dusty the place is and frown. The first thing to be done is cleaning from top to bottom. I refuse to live in a dirty, dusty home. I quickly explore the cottage, finding a large room with cleaning supplies that looked to be a laundry room as it contains a state-of-the-art washer and dryer waiting to be used. The idiots in charge of maintaining the Breeder cottages remembered to stock up on cleaning supplies but forgot to clean the place, typical. I smile sadly and leave the cleaning supplies where they are to continue exploring the other rooms.

The rest of the cottage has a new modern kitchen with a fully stocked refrigerator and pantry, three plain bedrooms, a master bedroom with an ensuite bath with a small bathroom in the second-floor hallway intended for others to use. I am actually quite shocked to see how big the cottage actually is inside, but sad that there is no basement. It would have been nice to turn the basement into a workout room now that I am trapped here.

Making my way back towards the laundry room, I come to another door just beside the entranceway and peek inside, shocked to find a garage. I guess the wall covered in vines on the outside is actually the garage door. With a smile, I decide to turn this into my home gym. I will need some place to keep me in shape if I am to have multiple children. Filled with excitement, I begin getting to work and run through the two-story cottage once again, searching through all the closets to find linen, bedspreads, towels, and any other textiles that would need to be cleaned. After a few trips, I soon had everything gathered in the laundry room sorted into multiple baskets with a load already in the wash. I had a lot of work to be done.

With the laundry started, I begin to rush around once more, opening all the windows and the glass door to the backyard to allow fresh air to blow inside while I start cleaning. I know the clothes I am wearing would be ruined with the deep cleaning I plan to do, but I would rather have a clean prison than clean clothes. I can always change later when my clothes are sent to me. I hate knowing that I only have three days to clean and prepare my new home but it is what I am given and I need to make the most of it. With determination, I make a promise to myself that no matter how late I get to a bed today, I will make sure this place is clean and dust-free. It sucks, actually every thing sucks right now, but the cleaning must be done.

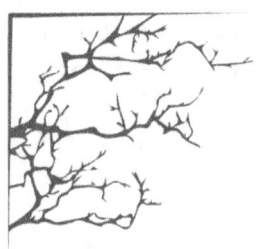

Chapter 3

I lean against the marble counter, a glass of red wine from the bottle I found in the pantry in my hands. Taking a sip, I turn to look at the time on the microwave—ten o'clock at night. I know that as a sixteen-year-old, I'm three years underage to legally drink in Canada but fuck it, I really need something strong after the day I've had. Chris always limited me to one glass of wine at functions, so the alcohol has little effect on me. It has been an exhausting day, from being designated as the new Breeder to my small breakdown outside and finally having to clean an entire cottage all by myself. I should have made a stupid guard help me clean since their job is to basically keep me locked in this property. Still, the thought of one of the wolves outside stepping into my designated space causes the anger to swell inside me at this unjust situation. The kitchen had been the last place for me to clean as I knew that with all the dust and grime from all the other rooms floating around, I would have to clean the kitchen twice if I made this the first room I cleaned. At least now I can wake up tomorrow morning and cook breakfast without worrying about dust.

Suddenly, something vibrates against my leg, causing me to jump and nearly choke on my drink. Remembering that I had stashed my cellphone into the pocket of my skirt earlier this morning, I place the glass on the counter and proceed to take out the device. My screen flashes with a picture of me and my best friend Abby, and a small smile plays on my lips as I slide my finger across the screen to answer her incoming call.

"Hey, Ab-" I begin, heading upstairs as she cuts my greeting off.

"Is it true? Are you the newest Breeder?" I wince at her words and sigh—something I've been doing all day—telling her to give me a moment since there are guards outside my cottage. Heading towards the master bedroom, I make my way towards the bath and turn on the shower, letting the running water mask our conversation.

"Yeah, it's true, sadly," I reply after a while, sliding down the wall to sit on the cold tiled floor. "We have to save you!" My best friend exclaims, worry evident in her voice. The tears start to pool in my blue eyes and escape down my cheeks.

"You can't do anything. Think about your mate. He's the Beta here, and if Alpha Sam finds out you tried to free me, imagine what would happen." My voice cracks as I begin to sob again for the second time today. I make a quick decision and tell my best friend all my fears and worries about my new position, about how I wish I weren't chosen as a Breeder at all and wish I had met my mate before today since mated females are safe from becoming a Breeder. By the end of my sobbing rant, I feel better with a clearer mind. Talking to a friend really helps.

"I know I'm allowed to come to see you tomorrow to help get the house decorated, so I'll bring you some essentials. What do you want?" Abby says quietly, trying to distract me from the current situation. I smile and let out a chuckle at her antics. As the Beta Female and surrogate Luna of this pack, my friend has a say in what happens with the new Breeder, and it is her job to help the Breeder settle in on the second day. I somehow got lucky with our packs Beta Female being my best friend. I can request items I will need and know without a doubt that she will do everything in her power to help me out.

"As many clothes as you can grab from my closet, lots of chocolate to help my emotionally unstable mind right now and my phone charger, please. Talk to my cousin and his mate about stuff to bring for me." I rattle off a list, glad that my friend's status allows her to visit me whenever she wants.

"Okay, I will see you tomorrow then." She reassures me as we say our good nights and end our phone call. I turn off all sound on my phone, not wanting the guards to take it away from me in case I need to reach Chris or Jack in an emergency. I turn off the shower, and silence resumes. Trying to think of a hiding spot in my room where no one will find my cellphone, I leave the bathroom and make my way towards the nightstand beside the bed and pull open the top drawer, a wide grin spread across my face. What looks to be a simple empty drawer actually holds a pleasant surprise: a false bottom that I had discovered in my mad cleaning session. It was something I guess the previous Breeder had created using a piece of wood matching the nightstand since she had left a leather notebook containing what I assume to be a biography or note for the next Breeder now sitting on the nightstand. I plan to read it at some point to see just how the Breeder who once resided here lived daily. Hopefully, this book could give me details on how to survive and what I can do to make my life less miserable as a Breeder.

Once my cellphone is secure in its hiding spot, I look at the leather notebook and debate whether I should read it or not. Curiosity wins out as I grab it with one hand and sit cross-legged in the middle of the bed, taking the time to read what my predecessor wrote. I decide that reading everything in one sitting is a bad idea and focus on the first few pages. I quickly discovered that this notebook is actually a diary. My focus is captivated by the first entry from twenty years ago when she was forced to become a Breeder and what transpired on that day. My heart breaks for this she-wolf who remains nameless in her entry, as she wrote about being immediately dragged away to the cottage without a goodbye to her family. She was thrown into this cottage that was completely empty compared to what it is now—save for a bed—and this she-wolf spent her night cold and lonely. I felt better knowing that the treatment this she-wolf went through is different from what I went through today. At least I had some food in the fridge, and there is some form of furniture and bedding for me to use, even if the other rooms were empty.

Taking the time to read the next entry, my eyes widen in horror. Instead of the she-wolf having a few days to settle into her new role, the breeding process started the next morning. She had lost all her rights as a regular wolf right away. My heart drops in horror as I read of her being awoken and promptly raped by the Alpha and another Warrior. There was neither the courtesy that we experience now nor any humane treatment.

Placing the leather book down, I take a deep breath and re-evaluate my situation. I could settle into my new role, knowing I have a few days to take everything in and focus on any plan I could, or I could fight back and possibly be injured. I decided a shower would do me well with the new information from the diary and make my way to the bathroom, turn the shower on and undress while the water comes to a temperature I prefer. Stepping into the spray of warm water, I allow my thoughts to circulate with the rules I was told of being a Breeder, what the next few days will be like for me as well as the two entries from the Diary. If I want to survive, I will have to be obedient as a Breeder for now and do what I am told.

Accepting my fate for the moment, I pick up the loofa and scrub away the grime from cleaning off of my body. My mind wanders to the thought of what to do with this cottage. I think of what to do with the other rooms since I have no choice but to perform this role as the pack's Breeder. Since I would need a nursery for the many newborns I will be forced to have and a room for any toddlers, I would have to decorate those rooms first. The time ticks by, and I force myself to stop thinking. Anything that needs to be done can be dealt with tomorrow.

With the water turning cold, I turn off the water and step out of the shower, wrapping myself in a towel that envelops my small body. I slowly open the bathroom door, the steam escaping the warm room and shiver from the cold breeze that rushes to greet me. Quickly, I run to the walk-in closet, taking the oversized, long-sleeved shirt and boy shorts I had found and cleaned earlier and quickly towel-dried my body to put the fresh set of clothes on.

Padding quietly into my room, I shiver once again, remembering that all the windows were opened when I began cleaning earlier. I want nothing more than to fall into the queen-sized mattress and allow sleep to take over but instead I rush around the cottage, closing all the windows and the back door. Even though it is late spring now, the night is chilly almost like the end of winter since we are located in the northern part of Ontario, close to the Hudson Bay. Checking the thermostat to make sure the cottage warms up; I finally head back upstairs and into my new room where I climb into bed, wrap the warm, soft blankets around me and letting my exhausted body relax as the scent of the lavender fabric softener surrounds and soothes me into a deep, dreamless sleep.

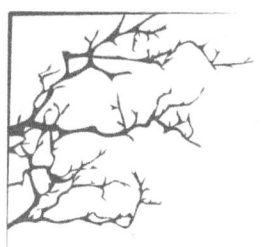

Chapter 4

Early in the morning, I wake up with sleep-filled eyes, taking in the blurry surroundings. For a moment, I panic, thinking that I am in the wrong house. Before long, the events of the previous day flood into my mind. Taking deep, calming breaths, I push the covers off of me and stand, stretching my sore body. I must have cleaned a little too hard last night to be so sore and drained. Looking around the room, I frown and wonder if today Abby can help me find some decorations that will make this prison a little more bearable. With her arriving today with my belongings, I have a feeling she will take me shopping and I plan to use the pack credit card to my advantage. If I am to be a Breeder, then I will make Sam's wallet bleed for this in-humane role.

Sighing yet again, I stumble out of my bedroom and make my way downstairs into the kitchen deciding breakfast will be a great idea. I already know what I want and take out some ingredients for my classic comfort food—banana-chocolate chip pancakes. I figure Abby will want to eat with me, and boy, can that girl pack down food like it's nothing! So, I triple my usual recipe and happily allow my mind to focus on this task at hand then my impending breeding.

As soon as the pancakes are done and the stovetop is turned off, I hear the doorbell ring with a visitor's arrival; I make my way over to the front of the house, opening the blue wooden door to see Abby standing there accompanied by four Warriors. The giant, burly Warriors are each holding a bag and boxes with "Laina's stuff" written on them in black Sharpie.

"Morning, girl. Do I smell.. pancakes?" Abby grins as she pulls me in for a long hug. The Warriors head inside, taking my things up the stairs. I tell them to leave everything in the master bedroom before ordering them all to leave. As soon as they leave, Abby winks and holds a tote bag out to me. I can't help the grateful smile I send her way as I take the bag and look inside, happy to see my phone charger, wallet, and other essentials that a Breeder isn't allowed to have. I'm so happy that my friend snuck these in for me.

"Thank you, Abby," I whisper. The two of us head into the kitchen, where a heaping stack of pancakes awaits us. We gather some plates and utensils and begin to dig into the scrumptious breakfast and catch up. Abby goes on about the gossip around the pack, thankfully steering clear of mentioning any rumours about me. It felt normal to be in the kitchen with my best friend, scarfing down comfort food and chatting like regular teenagers. Abby offers to clear the table and load the dishwasher while I head upstairs to get changed. Looking through the boxes and bags in my room, I manage to find a pair of leggings and a comfy cropped hoodie to wear with black sneakers and my purse. Fully dressed, I make my way to the foot of the stairs, where Abby waits.

"So, I have the go ahead to take you shopping without an escort." Abby explains, holding out a black card to me, one I take happily.

"It's the pack card. Make Sam regret making you a Breeder." She states with anger in her eyes. I thank her, tucking the card into my purse as we leave the cottage, Abby glaring at the warriors that try to stop me and ordering them to back off. I already know the first stop on our shopping trip and that is the closest sports store for my home gym equipment. I plan to buy the most expensive items I can and then work my way with Abby down the list. I plan to save shopping for pups last as right now I need to feel normalcy.

༄

"That's all for shopping." Abby exclaims. We left the cottage around eleven in the morning to make it to the nearest mall. Much to Abby's protest and thinking I am insane for wanting a home gym, I had her stop at the nearest sports store after pointing out that I will need to stay in shape for my new role and she quietly agreed with me. I made sure to take my time testing the equipment before ordering the most expensive models, I could practically see dollar signs in the poor clerks eyes as I paid for everything and Abby signed for delivery. After that, Abby dragged me from store to store, some being clothing, some furniture, some a paint shop that promised to deliver my chosen colours within the hour. Every other store we went to promised me the rest of the furniture would be delivers to the pack house where it will then be promptly brought to my cottage curtesy of a few Omegas and Warriors. Despite the thrill of shopping, I can't help the sadness that creeps in thinking that the first house I'll ever decorate is the prison of the Breeder's cottage.

"Now, it's time to get home to all the paint waiting for you to paint each wall." I can tell Abby is trying to stay cheerful, but her words are really starting to annoy me. She sounds more formal than friendly. I know my job as a Breeder means that Abby will have a say in what I will have to do as the Beta Female of the pack, and smiling around her soon becomes harder and harder. It felt like each sentence she said throughout the day became more and more insensitive. At one point, she told me, "Just choose a damned crib and let's go!" seemingly because it wouldn't matter what I chose anyway. The baby will be whisked away from me as soon as they're able to eat baby food. I guess my mood must have shown as I spot Abby roll her eyes at me while we climb into her car.

"It's going to be fine. Besides, I hear that Max is your first Warrior, and knowing him, he won't do anything with you. He's saving himself for when he finds his mate." Now, Abby's words do reassure me to some degree. Everyone knows that Max is an honest wolf. He grew up with the notion of "saving himself" for his mate, and, to this day, he's still a virgin. Part of me hopes he doesn't find his mate until I figure out what to do, but maybe, just maybe, I might be his mate. The only hope of getting me out of this situation is if one of the Warriors meant to breed with me is my mate.

"Thank god for that." I grumble a half-hearted reply, looking out at the scenery flashing by. Abby laughs at my words while she turns up the radio volume, singing along to whatever song is playing. I don't feel like joining her; her mood is a little too happy while she takes me back to the baby-making prison, I will be stuck in. I hate this.

Soon, her Land Rover crosses our back borders, and the familiar houses and forest pass by. The road to the breeder section greets us, and my cottage comes into view. Part of me wants to run away at this moment, but the consequences would be dire. As Abby pulls into the driveway, I feel the dread settle in even more. The situation is becoming all the more real and hopeless than ever right now.

"Well, where would you like to paint first?" Abby asks, shutting off the engine and turning off the racket coming from the radio, enveloping us in silence.

"The nursery. I want to paint it powder blue." I answer. It will never be the design I want for my babies because it will never be theirs for the rest of their lives, and I will never raise them and watch them grow up. A trail of warmth flows down my face, and I reach up, feeling fresh tears on my skin. I don't think I could do this at all.

"Laina, are you okay? Seriously, you need to pull yourself together because you're a fucking Breeder, and it's your job. Get used to this and stop crying." Abby gives me a sideways glance, with a look of utter scorn and annoyance on her face. I stare at my so-called best friend in disbelief for a moment, about to challenge her vicious glare. Is this how she really feels about all of this, considering I'm supposed to be her best friend?

"Does it look like I'm okay, Abby? Does it look like I'm used to this fucking situation already? My life got turned upside-fucking-down yesterday, and you're telling me to get used to it?!" I shout, my voice shaking. I've finally snapped at her. I can't believe how insensitive she is being right now, this last statement from her being the proverbial straw that broke the camel's back after all her snarky comments from our day-long shopping trip.

"You get to live a happy fucking life with a mate who loves you, and you get to have pups that YOU will raise." I scream, the volume blocking her from saying anything while I slam my fist into her stupid Land Rover's dashboard. It dents with my strength from my rage. My fists feel like they're burning as I control myself and stop the shift that wants to take over. I know my wolf form will not fit in her car.

"Do you want to know how long my pups will be in my life?" I ask, watcher her face as she winces from the power surging in my blood.

"Two fucking years. That's it!" I continue, feeling the tears flow faster.

"I don't get to be the mother my pups deserve. I don't get to see their first steps or first words. Their first day of school will be with their adoptive family, the family who rips my children from my arms to raise them. I get nothing, and all you can do is help me get this place ready for me to be raped in and tell me to get used to my job." I can feel the anger radiating off my friend, but I allow the power in my blood to radiate off of me in waves to cover her, watching her cower before me once more. I know Abby envies my bloodline having Alpha and Beta blood. She knows full well that her heritage is that of a Breeder's pup with an unknown father and hates her bloodline even though the wolves who raised her treated her like a princess. I guess she likes knowing my so-called "perfect life" she always made comments about came to an end now that I am a Breeder. I would be at her beck and call with her position as the Beta Female. I never noticed how much of a snake Abby is until today, and I start questioning her real motives for being my friend. I start questioning everything she has ever said or done while being a part of my life.

"Geez, Laina, tell me how you really feel?" Her sarcastic remark and glaring eyes filled with hatred simmering in waves towards my direction causes a low warning-growl to escape my lips. She may be a Beta Female and I but a lowly Breeder and inferior in comparison, but she knows I could have her head with my strength at any given moment. At the end of the day, my bloodline is superior to hers.

"Stay out of my life from now on." I reply as I violently push open the car door to get out and slam it shut. I hear the sound of the metal grinding together, knowing that the car door will never open again. I guess this bitch will need a new car. I think as I make my way into the house and the squeal of tires fills my ears. I scoff, knowing that Abby is running away both in fear and humiliation, and wonder how she even managed to become the Beta Female. She could never handle having someone yell at her the way I just did and was probably on her way to complain to her mate.

"Miss Laina?" One of the guards calls out to me while I try to calm the anger and indignation swirling inside me. I smile meekly at his worry-filled gaze, hoping that he doesn't see through my thoughts.

"Don't worry about it." I whisper, and he nods unconvinced before handing me a handkerchief.

"My mother was a Breeder. I knew that the people who raised me weren't my real parents. It just didn't feel right. One day, while we were school shopping, a woman came up to me and said my name. Everything about her seemed so familiar, and the next thing I knew, I was hugging her and begging her not to leave me. My adoptive parents finally told me who she was that night, and after that, I met my siblings. My mother and I still talk to this day, not the one who raised me, but the woman who was forced to give me up—though I still talk to my adoptive parents" The warrior begins as I wipe the tears form my face.

"I know what your children will go through. Just remember that if I can find a way to get you out before it's too late, I will." My eyes widen at the guard's confession, and I hug him without thinking. Part of me instantly feels safe with this guard, and I can't help but show weakness in front of him, something I hate showing but have been doing lately. His past is similar to Abby, but while she shows her true colours like a royally spoiled bitch - even when her adoptive parents did their best to give her everything she wanted - this guard shows sincerity and friendship. The wolves who raised him did well in raising this wolf that stands before me into a well-mannered man.

"I'm Alex, by the way." He laughs out loud, reassuringly patting my back.

"Well, Alex, I'm recruiting you to paint the rooms with me." We laugh together as I release Alex from my hug, motioning for the Warrior to follow me inside, where cans of paint are waiting to be used up. I wipe my tears once more and take a deep breath to calm myself down before rolling up my sleeves. For the rest of the day, we spent the hours painting each room.

Alex is a great help, with him being so tall and able to reach the top of the ceiling. It felt nice doing something mundane and not being looked at like a piece of meat that the other guards want to take a bite out of. The next day, Alex arrives early, just in time for the breakfast I made for the two of us before we get to work. I let him know that the furniture will arrive today and ask if he knows anyone he trusts who would be willing to help bring it to the cottage and move it around. With a grin, Alex leaves the room and makes a call before returning to the table to devour his breakfast.

Soon, I meet his half-brother Matthew, a dark-skinned wolf with a carefree smile. He, too, is a Warrior, and I learn that the two of them have been secretly helping Breeders escape when the chance is given to them. Hope flashes briefly in my heart when they agree to help me out when the opportunity arises.

Matthew brought along his mate, Milly, to help decorate with a woman's touch. Neither of them brought up the fact that I'm the newest Breeder. They treat me with respect, and it feels nice being treated as an equal and not a slave used to increase the population. Of course, once all the furniture is arranged and built and the walls painted, Alex and Matthew escape into the garage's home gym for a good workout. Milly and I are left to roll our eyes at them and spend the evening with wine and snacks. The only thing that surprised the two wolf-brothers is me being sixteen, apparently, the youngest she-wolf to be chosen as a Breeder.

"You know, it's been fun hanging out with you." Alex says, the two of us sitting on the back porch with hot cocoa in our hands. Matthew and Milly had left about three hours ago, leaving the cottage to feel slightly empty without their presence and laughter.

"It's been fun hanging with you too." I laugh, a genuine smile on my face. Part of me envies Alex's mate, whoever she or he might be, as Alex really is an outstanding wolf. Being mateless, Alex always talks about his hope of finding his mate and spending the rest of their lives together. I know he will make some wolf happy one day, and I hope that day comes soon for him.

"Well, I should let you go rest. The Alpha comes to check on you tomorrow." He kisses the top of my head gently, reminding me of how Chris would kiss me when I was worrying too much, and heads inside. I can hear the sink running as he cleans his mug and calls out his goodbye. Soon enough, he is gone for the night.

Sighing, I head inside and start getting ready for bed, taking a shower and making sure everything is ready for tomorrow. Whether I like it or not, the Alpha will take my virginity tomorrow, and I will fully become a Breeder. Four days after tomorrow, my job will begin, and the first Warrior to be my partner will show up and do what he has to do to make me pregnant. Dread fills me as I try my best to fall asleep, but if Abby was correct the other day, Max will not touch me.

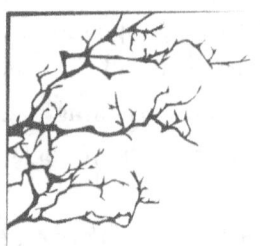

Chapter 5

Turning off the tap to the sink as I finish cleaning the dishes from breakfast, I turn my head just in time to see Alex sending a sad smile in my direction before quietly leaving the cottage to patrol the perimeter. No one else is allowed to be in the cottage after ten in the morning until the Alpha and the Doctor arrive to conduct their business. The Alpha will stay all night to do with me as he pleases and prepare me for my new role. Anxiety and nerves take over as I wring out the dish towel, trying to find something to do other than smoothing out the non-existent wrinkles in my outfit.

I am dressed in a simple white lace dress with a matching bra and thong, something one of the guards told me to wear considering I am still pure - still a virgin. It scares me to think that today Alpha Sam will take away something I wanted to save for my mate without a care in the world and without any consideration for my well-being; this will be nothing at all like the Sam I grew up with. Another hour passes and I find some things to clean in the already spotless cottage, trying to distract myself from the inevitable that is soon to come. I started thinking that maybe the Alpha had forgotten about today. Forgotten his job of taking away my virginity, but my hopes are soon crushed when the front door swings open and he and the Doctor waltz in.

"Good morning Miss Laina. Hope you are doing well." Doctor Freelan greets me, his eyes roaming my body. I suppress a shudder and smile as sweetly as I can, bowing my head in submission. As a Breeder, I have to be good and obey these two males or risk being punished each time I disobey them on their visits. I once saw a Breeder be punished about two years ago. Apparently, she tried running away from her role, only to be caught. The Warriors in charge of guarding her took a silver whip—silver being our Kryptonite—while another set of Warriors tied her hands to a pole. The attempted escape happened two days after being assigned her new role. The guards took turns raising the whip and lowering the ends onto her back as

I watched on in horror as the silver tips shredded the fair and delicate skin, and blood dripped down her body to pool onto the dirt floor below her. No one knew what happened to this Breeder but the memory of her screams and pleads for mercy on that day reminded me that Breeders are nothing but slaves.

Now, as a Breeder myself, I will have to bide my time if I want to survive with the possibility of escape.

"Good morning, Doctor, Alpha." I greet politely, welcoming the two into the living room as if the thought of escape never crossed my mind. The Doctor wastes no time after initial greetings, and the morning passes quickly. I am weighed, measured, and had blood and urine samples taken for the Doctors at the Pack Hospital labs to run their needed tests on. Thankfully, I will have to wait for those tests to return before the Alpha can touch me.

Doctor Freelan leaves with his bag full of notes on my health and the vials to be tested, leaving Alpha Sam and myself alone in the cottage. Nerves once again take over me, and I excuse myself to hide away in the kitchen to cook. It would be unwise to deal with a hungry Alpha, and this task gives me something to keep my nerves at bay. After a quick lunch with Alpha Sam, Doctor Freelan returns with a beaming smile and joins Alpha Sam and I at the dining room table.

"You're fit and strong. Your pups will be amazing." He announces with delight. I groan internally while my outer appearance displays a grateful expression. Never show weakness to those you consider your enemy. I repeat in my mind.

"Thank you so much," I reply, faking a relieved breath, getting ready to kick the Doctor out of my cottage. It will be quicker to get the deed over with and done and allow the Alpha to take my virginity away now without any fight.

"I am not done yet." Doctor Freelan continues, making it hard for me to hold in the sigh of irritation that builds with each moment the Doctor stays in this cottage. I jump when Alpha Sam clears his throat, forcing me to turn my body in his direction to give the wolf my full attention.

"As you know, since becoming Alpha six years ago, I haven't found my mate, and I need an heir by this time next year. Otherwise, my brother and his mate will take over as Alpha and Luna." I nod with confusion, not understanding where this conversation is going.

"The pack Elders and I have decided that the first pup you will bear will be my own. If you can produce two pups for me, then your position as a Breeder will be nullified, and you can become a female Warrior or Acolyte. The choice is yours." He continues, causing my mind to reel with shock. This offer feels too good to be true but at what cost? Would his mate even accept his pups from a Breeder? A moment of silence settles between all of us as I take a moment to think. I could weigh the pros and cons of this offer all day if I wanted, but I had a feeling they would want me to answer now. Finally resigning to my fate, I look at Sam and give him a small smile.

"Do I even have a choice?" I ask in a small voice, already knowing his answer.

"No." Both men say in unison. I sigh, resigning myself to my fate and turning to look at the Doctor.

"So what role do you play?" I ask, watching a sadistic grin spread across his wrinkle-filled face.

"This one!" He exclaims happily, opening his bag and producing a needle with the point gleaming evilly in the light. A liquid sloshes around in the glass tube, the amber colour sending a sense of foreboding through me. I have a feeling I am not going to like what he is about to do.

Before I can comprehend what is happening, the Alpha has his hands on my arms, holding me in place as the Doctor moves quickly, shoving the point of the needle into my left arm with such accuracy that I feel he has done this hundreds of times already. A tingling sensation courses through my body as the Doctor removes the needle after making sure every last fluid in the syringe is injected into my body. I want to feel fear or the urge to fight my way out of their grasps, but none comes. Only shock fills me with what these men have done.

"You have a week to get her pregnant with this serum. Her sex drive will be hyperactive, and it will feel like she is in heat, so have fun." Doctor Freelan gathers his things after these instructions and leaves my cottage. My skin slowly blooms with a slight blush as I begin to pant for air. The room begins to feel hot and humid on my sensitive skin, and the Alpha grazes his fingertips across my arms, causing me to let out a loud sensual moan.

"Guess it's starting to work." The Alpha's smug voice fills the room, and I feel myself being lifted into his strong arms as he forces me to straddle his lap. I watch as his lips descend onto my neck, sending torturous kisses and nips on my now-sensitive skin, causing the valley between my legs to drip with wetness. I gasp as his lips find a sweet spot just on the swell of my breasts, his kisses moving the clothes aside as he exposes the hard bud of my nipple. He sucks my nipple into his mouth, causing me to moan and grind myself against the bulge in his pants. I need to feel some form of release, feel something inside me.

"This is going to be fun, Laina." He growls. His lips smash onto my own, and his hands cup my ass as he stands from the chair, my legs instinctively wrapping around his waist. I can feel him moving towards the stairs, hear the thud of his foots on the steps as he carries me to the second floor. Moments later, I find myself being lowered onto my bed, the Alpha on top of me and between my legs. I feel him slowly grinding himself into the thin material of the lacy white thong that I know is just soaking wet with my cum.

"Alpha!" I whimper out in pleasure, grinding back against him. Everything in me knows this is wrong – that this is not supposed to happen. But the primal instinct of my wolf side wants nothing more than to be mounted and pounded into by the man above me.

"Call me Sam, baby girl." Sam's husky voice fills my ears as his strong hands tear my dress apart, leaving me in nothing but the push-up bra and soaking thong. His lips once again descend onto my skin, kissing, sucking, biting me, causing me to grind harder into him and moan. My body is burning with desire by now. The drug injected into me is doing its job as Sam rips my bra away. He wraps his lips around the hard rosy nipple, sucking and biting hard on it. His callous fingers find their way past the thong and into my pussy, slowly stretching me and moving against the wet flesh. Pressure soon begins to build inside me; my moans and screams fill the room as I clutch at my bed sheets, my hips moving in sync with Sam's fingers deep inside me. Finally, my insides clench, constricting against the three digits that Sam manages to squeeze inside as liquid oozes out and onto my thigh. I gasp for air, but the feeling of wanting more fills my mind as I hazily look up at the smirking male before me.

"Now that you've had your first orgasm, I want to feel your pretty little mouth wrapped around me for a moment." Sam orders, his hand - still wet with my juices- leaving me as he undresses to reveal a well-built and muscular body for my eyes to feast. I gulp when I catch sight of his hard, thick cock ready to be plunged inside me. He reaches for my head and wraps his fingers in my chestnut locks, pulling my head forwards until my lips brush against the tip of him.

"Open up and suck, bitch." He orders. My mouth opens upon his Alpha command and he quickly pushes his length inside me, causing me to groan. My pussy still twitches, wanting more pleasure, but I have to do what I am told. One hand reaches out to steady my body on the bed while the other grasps the base of Sam's cock, moaning as I begin to suck and caress my tongue against him. I watch as he grunts and groans with pleasure, his eyes glazing over as he rhythmically thrusts into my mouth. Sometimes he would hit the back of my throat, causing me to gag on him, which only encourages Sam to continue that movement over and over again. Suddenly, he pushes me back out of nowhere, his cock leaving my mouth with a pop sound. Confused, I look up at my Alpha as his hungry eyes takes in my naked body.

"I'm close to cumming, Laina, and I am far from done with you." Sam forces me onto my back and spreads my legs, positioning himself just at my entrance and rubbing the tip of his cock just against my wet folds before pushing into me without warning. I cry out from the pain of his rod penetrating my hymen and taking away my virginity. He thrusts hard and fast inside me without a care for my own comfort as the pain pulsates inside me. But it doesn't take long for pleasure to take over pain as he wraps his hand around my throat. The hours pass, and I scream in both excruciating pain and the most blissful pleasure, feeling his muscular, sweaty, naked body on top of mine while he plunges into me. Sometimes he would flip me onto my hands and knees, taking me from behind and smacking my ass or yanking my hair, calling me his filthy whore, his girl, as I let him take my body any way he pleases. At some point, I lost all senses, only able to feel the wolf inside me, begging for more. Finally, we finish, and I lay pressed to his side, panting, him still inside me as his seed continues to flow inside for the ninth time tonight.

"Soon, you will give me an heir." He whispers, his hand rubbing my back. My mind is screaming. This is still wrong. This is against the rules. But my body craves for more. I curse whatever the Doctor injected into me.

For the next week, with each time the Alpha visited, my body always craves him the moment he steps inside the door. My bedroom begins to hold a permanent scent of sex and sweat. I lost count of how many times Sam came inside me. It is ludicrous, but it is my job now, and I have to do what I am told or else I would end up with torn flesh like the Breeder from two years ago.

My job now is to produce heirs for Sam.

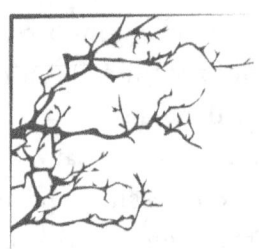

Chapter 6

I stare at the small stick in my hand both in disbelief and dread before realization sets in. It has been a week since Sam came and begin to breed me with the intention of producing his heirs and the result on the stick is one I had prayed would never come. As the realization sets in, I find myself unable to stop the tears the flow and cry my heart out; not because I am happy, but because my life has taken a sharp one-eighty turn with no end in sight. It will be six months until this pup is born. Six months for me to be locked away and pregnant . Then I will only have two years with my pup before Sam takes away the wolf inside me and raises his heir without me in this pup's life.

"Laina?" Alex's voice floats through the door and I jump, flushing the toilet and throwing the evidence of my pregnancy away in the trash bin. I do not want anyone to find out that I'm pregnant right away. Hell, part of me is ashamed for how I acted like a wonton whore who only wanted to be fucked over the last week with the Alpha. I curse the Doctor each time I am left alone in bed, as the Alpha leaves my used and bruised body that he has just filled with his seed for the umpteenth time to do pack work before returning to make me his own little sex toy once more. Washing my face with cold water, I compose myself and force the thoughts of what I was forced to do for the past seven days from my mind. When I feel like I am composed enough to face my friend, I leave the safety of the master bathroom.

"You okay?" Alex asks as I walk past him.

"Yeah, I'm just overwhelmed." I smile as best as I can at my friend and usher him out of the room.

"I'll see you in a few, just want to tidy up." My friend nods and closes the door giving me a moment to myself.

I have to focus on putting together a bag of essentials if I want to run away soon. Alex and Matthew will help me if I tell them about what Doctor Freelan and Alpha Sam did to me, they detest the Breeder system and most likely will do everything they can to keep me out of our Alpha's grasp. Grabbing a small pink notebook, I take out my hidden phone, writing down all important contacts before I start making a list of things I will need as well. I will have to leave my cell phone behind or risk being tracked by Sam and his Warriors. Since it has been a week and the drug that was injected into me is out of my system, my mind feels much clearer and more refreshed than it has in days. This means that today is my best option for running away. I know that the Alpha is gone for the whole day due to pack business and will only return tonight with Doctor Freelan to give me a check-up, he told me himself last night after making sure I was filled with his cum, this means I have time to plan. It is now or never, and part of me knows that Alex and Matthew will help me like Breeders before when I inform them of my plan to escape.

I smile at the one good thing Abby has done to help me, her bringing my emergency money and wallet with all my cards and I.D. inside. I haven't heard from or seen that bitch since she left me here, but Milly said she has been gloating about the mighty Laina Starcrest becoming nothing but a fuck toy. I'm glad I dropped her as a friend when I did, who knows what she would have done if I allowed her to continue coming to this cottage.

I stuff my wallet into a large black duffle bag I kept by the bed and begin to rummage around the room, picking and choosing what would be essential to bring with me, including practical clothing and an extra pair of running shoes. With the duffle bag packed and leaving enough room for other things like food, water, and medical supplies, I slowly open the door to the bedroom and heighten my wolf hearing, taking the time to see if Alex is in the house. He isn't, thank the Goddess. Right now I do not need him asking me what I am doing and risking his partner hearing my plans of escape.

I smile before making my way downstairs and into the kitchen, grabbing a handful of protein and granola bars, several bags of jerky, and dried fruit while throwing them all into the bag with my stuff. I then make my way towards where the first aid kit is kept under the kitchen sink. I choose what I will most likely need on the run, placing bandages, gauze, medical tape, pain medication and disinfectant spray into a large Ziploc bag, making sure everything is secured in the bag. The last thing I add are a few water bottles, knowing that I can fill them at restaurants on my way to finding someplace safe before I rush outside to hide the duffle bag by the back gate. If all goes well, Alex and his brother can sneak me out during the shift change.

Smiling triumphantly, I turn towards the cottage and take in the building and its surroundings. This place will never be my home if I have a say in it, but for now, I need to act as if it's just another day. After making sure the bag I've hidden won't be seen, I make my way back inside and head straight for the kitchen. I need to eat something filling today and decide on some comfort food—lasagna sounds like a good idea. I busy myself preparing the Italian dish, making sure each layer has enough meat and cheese with a little bit of sauce, before placing it in the oven to bake. As a last-minute addition, I add a baking sheet with some garlic bread alongside the lasagna. Meat and carbs are a werewolf's best friend when planning to run any distance, whether for training or running away.

"Food smells good," Alex says as he enters the kitchen from the back door. He heads towards the table, taking a cookie from the plate that is already waiting to be eaten while I place the garlic bread beside it. The timer dings, letting me know that the lasagna is done and I quickly retrieve it before bringing it to the table and settling it on the pad set between our plates.

"I have something to talk about after we eat." I manage to lough out after rolling my eyes at my friend's enthusiasm for food.

"Sounds serious. Good thing there is good food first." Alex agrees instantly, his focus on the food before him as he scoops a healthy portion onto his plate.

[Laina, the Doctor and I can't come over today, we have urgent pack business at the pack house. Stay inside!] The Alpha's voice rings clear in my head as he links me with a hint of urgency in his voice. I sigh in relief and sit down at the table, digging into my food, my mood becoming lighter. With this information, the check-up seems to be cancelled, and I can't help but grin. My chance for escape increases, knowing that the two males who have made my life a nightmare for the last seven days will not make an appearance tonight. If the check-up had gone as scheduled and if I weren't pregnant, I would have most likely been dosed with the serum again and repeated the process with the Alpha once more. Luckily, neither of those options will happen. But a nagging feeling fills me. Why would the Alpha still be on pack lands when he had gone out this morning?

"Good news?" Alex asks. I nod, giving him a full smile as I shove a fork full of delicious pasta into my mouth.

"He isn't coming today; neither is the Doctor." I mumble through a mouthful of garlic bread, catching sight of Alex as he lets out a relieved sigh and his body relaxes.

"Good. As taboo as it is to say, I hate the Alpha." He says. I laugh, almost choking on my food. I love how honest my friend is with me.

"Don't worry, I hate the Alpha too!" We continue our lunch, the mood lighter with the knowledge Alpha Sam and Doctor Freelan will not be making an appearance today, giving us time to catch up. I hesitate to tell Alex my plan, knowing that even though he has helped other Breeders escape this fate, I am a special case. I carry Pine Paw's heir now.

"Alex, we have a problem!" James, the other guard in charge of keeping me prisoner to this cottage, shouts. I can hear not-so-distant growls and howls coming from behind him and instantly place a hand over my flat stomach.

"Rogues." Alex says hurriedly as his body tenses, ready to fight. He rushes over to the back door and looks outside before coming back to my side with hope in his eyes, hope that ignites the fighting spirit inside of me.

"Our job is to protect you, so run and hide. if we "lose" you in the confusion, it's not our fault, but the rogues." I take the hint instantly, knowing what my friend is implying and hug Alex tight, tears stinging my eyes. I can see that he has been waiting for an opportunity like this to help me, and I'm grateful I extended an olive branch of friendship to this wolf over a week ago.

"Thank you." I whisper, feeling his arms wrap around my waist.

"Don't worry, just protect your pup." I pull away, shocked as he taps my nose, a bemused smile on this wolf's face.

"I smelled the chemicals from the test. I'll get rid of it for you later. Just stay safe. Also, your cousin asked me to send this to you. I slipped my number in there. You can call me when you find somewhere safe, and I will find you, Laina. You're like a little sister to me now, and I've been waiting to find a reason to leave." He hands me a letter, and I nod, speechless at how much help he is giving me. He hands me a jacket and pushes me out the back door before he runs out the front. I take the opportunity to run, putting my jacket on and grabbing the bag I had stashed outside the back fence and keep running. The sounds of wolves fighting fill the forest, but I did not chance to look back. I can't look back, or else I will be captured and taken back to the cottage to resume my life as a Breeder. Being pregnant means I will not face punishment, but the security would be doubled around the cottage.

The soles of my shoes slap against the forest floor, and I clumsily make my way through the underbrush. The sounds of fighting drown out the sounds of my escape. Multiple times I find myself changing directions to avoid the clash of wolves who fight tooth and claw to the death, with clumps of fur littering the ground. The closer to the edge of the territory, the quieter the forest becomes. With the sounds of fighting far behind me now, I make it to the edge of my pack's territory in an hour and stop before crossing it. Now, while everyone is busy with the rogues, I take the time to catch my breath. The forest is quiet away from the rogue attack, giving me peace of mind I haven't had in a long while. Remembering the letter Alex gave me, I take out the envelope I stashed into my jacket pocket carefully putting away the slip of paper that contains Alex's number before reading through the contents of the letter.

Lainy,

I hope you would read this before you got pregnant, and if you are, then I hope that it's the first set of pups you have.

Head to the treehouse we used to play in as children and grab your pink duffle bag. I know that your mind wasn't in the right place the day you were made a Breeder, but now I want you to do one thing, RUN.

Keep running until you find a mate because he or she will save you from being a Breeder.

This is the law the great Elders set out.

Stay safe and know that we love you.

Chris and Jack

Tears flow down my face again while I read and re-read the letter. It still smells like Chris with his neat handwriting filling the paper. I estimate that I had about an hour run in human form towards the treehouse, but luckily it is close to the pack border. This information makes this whole running away thing a hell of a lot easier. With a smile, I take a risk and strip my clothes off, stashing them into the duffle bag I carry now before shifting into my wolf form. Gingerly, I pick up the straps of the bag with my muzzle before dashing through the forest. I know shifting is taboo for pregnant werewolves, but now it is a desperate situation. I need speed to make my escape, and my human form is not as fast as my wolf form.

The old oak tree comes into view after about forty minutes of running and I let out a sigh of relief, dropping my bag and shifting back to human form. After quickly dressing into the clothes I wore earlier, I make my way to the ancient oak tree, the ladder to the treehouse greeting me. The scent of wolves lingers in the area, and I can't help but smile at the thought of pups still playing here. Looking around the base of the tree, I search for the little hollow I used to hide in, spying my all-too-familiar pink duffle bag ready and waiting for me. I know that Chris and Jack would stock the bag with things I would need, so I decide not to bother with checking the contents. Right now, I need to leave; when I find somewhere safe, I can look inside the pink duffle bag.

The border is just a few feet away from me, waiting to accept me into the unknown and escape this cruel fate given to me. If I renounce my status as a member of Pine Paw, I will become a rogue, and so will the pup inside me. Slowly I walk towards the border, my toes just on the line as I feel the power rushing through my sneakers. I know what I have to do.

"I, Laina Starcrest, renounce my membership of this pack and henceforth become a rogue until I find my mate or a new pack to call my own." I take a step over the border and feel the snap as the connection to the pack breaks. Since my pup is only just conceived, it will have no ties to any pack until I join one. I smile and continue to run, moving wherever is farthest from my old life. I will miss my cousin and his mate, as well as Alex, Matthew, and Milly, but I need to do what is right for me and for the little one inside me. I need to find a place where there is no Breeder status and be free once again. Once I have found a place to call home, I will send for those I love to come join me.

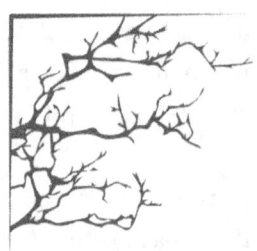

Chapter 7

Four Months Later

The sounds of their howls were closer than the last time. I am slower than when I first escaped Pine Paw with my now-protruding stomach filled with them, the twins. But for their sake, I will keep going. I have to keep going.

Currently, I'm in no man's territory where rogues like me bounce from town to town, trying to find a place where we belong. It's a region where rogues are supposed to be safe, but my pursuers tell me otherwise. The sounds of town life reach my sensitive ears from the safety of the forest trees, and I try my best to run faster. Just a few more kilometres, and I will be safe from my pursuers, from the wolves of Pine Paw who are just a stone's throw away from me.

I can hear the sounds of both wolves and humans now chasing me, realizing that some have shifted, probably to make it easier to try to persuade me to come back. Hell has a better chance of freezing over than me going back to Pine Paw.

"Don't hurt her. She is carrying my pup." Sam calls out to the wolves behind him. He knows I am pregnant. Most of my old pack knows; I guess Alex never had a chance to dispose of the pregnancy test. But no one understands why I would run away from Pine Paw, run away from being a Breeder. I left everything behind to protect my pups. I may be sixteen, but I know what is right and what is wrong. Being hunted and chased by these wolves is wrong. Being forced to accept my Alpha's seed and produce his heir is wrong. Becoming a Breeder is wrong. Everything Pine Paw did leading up to this moment is wrong. It is because of all these wrongs that I ran and will keep on running.

The safe-haven I call the town line finally comes into view, bringing renewed hope into my being. I take the chance to pick up speed and rush into the safety net. I feel some resistance at first as if some invisible force is trying to keep me out, but I keep pushing forward, and soon I am safely across, relief causing my nerves to settle down and with a sigh, I stop running and catch my breath. I turn around to face my pursuers with a smug grin, slowly walking backwards as I take in each of their faces.

"You will never have this pup, and I will never be a part of your pack again!" I growl out at Sam, wrapping my arms around my stomach protectively as I continue to walk backwards. So far, he only knows about one pup, and I would be damned if I let him learn that I am carrying twins.

"Look, Laina, we can talk. Just come back to the pack." Sam pleads, his body nervous as he keeps looking around. Something is off about him, but then again, I have a feeling that Sam isn't playing with a full deck of cards in his mind and that he hasn't had a right and stable mind for a while.

"How about no." I smile triumphantly and turn on my heels, walking down the road towards the town. I can hear Sam and his warriors calling out to me. They are begging me to return to them and stop walking to town—I ignored them all. I know they just want me back because of the pups inside me, believing I am only carrying one. I am in no mood for their tricks and mind games. Instead, I want a poutine.

I travel along the side of the road, coming up on the sidewalk when I find one, and take in the forest surrounding the roads. It is a pleasant walk, and not having to worry about being pursued for the time being makes it easier to enjoy the fall-coloured forest. I enter the small town with my two duffle bags and keep an eye out for anywhere that might sell poutine. Many of the places were commercial restaurants like McDonald's and Tim Horton's, but neither could give me the satisfaction I needed. Then I see it and begin grinning like a Cheshire cat when the colours of a red and white checkerboard sign of a vintage-looking diner appear like some form of Messiah. I walk into the small place with lighter steps and sit at a booth, placing my bags beside me and taking out my worn-out leather wallet and placing it beside me on the table.

"Long day?" I jump when a waitress quietly comes up on the other side, her face sympathetic as she takes in my tired appearance and worn-down bags. I take in her pristine white apron, her brunette hair pulled into a large bun on top of her head and a short, long-sleeved checkerboard dress that compliments her figure perfectly with her red high heels.

"Very, being pregnant is hard work." This gets the girl laughing, and I couldn't help but smile. It felt nice talking to someone not trying to capture you.

"I have three of my own, so I know the feeling. Do you know what you're having?" The waitress's friendliness brings whatever frazzled nerves I have remained down to a calmness I've missed. Being on the run for four months of my pregnancy took its toll on me.

"Twins, that's all I can tell you." The waitress nods and flips open her book, taking the pencil from behind her ear.

"So what do you want, darling?"

"Poutine with extra cheese, a vanilla milkshake, and plain cheesecake, please." She smiles at my order, shaking her head in amusement as she takes it down on the notepad in her hand.

"That's what I got all the time when I was pregnant with my kids. It'll be ready in a few." With that, she leaves to ring in my order and I heave another sigh while relaxing in the booth. From what I can tell from my walk into town, this small town is quiet with a peaceful community, and it looks like my old pack can't come here. It is a paradise in a world of darkness that sends a light of hope just made for me. Maybe, just maybe, I can find a home of my own and raise my pups.

"What do you think of living here?" I ask my protruding stomach, rubbing it gently and smiling when I feel some movements.

"Yeah, I like the idea too." I laugh. The idea that I have found a place I can call home and raise my babies in has my eyes watering with tears of joy. Pack or no pack, I will make it on my own and raise these babies, and if being in this town means I can do so here, then so be it. I felt safe the moment I crossed the town line, and this feeling of being safe is what I need in my life. I can send a message to the college I applied for, explain my situation and hopefully transfer to a nearby community college to get my degree.

"Talking to yourself?" The same waitress returns and sets my milkshake down in front of me with a friendly smile. I nod, my focus on the milk shake and reaching for the creamy goodness before inhaling it, quenching my thirst.

"I figured you were thirsty, so I brought two for you." She chuckles as she sets a second glass down in front of me, shaking her head as she looks at me with amusement.

"Thank you." I thank the waitress, reaching for the glass and setting my empty one aside as I slowly sip on the second milkshake.

"No problem, darling. Now-" She stops mid-sentence to sit down across from me, folding her hands on the table and looking me right in my eyes. Her posture states that what she is going to say next might ruin my day, but as long as it doesn't stop me from moving into this town, she can say all she want.

"What is a rogue doing here on my pack's territory?" I freeze with her words, fear taking hold while I sniff the air, smelling her carefully. My eyes widen when I finally take in her scent and learn that she, too, is a werewolf.

"It's not what you think. I was running away from my old pack." I state, and she just stares at me with squinted eyes, not believing a word I say. But as a rogue, I know that trying to convince anyone of my innocence will be difficult. All I can do is tell her the truth.

"Your pack probably has Breeders like mine, and I was forced to be one, so I ran." I continue my explanation, hoping to gain her sympathy and help to settle down. I am tired of running and need a place to safely raise my pups.

"Breeders are illegal now. The Great Elders told all Alphas this new law two years ago." The waitress nearly shouts, and I'm happy that there was only one other person here in the dining area, and he had disappeared to what I assume is the washroom a little while ago.

"B-but that's impossible. The pack I'm running from always had twenty at a time." I exclaim, my brows furrowed in confusion. If Breeders are illegal now, then why did Sam continue it?

"Listen, I am calling my Alpha. Then we are going to get the Elders, and we are setting that pack straight." The waitress states with a small growl, running a hand through her hair.

"Don't worry about paying for your food. It's on the house. You have been through a lot already, and you need a break. If you need anything, go to the counter and ask for Eeva, that's me, and I will come see what I can do." Eeva offers me a smile as her once suspicious eyes turn to ones filled with sympathy and sadness for me. Her hand reaches out for mine and squeezes it in a reassuring way filling me with all the hope I had lost over four months ago.

"O-okay." I stutter slightly as Eeva stands and leaves me alone to my thoughts. She disappears to what I assume is an office, hopefully calling her Alpha. I put my wallet away and sip at the milkshake, sighing slightly. What had happened to me was illegal, and yet it still happened. The thought that I was forced to be bred like an animal for someone's own gain causes a shudder to travel down my spine. I spent several days in a drug-induced state for something that was abolished two years ago. Another waitress brings me out from my swirling thoughts, placing my meal on the table. I thank her before I dig in, savouring the warmth of the poutine. I was almost done when the door to the diner opens and the bell above chimes at the arrival of a newcomer. Now that I know I am on someone else's pack lands, I make sure to pay attention to the coming and going of customers and take a deep breath, inhaling the new-comers scent. The scent of an unfamiliar male floods the diner, causing slight tingles to run down my spine and confusion to swirl once more inside my mind. Something tells me this is the Alpha, but there is something else, something that tugs at my mind, body and soul.

"Alpha Tate, this way." Eeva's voice rings clear through the diner, and my eyes widen. The reason why Sam had been terrified earlier stands just inside the door to the diner, and dread settles inside me once more for the umpteenth times this month. I am in Bloodsvain territory, and the man that just walked in is Tate Randall-Silvermoon - the Blood Alpha. The man who slaughters packs that anger him, who is possessive over the she-wolves he dates. The only other mate-less Alpha in Canada that is feared by all but wanted by she-wolves. And he now blocks my way of escape.

I feel the power radiating off of the Alpha, feeling it get closer and envelop me as Eeva and Tate near my booth. Shivers continue to run down my spine, some are shivers of fear, but the rest are a strange feeling that I couldn't put my finger on. The Alpha's scent wraps around me, causing my body to unconsciously relax even though part of me wants to run away and move on to a new town.

"Alpha, this is the girl I told you about on the phone earlier." Slowly, I stand and turn to face her Alpha, my head bowed in submission. I am on his territory and need to show that I am not a threat if I want him to help me.

"You don't have to be afraid." His voice is gentle, something I did not expect from the infamous Blood Alpha, whose hands have been covered in blood on multiple occasions. So is his touch, as his fingers are gently placed under my chin while he raises my head, causing me to look him in the eye. My eyes widen in shock as sparks of electricity trail from his fingertips, down from where his skin touches mine and right to my toes. My breath is caught in my throat when I see his dark green coloured orbs staring back into my own, and a trace of possessiveness flickers through his gaze.

"Mate." He growls out, pulling me closer to his body, barely giving me time to press my hands against his chest to leave some room for my protruding baby bump.

"Tate, be careful. She is pregnant." Eeva warns, only to get a possessive growl from the Alpha who holds me like some delicate porcelain. I feel his arms release me for a moment, only to watch as Tate moves my bags to the other side of the booth and sits down, pulling me down carefully beside him and wrapping a protective arm around my shoulders.

"Don't be so possessive." I state boldly, glaring at the wolf before me and hating how within our first meeting he stakes his claim on me as if we were a bunch of barbaric beings.

"I can, and I will. You are mine." He retorts back with a bemused expression on his face as if what he says is the right answer.

"I belong to no one." We both glare at each other for a moment, neither of us wanting to back down, as the idea of him staking his claim on me rubs me the wrong way. Not realizing that Eeva had disappeared until she returns to the booth, she breaks us out of our staring contest with more milkshakes and a tray full of pastries and cookies that she slams onto the table to gather our attention.

"Look here, this girl is pregnant and already had a rough day. Now baby brother, let her be and give this woman some space." Tate growls at her words and Eeva growls back just as threateningly. The power of two Alphas cascade over me like flowing water and the fear I felt earlier is gone knowing that I am mated to Tate. I smile as I grab another vanilla milkshake and a chocolate tart, taking a bite and letting myself relax once more. Tate's arms loosened from around me while Eeva takes his attention. The two stare at each other for a moment, linking each other from how their eyes glaze over, while I continue to eat the treats before me. I guess Eeva won whatever silent argument they were having as she sends a smile my way and takes my hands in her own, giving me a concerned smile.

"Now, sweetheart, what's your name?" She asks. I can feel Tate's eyes on me, waiting patiently to learn his mate's name. I guess if I want help, especially from these two wolves, I will have to speak.

"My name is Laina Starcrest. I came from Pine Paw pack under-"

"Samuel Lightran's rule." I nod as Tate finishes my sentence, hearing him growl loudly. Something inside me tells that Sam and Tate have a history that most likely ended badly.

"He knew about the new law and didn't stop Breeders. Tell me whose pups you are carrying." I stay silent and look down at my hands, tears forming in my eyes. They asked me where I was from, and I answered as this will help me and the twins in the long run. I did not expect some Alpha with a high and mighty attitude to start demanding things from me. I feel shame bubbling inside me. I had wanted to give my first everything to my mate, from my first kiss to my first time. Now would Tate stay with me knowing that I was forced to be a Breeder and pregnant with another wolf's pups.

"I said tell me!" He bangs his fists on the table in anger, and I flinch, the tears now falling down my face. I couldn't bring myself to tell him, but I knew deep down I had to. Tate deserves to know the truth.

"Tate, you're scaring her. I thought you said she is your mate." Eeva scolds the angry Alpha beside me, and I sense her move from across the table where she sat to my side and pull me into a hug. My body shakes as sobs wreak havoc through me, and the protective feeling that comes from the she-wolf beside me gives me the courage to speak.

"They're his. He forced himself on me to have heirs." I whisper through the sobs, feeling both of them stiffen. I knew this information must be shocking even for a normal wolf, as a rule to the Breeder is that the Alpha is forbidden to take part in producing pups. Soon, I spill the details of four months ago and what the Doctor and Sam did to me. I find myself situated in Tate's lap not knowing when I had been moved, my hands clutching his shirt as I slowly take in his scent that seems to calm my nerves.

"I'm going to-" He begins saying through clenched teeth, his hands tightening their hold around my pregnant body.

"Take Laina to your house and get her settled and cleaned up. Then, we can contact the Council and deal with this situation the right way. You know you can't slaughter the pack until they give you the go-ahead." Eeva cuts her brother off, giving him a warning glare that I catch from the corner of my tear-filled eyes. This time, I stiffen and pull away from Tate to look him in the eye, fear taking hold for those I care about being at the hands of his mercy.

"Not everyone is bad. Some of the Warriors refused to take part in it, and others helped me escape, like my cousin and his mate and the one Warrior who guarded me, his half-brother and sister-in-law. You can't kill them all." Even I could tell I am begging with my desperate attempt to protect those I care about. But I had to beg. I couldn't let the innocent die because of my escape. Tate relaxes against me, pulling my head to rest on his shoulder and playing with my hair.

"Make a list of those who were good to you and the other Breeders who you know of, and they can join the pack in the end. Wolves with families will be left alone. The Warriors who love partaking in the breeding will die, and so will Samuel. That's a promise, Laina." I feel his arms tighten around me. For once in a long, long time, I felt safe. I felt protected. The very thought of letting this male protect me, the wolf who seems to have more mood swings than I, a pregnant woman, have in a day, seems to be something I can consider.

"Now, let's get you home and relaxed. You need a good rest with what you've been through." He adds, pulling away and smiling at me with the most amazing smile ever. I couldn't help but be engrossed by Tate while I nod agreeing with him.

"Okay." I smile back shyly, hearing him chuckle at my reaction while letting me slide out of the booth. He takes my bags in one hand and leads me out of the diner with his other hand protectively at the small of my back. Maybe being his mate isn't such a bad thing after all.

"Wait, take these." Once again, I hadn't noticed Eeva slip away, but she held out a bag with small boxes inside and I could smell the delicious treats. Eeva truly is an angel sent to help me in my time of need.

"Tomorrow, we can go shopping if you want." She adds. For once, I was happy to have come here.

"Can it wait until I get her settled in?" Tate asks, his eyes darting between his sister and me. I hear a tinge of jealousy in his voice and try my best to stifle my laughter but fail as giggles erupt from my mouth.

"Sure, get some rest, Laina." I hug Eeva, my new friend and sister-in-law, and follow Tate out the door towards a black Jeep. I climb into the passenger side and let Tate drive me to wherever "home" is. The prospect of belonging to a pack once again fills me with a sense of security I lost in Pine Paw.

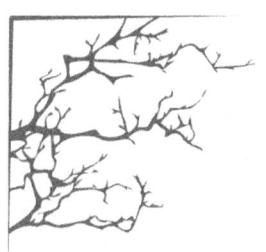

Chapter 8

The drive is longer than I expected as we slowly leave the small town behind, and I can't help but smile contentedly when the buildings give way to the beautiful forest. The leaves are changing to the lovely colours of red, oranges, and yellows you would find in fall and the thought of running through the forest after my pups are born brings has my smile growing wider. Inside the Jeep, Tate turns on the seat warmer for the passenger seat, and the warmth underneath me causes my eyelids to feel heavy as I drowsily continue to watch the scenery fly past me. Its been so long since I felt this safe and comfortable, that I have felt this relaxed and no longer feared being caught.

Some time during the drive to Tate's house, I must have dozed off from the quiet and warm peaceful drive with my newly discovered mate watching over me as I rouse sleepily to strong arms gently unbuckling my seatbelt and lifting me into their embrace. Groaning, I turned my head into who I am positive is Tate, his scent of juniper berries and stormy night wrapping around me while I do my best to hide my eyes from the light above.

"Shh, Laina, go back to sleep, little one." A deep gentle voice whispers in my ear. I oblige, letting the darkness of a comfortable, dreamless sleep take over once more while listening to the steady beating of Tate's heart.

Light falling across my eyes has me waking feeling energized and relax. It has been so long since I had a peaceful sleep and I can't help but sigh as I snuggle into the soft mattress below me until realization that this is not my bedroom, nor a room I have ever been in. Pushing myself up from the bed, careful of my pregnant belly, I look around the unfamiliar room and try my best to quell the building panic that rises inside me. Late morning light tries its best to filter through the soft, blue curtains, giving some light to the otherwise dark room showing the outline of three doors. One appears to be a closet, the second what I assume is the exit into the hallway, and the third is a bathroom as it is open and reveals the hint of a toilet and bath tub.

I notice my bags right away in front of the room I assume is the closet door and scramble to my feet in a panic, going through every pocket and finding the bags completely empty. I open the door behind my bags and discover a walk-in closet, finding the minimal clothing I own cleaned and hanging nicely on one side. Exiting the closet, I notice a vanity sitting just beside the large window with a brand new Kate Spade purse sitting on top with a piece of paper attached to it. Curious, I slowly walk towards the vanity, my hands reach for the paper that smells like juniper and stormy night and realize that the note is from Tate.

Laina,

Sorry for intruding on your things, but you were in a deep sleep. I hope you like this new purse. I thought it would suit you.

Tate

I sigh with relief and a bit of giddiness as I look inside the purse, noticing a new and the pink booklet of numbers inside. Tate has a notorious name in the werewolf community as a ruthless wolf who demolishes and massacres packs that anger the Blood Alpha. But this big bad Alpha wolf seems to be a softy when it comes to me. Putting the note away in the new wallet, I happily discover that my old wallet is behind the purse and begin to transfer everything into the new one. Once my new purse is organised, I continue to explore the room.

My next stop is the bathroom I spied earlier, finding a clawfoot bathtub to soak in and doing a mini dance of triumph. I missed the clawfoot tub back in the home I grew up in and the thought of soaking in this one brings me so much happiness. After relieving my full bladder that the twins press against, I turn the water on and begin to fill the tub and search the bathroom for some bubble bath finding a vanilla-scented bubble bath that I instantly use half the bottle of. Foamy bubbles soon cover the surface of the bath water. The vanilla scent fills the room and I sigh, enjoying the soft smell that makes me want to melt. I carefully undress and climb into the clawfoot tub, the scent of vanilla wrapping around me. The heat of the water is comforting, and my sore muscles begin to relax. The twins must have agreed with me as they gently move inside me, causing a soft smile to spread on my face.

"What do you think of this Alpha?" I ask my stomach, gently rubbing the baby bump. I giggle when they kick at my hands harder than earlier, taking their movements as a positive response. Maybe being here is turning into a good thing. The quiet bathroom fills with steam and the scent of vanilla, causing my still-tired body to become slightly drowsy again. I decide that now would be a good time to scrub my body clean and rinse off the suds with the shower hose before I doze off into dreamland and accidentally drown in the water.

Once fully cleaned and the sore muscles from being on the run relaxed, I climb out of the now empty tub and wrap a large, fluffy, black towel around my body. Part of me did not want to leave the warm room, but my stomach is starting to protest its need for food and I need to find something to eat soon since I am eating for three. After towel-drying my hair, I exit the bathroom and head into the walk-in closet to pick out a pair of leggings and a baggy long-sleeved shirt. I couldn't help but sigh, knowing that the shirt I'm wearing is a little too snug, but there is nothing I can do until I go shopping for proper clothing to fit my growing body with Eeva later.

Exiting the closet I am about to try and find Tate when a knock on the one door I have yet to open catches my attention, causing me to turn towards it with suspicion. Taking a deep breath to steady my nervous heart, I reach for the nearest object I can do damage with—a lamp—and position myself just to the side in a defensive stance, ready to attack whoever is on the other side of the wooden door.

"Come in." I call out, watching the door open to reveal Tate, his scent instantly over powering the vanilla from the bubble bath.

"Good mor- Wait, were you going to hit me with that?" I sigh with relief and put the lamp back on the night stand before facing my mate who gives me a puzzled look.

"No, I was going to hit whoever I didn't know with it." I correct, getting a chuckle from him that sends my heart fluttering.

"Technically, you don't know me." He points out with a smirk, making me roll my eyes as I cross my arms over my chest, noticing how his gaze watches my movements.

"Anyways, I thought you would like to know that food is ready, and I brought you a shirt since yours looked too small when I was cleaning your clothes." I smile at Tate's considerate thought, thanking him while I take the offered shirt. Slipping out of the tight long-sleeved shirt, I pull on the soft, cotton, black long-sleeved V-neck that smells faintly like him. Now feeling much more comfortable, I stretch, loving the fact I can move freely once again.

"Not shy around guys?" It wasn't a question, but how Tate words his statement causes me to blush slightly in embarrassment.

"Sorry. I am used to changing in front of my cousin and his mate because they're gay and everything. You should have seen their faces when they would bring me back new clothes and have a fashion show in our living room." I apologize, giving Tate an explanation at my comfort around men I put my trust in. I squeak in surprise when strong arms pull me towards a chiselled chest, Tate's scent enveloping my senses as he tenderly holds me.

"Don't apologize to me. You are my mate. You should be comfortable around me." He says, kissing the top of my head. I can't help but snuggle into him, the sense of security I felt when we left the Dinner returning. If this is how a mate is supposed to be, then count me sucked in and give me a contract to sign.

"Now, come on. Let's go eat." He lets go of me and I instantly miss his warmth. He must have noticed my disappointment as he suddenly takes my hand and leads me out of the room. The hallway he leads me down is a light grey colour with pictures of Tate, Eeva, and three young boys placed every now and then. Being led down the dark wooden stairs, I try my best to take a peek around the front entrance and the next hallway until I stand in a large, bright kitchen. I can't help but smile at the thought of baking inside here while I look at the large counter with a high-end stove and a door to what I assume is the pantry. The thought of the recipes I love so much filling the house with their delicious scent and children running around is feeling I know is close to becoming a reality.

"Sit over there, and I'll bring you some food. I know you've had a rough time, so I want you to get some rest and take it easy for now." Tate directs me to a breakfast nook in the corner of the kitchen, situated under large windows on either side. I smile at how pampering he sounds. The image of a cruel Alpha I once imagined him to be is slowly dissolving into this sweet mate image he displays now. I sit down and take the time to fully look at my mate now that my fight or flight instinct has died down. He has dark chestnut-coloured hair, similar to my own, with lighter natural highlights thrown about. His hair is cut short and styled messily causing my fingers to itch with the need to run them through his hair and feel just how soft his locks are. His broad shoulders connect to solid muscular arms, the same arms that have held me multiple times since meeting yesterday. One thing is for sure, Tate is fit and lean, his body radiating power as an Alpha's body should. His dark green eyes reminded me of the forest in the summer, warm and welcoming with cool undertones. I know that if I stare too deeply into these eyes of his that I will lose myself to him.

"Here you go. Over easy eggs, bacon and hash browns." Tate's voice breaks me from my thoughts as he places a full plate in front of me. My stomach grumbling from the wonderful aroma.

"And some blueberry vanilla tea." He adds, chuckling at my reaction to the food.

"Thank you." I smile graciously at my mate, taking a sip of the herbal tea before digging into my eggs. Tate soon joins me with a plate of his own and adds two pieces of toast to my plate, which I use to soak up the warm egg yolks. The distinctive smell of coffee hits my nose from the green mug Tate sips from, his eyes looking everywhere but at me as my nose scrunches up at the strong scent. Thankfully, the strong smell doesn't cause my stomach to turn as we sit there in silence for a moment before he sighs and looks at my stomach. I see the reluctance to accept my pregnancy reflected in the depth of his eyes and wonder what he is thinking.

"You really did not know about it being illegal, about Breeders being illegal?" He asks with concern etched into his face. I couldn't help but put my left hand on my stomach, nodding yes to answer his question and receiving another deep sigh from Tate.

"I guess only a few knew about the new rule. The Beta pair probably knew. Most wolves probably just decided to ignore it to get free sex." I reply quietly as I think about Abby and her attitude. It all makes sense with how her behaviour took a one-eighty that day.

"They are a bunch of morons if you ask me." Tate growls out in frustration, rubbing his hand against his face.

"Not all of them." I look up to see him staring at me, his eyes filled with love and jealousy. I start to have doubts and wonder if Tate would protect my pups as his own or if I would have to leave this wolf behind. The thought of the latter causes pain to rip through my heart but I will do anything for my babies.

"I will protect you, but I don't like the fact that the pups you are carrying aren't mine." I sigh at his angry words, looking down at my empty plate. I get he must feel terrible knowing that the mate he has waited for is pregnant for someone else, but it's not like he waited for me. Everyone knows of the many girls he had dated before becoming an Alpha. I used to feel sorry for the wolf who would end up as his mate, but seeing how concerned and gentle he is with me makes me happy in a weird way.

"Look, Tate." I begin, deciding I need to stand my ground. I am his mate, his equal, and It's time I start acting like the strong blooded she-wolf I am.

"I am not in the mood for arguing. We just met. I want to get to know you and for you to get to know me, but whether you like it or not, I am keeping these babies." I state clearly and carefully, standing up to put my dishes in the sink. I feel his eyes on me as I make my way out of the kitchen and into the next room that turns out to be the living room, the soft and welcoming sofa making me want to flop onto them as the fireplace in front warms the room. But I there are things I need to do today and Eeva promised to help me. I scan the living room, hoping to find what I am looking for and smile when my eyes instantly locates the house phone located just on the desk by the large bay window. I walk over to pick it up, taking the time to scan through the contacts until I find the person I am looking for—Eeva.

"I told you to let her sleep, you idiot. She's pregnant, for Goddess' sake." Eeva answers - more like yells - into the phone before I could say anything.

"Um 1- My ear!" I shout back, switching the phone to my left ear while I massage the abused right ear.

"And 2- Want to go shopping? I need clothes for my ever-expanding baby bump." I continue, offering an olive branch to the wolf that is now my sister-in-law.

"Sorry about that, Laina. I thought you were Tate calling." Eeva instantly apologizes, causing me to giggle.

"The idiot has called me about ten times today wanting to wake you up since you've slept like the dead since last night." She continues, my mind wandering to thoughts of Tate pacing the house with worry, wanting to make sure I am okay. I smile at the thought, wondering if I was a little to harsh earlier and decide that I will apologize later.

"Anyways, I would love to go shopping with you Laina, you're my new little sister and need to look the role of a Luna. I'll be there in a few." With that, Eeva hangs up before I can speak a word making me roll my eyes at the phone before putting it back in its receiver. I make my way back up the stairs return to the room I woke up in and quickly grab my new purse. After washing my face and brushing my teeth, I head back down the stairs only to see Tate standing in the front hallway with a suspicious look on his handsome face.

"Where are you going?" He asks, his eyes looking at the purse in my hand while I look my shoes in the hallway closet. They weren't in the walk in closet in my room so I can only hope that they are here.

"I'm going shopping with your sister." I reply, finding my warn-out sneakers and slipping them onto my feet.

"I am your mate. I should go with you." He growls possessively, his arms landing on either side of my head against the wall I am leaning on. I can see his emotions swirling in the depth of his eyes as I wonder what his problem is. I get we are mates, but I needed this, some sense of normalcy again. Going out with a she-wolf brings this normalcy back.

"And I am a free person who can go anywhere I want, and I will not be treated any differently. I became a slave to my old pack before running away; I will not be treated as one in my new pack!" I retort, raising my voice and allowing the power in my blood to seep out. Shock fills Tate's eyes, replacing all of the other thoughts, as he stares at me in disbelief. A blush covers my checks when I realize what I have said, turning to look away for a moment.

"Wait? Your new pack?" He questions, his fingers tilting my head to look back at him.

"I figured since we are mates, I should join. If you don't want m-" My words are cut off as Tate's lips are pressed to mine. The kiss is sweet and gentle. I can feel his possessiveness and care he pours into this single kiss as his hands move to wrap me in an embrace.

"I want you." He says when he pulls away, kissing my forehead. My face breaks into a wide grin as he tucks my head under his chin, holding me close to him and running his fingers through my hair.

"Just get yourself a cell phone so that I can reach you and so you can call me until we can perform the initiation ceremony." He adds with a sigh. With a nod, I agree instantly and mentally fist bump as I won my time to go out with Eeva and get away for a bit with these words. The front door swings open, and Eeva sticks her head in, looking around as if she is afraid of being caught.

"Sorry, I was waiting for the yelling to stop before I came in." Eeva states, and I laugh at her as Tate and I pull away from each other to look at the she-wolf.

"So, my mate has the punks for a few hours; you have a meeting to go to Tate and don't worry, Laina is in good hands." My new friend states as she pulls me from her brother's arms and leads me to the front door.

"Bye, bro. Love you." She says in a singsong voice, pushing me out the door and out of his reach as I laugh at her antics.

"Go, go, go! He is possessive and did not like the way I took you away from him." She says as if she is a soldier ordering me about as I climb into her Hummer. She speeds out of the driveway just in time for a pissed-off Tate to run out after us, his eyes glaring at his sister as he shakes his head.

"To the mall!" She exclaims as I sit back, clutching at my stomach that is slightly sore from laughing so hard.

"Hey, if you pass a Tim Horton's, can we stop so I can get a white hot chocolate?" I ask, the craving slamming into me like a brick wall.

"Sure, one thing about our lovely Canada is that Tim Horton's are everywhere." She answers, and I laugh again. I have a feeling that Eeva and I will be remarkably close, almost like true sisters.

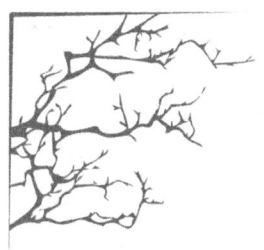

Chapter 9

"I don't need all these clothes!" I exclaim in frustration as I exit the changing room, only to spot Eeva throwing more clothes into the shopping cart. I can't help but shake my head at the brunette woman as she picks clothes for me from dresses to pants, casual to formal and everything else in between. I have a feeling if I let her continue like this, she will turn whatever savings I have into nothing.

"One, you do. I even threw in clothes you can use for after you deliver your babies." She begins, giving me a pointed look.

"Two, they are cute and will fit any occasion. And as the future Luna, you need them. And three, they fit you." I couldn't argue with Eeva's logic as all of the clothes she has chosen for me are in a style I like and many were close to the pre-pregnancy size that I can fit into once the twins are born. With a sigh, I follow behind Eeva as she pushes the cart towards the counter, her eyes scanning around if she missed any other article of clothing from this store that would suit me. It feels like she did not get out to shop much and is using me to enjoy the opportunity to shop until we drop. Heck, I even noticed her throwing in a few pieces for herself, winking at me and making me promise not to tell Tate.

"Come on, preggers, as much as I would love to stay here at the mall, we, unfortunately, don't have all day. You need to look good to see the Elders." I stop at her words, shocked at the mention of the Elders. Not many people can get an appointment right away and would have to wait months just to get anything changed from the leaders of the werewolves. The Elders—ancient werewolves from the first packs—are the ones who make the laws that we have to follow; even the Alpha King who rules over wolf kind needs to listen to these Elders to some degree. They approve of new packs and decide whether war between two packs would be a good or bad decision. They mainly focus on keeping the peace between the packs and presiding over the annual National meeting each spring.

"You managed to get their approval for an audience?" I ask in disbelief. Having Breeders at Pine Paw must have been a huge taboo for the Elders to push my case to the top of their list.

"Yes, I managed to get an appointment. It's easy considering Bloodsvain is one of the oldest packs in Canada." Eeva answers, her head held high with pride. I can't help but wrap my arms around her in a tight hug as best as I can. It dawned on me that running into Bloodsvain territory is the best thing I have ever done since being declared a Breeder.

"Okay, girly, enough sappiness. Let's go check out and head to the next store." She chuckles, hugging me back. I pull away from my new friend, her eyes slightly teary with concern for my well-being and the situation I had been forced into before we continue towards the counter. The store clerk takes each item Eeva places in front of her and scans them, the pile in the cart dwindling as the bags of clothing grow. I decide not to look at the total price, knowing that I will probably stress about how much money I would have to spend and proceed to fish my debit card out from my wallet.

"Should I put everything on the usual tab, Miss Eeva?" The Clerk asks as she continues to carefully fold and bag the clothing, shocking me and making me look up at the two ladies.

"Yes, please, Anne, that would be great. By the way, this is my sister-in-law, Laina." Eeva replies back, taking the many bags of clothing before ushering me out of the store after Anne greets me politely.

"I could have paid!" I state, slightly pouting at the feeling of being treated as a child. I preferred doing things for myself, something I had gotten used to with my parent's passing.

"I know, sweetie, but you are going to be a member of our pack and the Luna. You should get used to being treated like one of us. Besides, our pack owns the town that everything is located on as well as many other businesses in Canada. If you think spending money on you is going to cause Bloodsvain to go bankrupt, think again." Eeva explains with a smile on her face making me sigh in defeat. I guess being Tate's mate did bring benefits, but I still felt a little uneasy.

"But Eeva –" I begin to protest, wanting to voice my need for independence.

"No buts, Laina. As my sister-in-law and Luna, you will allow yourself to be pampered." Eeva cuts me off, her voice stern like my mother's used to be when I was being unreasonable. I sigh in defeat once again, deciding to agree with Eeva's reasoning. I will be the Luna of Bloodsvain soon, so I have to just accept everything that comes with it, including being allowed to spend Tate's money.

"Fine, but let's drop the bags off at the car before we continue shopping, okay?" I relent, seeing a wide smile spread across my friend's face.

"Sounds like a plan." She agrees, leading me towards the parking lot where we deposit the bags from the first store into her Hummer and continue our shopping. After two more stores, I convince the energetic she-wolf to stop at the nearest Chinese buffet for a late lunch. Honestly, I just need a moment to sit and relax my swollen feet.

"After lunch, do you want to head home?" Eeva asks, shoving a whole chicken ball into her mouth. I open my mouth to answer when movement from inside me catches my attention, and I can't help but giggle, placing my hand on where one of the babies kicks.

"One minute, give me your hand." I whisper in awe, taking Eeva's outstretched hand and placing it on my stomach. A couple of seconds later, two sets of feet kick out at us, causing wide grins to spread across our faces. Love blooms for my babies as we sit at our table in silence, the smell of Chinese food and the soft sound of a zither playing in the background, bringing back the sense of normalcy in my life.

"Would you like to shop for them? We could start their nursery." Eeva whispers.

"I'm positive Tate will be happy to see you smiling." She continues in a low voice, not wanting to break this serene moment. With a small smile, I nod, my eyes still on my pregnant stomach. Now free from my Breeder status, I can raise my babies in a room they can grow up in, a room I design and will be able to enjoy as the years pass. This thought brings tears to my eye and I can only blame my emotional state on the pregnancy hormones coursing through my body.

"I would really like that, please, but let's keep the colours neutral for now." I agree with Eeva's suggestion, letting my own wants be voiced. Eeva quickly agrees with me, her excitement for baby shopping matching my own while we finish our meal and leave the buffet to search for children and baby stores. I think back on the horrible shopping experience I had with Abby four months ago and compare it to this one with Eeva. Where Abby snapped at me after I took some time deciding on the nursery, Eeva spent the time comparing cribs and bassinets with me, answering questions I have as she already has her own pups. Having someone like Eeva who waited patiently while I search through every item the stores have to offer for my babies brought happiness surging inside me. I am grateful for how Eeva has treated me so far in these last two days.

She is kind, patient, caring, and sort of motherly, but not once did she pity me; only sympathy and concern are ever shown in her expressive eyes. Once everything is ordered and the delivery date for the twins' nursery furniture is set, Eeva and I make a final stop at the Bell store in search of a new cellphone for me. I find a Samsung phone that I like, and we set up a new account, finally ending our shopping trip.

"Let's not 'shop till we drop' anymore." I yawn, climbing into Eeva's car and clicking the seatbelt into place. My body feels sore and exhausted but I welcome it as it reminds me that I am safe and that this trip out with my new sister-in-law was a success. I never realized how badly I needed something as normal as a shopping day with a friend until now. As Eeva shifts the gear into drive, and we proceed to head back home, I let a soft smile grace my lips. Home. After four months of running I had found a home to live in and watch my twins grow.

"Okay, we'll just shop till we have what we need next time." My friend says sarcastically to my earlier complaint, causing me to roll my eyes at her. Knowing Eeva, if I let her drag me to another shopping spree she would keep shopping even well after I drop with exhaustion. I just hope that I can learn how to reign in this Alpha she-wolf before the next trip comes.

"Have you decided their names yet?" Eeva asks, motioning to my stomach. I smile down, rubbing my pregnant belly.

"No, not yet. I haven't learned their genders, so I am waiting until after they are born." I answer, catching Eeva nod understandingly.

"Well, you still have a few months left, so don't worry." She reassures me, and I smile. But my smile lasts for a few seconds before I turn my head to look out of the passenger window and sigh. There was one nagging problem at the back of my mind. One I've been wondering since running away with the thoughts of finding a pack to call home or finding my mate.

"Okay, ask it, Laina," Eeva says after two songs on the radio fill the silence between us.

"Do you think Tate will get over the fact that these aren't his pups?" I finally say with worry in my voice, my eyes searching Eeva's face.

"Yes, he will. He is just pissed off that you had to go through what you did." Eeva says quietly. I couldn't tell if she is trying to reassure herself or me with these words, but a hopeful smile spreads across my face. I know that things between Tate and me will be hard with my pregnancy situation, but I hope he will eventually accept my babies. I spent four months running away to protect them, and no one - not even my mate - will take them away from me.

Eeva and I both go into our own thoughts after that and I decided to take out my new cellphone from my purse, enjoying the feel of the latest Samsung device in my hand as the large screen comes to life. Taking the notebook I had stored the numbers of important wolves in my life, I begin to slowly add everyone into my new phone—starting with Chris, Jack and Alex—and text each person, letting them know it's me and that I am safe. I get replies back quickly, the three happy to hear from me as I tell them where I am and who my mate is which brings a mixed reaction from Chris and Jack and worry from Alex. As we drive out of the town and towards the forest road, I catch glimpses of wolves running through the trees, me smiling at them as they stop to bow towards us respectfully before continuing about their business. I can't wait to be able to shift and run with them.

"Hey, Eeva, what is your phone number?" I ask with my eyes still on the forest. A larger black wolf than the rest catches my attention, his forest green eyes turning to stare back. Something in me tells me it is Tate, and I can't help but take my phone and snap a picture to enjoy his majestic wolf form when ever I miss him.

"I think it's..." She trails off, thinking for a moment before rattling off the numbers. I quickly key in her cellphone number into my contact list, saving it and sending a quick text. She pulls off the main road and into a smaller dirt road before pulling over to quickly add my new number to her contacts, a grin on her face.

"There now we have each other's number and can talk whenever until we can link one another." I exclaim with a grin, laughing as she widens her eyes and places a hand over her chest.

"Oh darling, you make my life complete." She fake cries in joy, causing me to go into a laughing fit with her antics. To think she still has pup like behavior even though she is mated with pups of her own.

"You know, you look younger when you laugh. I mean for a twenty-year-old who is a soon-to-be mom you-" She muses, looking at me with a grin.

"I'm not twenty." I cut her off, watching her eyes widen with shock this time.

"You're not?" Eeva asks with skepticism.

"No." Is my honest reply with a grimace on my face.

"Then how old are you, Laina?" I could tell that Eeva is weary, her eyes showing even more sympathy than yesterday.

"As of May this year, I turned sixteen." I admitted, twirling a lock of hair with my finger. I look outside to watch the early October breeze rustle through the trees, feeling a little ashamed. Leaves fall in a twirling dance to the ground. The car is silent for a while, and I look to Eeva to see her eyes unfocused. I guess she is mind linking someone, Probably Tate. When her eyes regain focus, she starts driving once again, a frown on her face.

"You told Tate, didn't you?" I say, feeling both relieved and a little worried. What will he do knowing my age now?

"Yes. I'm sorry, Laina, but Tate needed to know that you are considered a minor here in Canada even if pack laws dictate wolves to be adults at sixteen." Eeva replies. I spy the worry in her eyes as I turn back to look out the window and watch the scenery.

"Thank you." I whisper as we pass by a few log cabins, cottages and houses that I assume are homes to pack members.

"For what?" She asks with a smile in my direction.

"For being a true friend and treating me like an adult."

"Why wouldn't I treat you like an adult or be a friend to you? You're practically my sister now that you're my baby brother's mate." She reasons, and I smile.

"I'm glad for that too."

"Me too, Laina. Even though Tate had girlfriends, he always kept searching for his mate. My brother has anger issues, but I haven't seen him lose control in the last two days since meeting you." Eeva adds. I could hear the relief in her voice as she talks about Tate. I hated knowing that he had other girls in his life before me but felt like a hypocrite considering I am pregnant for someone else. This whole situation is just fucked up.

Eeva decides to change the radio station, and we begin to belt out the songs we know. The mood lightens as she points out the pack house—a five-story mansion that I am told was built seven hundred years ago—and other important buildings in the pack. We pass by an elementary school for children, a pack hospital, and a library built to help the younger wolves study. Finally, we arrive home, and I take in the other houses scattered about that I missed in our mad dash to escape to the mall this morning.

"My brother's house has six bedrooms. I think right now you are in one of the guestrooms, so I'll wash your new clothes and the baby clothes, then bring it to your room." Eeva says as we enter the house with the bags from our shopping trip.

"I can help." I state, following her to the laundry room that is located on the first floor of this massive place just to the side of the kitchen—thank the Goddess for first-floor laundry rooms because I currently hate stairs.

"Laina, how far along are you?" Eeva questions as we set the bags on the floor in the pristine room, the machines all high-end and state-of-the-art perfection for the cleanest laundry possible.

"Somewhere between four to four and a half months." I say, placing a hand on my stomach.

"Well, a she-wolf gives birth to her pups at five to six months, so no work for you. You sit and look pretty while I help get you set up." Eeva orders with her no-nonsense motherly tone.

"But Eeva!"

"No buts, go sit." She cuts me off, ushering me out of the laundry room and towards the living room.

"Okay, fine, I will. But you call me if you need help." I concede as she hugs me and disappears once again into the laundry room, slamming the door shut as her response.

I smile and head to the kitchen to make tea, realizing that it is five-thirty in the afternoon. I figure that Tate will be hungry when he gets back from dealing with his pack, and I want to surprise my mate with dinner. Fluttering around the kitchen, I familiarize myself with where everything is placed as I gather the ingredients and equipment I would need from the fridge, cupboards and pantry.

"What are you making?" Strong arms wrap around me, and soft lips find a spot on my neck as a warm body that sends happy shivers down my spine presses me against it.

"Chicken and waffles." I reply, a smile on my face as I lean into Tate. His scent wraps around me as his body tenses slightly with our contact before he relaxes into me once again. He towers above me, my head just reaching past his shoulder, making my frame feel small and safe inside his embrace.

"Sounds delicious. Do you want any help?" He asks, his lips finding my neck once again as he plants soft, gentle kisses.

"S-sure, do you know where the waffle maker is?" I lush at the flustered tremor in my voice with his close proximity, knowing that he heard it as well. With a chuckle, Tate lets me go and walks to a cupboard I have yet to go through instantly making me miss his warm touch, the mate bond between us simmering gently in the air. Returning to my side, I begin to instruct Tate on what to do with this recipe, watching his large hands skilfully mix the waffle batter as I work on breading and shallow pan-frying the chicken.

"So, what were you learning in school before you..." Tate asks once we engross ourselves in the task of cooking. His voice trails off at the end, neither of us wanting to bring up the Breeder subject.

"I was going for interior design at the local college. I always loved creating and decorating when I was growing up. After my parents' death, I ended up shutting myself off from everyone and focused on school. It allowed me to by-pass grade school and took me about two years to finish high school courses since I took courses in the summer and online. I never felt like a normal teenager as many kids my age were hanging out with friends and partying, and all I wanted was to help out my cousin and his mate." I answer with a shrug, smiling as I think about my cousin.

"Chris took me in when he was eighteen. I felt that he had to raise me and thought I would build a career to help him out. He surprised me by enrolling me in the college courses on my sixteenth birthday. I would have started school last month and only two years away from getting my degree before being told my role..." My voice trails off as I let out a long sigh, thinking about the career I could have had and what I could have done. I wish I could bring my sketchbook from my room in Chris' house to show Tate the work I put in, but I know that that would probably never happen. My fingers itched for a sketchbook, some sketch pencils, and a sturdy ruler to come up with concepts and designs for the rooms in this house. I notice that it has more of a cold, distant feel to the living room, the front hallway and the entrance, and I guess that the other rooms that I have yet to explore are empty and cold and in need of redecorating. This house definitely needs a bit of a makeover and a woman's touch.

"If you want, there is a study down the hall with a computer. It's my office, and you can use it to take courses online from your college while you redesign one of the rooms upstairs for your own office." Tate offers, his face lowered in a bashful way while a slight pink tinge colours his cheeks. My eyes widen as I process his words before I fling my arms around him as best as I can with my pregnant belly protruding out. The rumours of Tate being a heartless monster seem to vanish with how warm and caring he is towards me. Stretching up on my toes, I pull Tate's head towards mine, kissing him quickly with a peck on the lips in my excited state.

"Thank you so much!" I say happily when we pull away, surprise and shock on his face as he holds me in his embrace.

"Anything to make you happy, Laina. I can't wait to see what you do with the house to make it more like a home. To be honest with you, I usually stay at the pack house to do work. I haven't had a reason to stay here other than to grab clean clothes until you came around." I watch as another blush creeps across his face, the butterflies fluttering around my heart at his confession. We go back to cooking our dinner as we talk about our day. I laugh when I tell Tate about all the stores I went to, and he sighs.

"I have a feeling Eeva went overboard with shopping and snuck stuff in for herself, didn't she?" He questions, and I grin mischievously. He was right, though, as Eeva had spent some time shopping for herself, but I refused to snitch on her as I promised not too, even if Tate is her brother.

"Finally getting along?" Eeva asks as she walks into the kitchen just as Tate and I finish cooking. She helps us set the table as I stretch my tired body.

"We always get along." Tate answers, pulling me to his side and rubbing my back. I lean into his touch, enjoying the small massage as my tense muscles relax with the small pressure.

"Well, that's good to hear. Laina, I put the clothes in your room and the baby stuff in a basket for when you find a room to decorate." Eeva states, snatching a piece of fried chicken from the plate and snacking on it.

"Now, I have to go. My mate and the pups have a surprise waiting for me. Enjoy your meal, you two." With that, Eeva saunters out of the house. Tate sigh with relief, a boyish grin on his face as he helps me sit at the breakfast nook in the kitchen.

"I love my sister, but Hurricane Eeva can be too much to handle." I can't help but laugh at his helpless look and agree with my mate as he walks towards the fridge and brings a jug of orange juice and two glasses to the table.

"Now, let's eat!" He exclaims excitedly like a little pup, pouring each of us a glass of orange juice. It doesn't take long for the both of us to load our plates with the soft and fluffy waffles and crispy chicken. After a moment of comfortable silence and the sound of cutlery clinking across the plates, I look at Tate with a shy smile.

"Do you want to get to know each other and play a round of questions?" My question comes out quietly, almost a whisper. I can see the smile spreading on my mate's face with my initiative in getting to know him as he takes a bite of a piece of chicken dripping it in Canadian maple syrup.

"Sure, what's your favourite colour?" He questions back, a grin spreading across my face.

"It's a deep green, like your eyes. They remind me of the forest." I answer, smiling at the thought of being able to run in the forest again and watching his eyes widen in surprise.

"What's your favourite food?" I ask, wanting to know what I can cook up for him in the following days.

"Believe it or not, it's actually chicken and waffles. Eeva would have it ready for me every time I enter her diner. But now I think yours are actually the best I've ever had." I feel my face heating up with his compliment at my recipe, smiling at the memory of how I learned it.

"It's a recipe my mother taught me. I have all of her recipes memorized." His eyes soften with the mention of my parents as he mentions he would love to taste all the recipes eventually. Our game of "Questions" continues while the pile of food slowly disappears between us, the two of us enjoying our second day of knowing each other happily. Eventually we decide to move to a more comfortable area and make our way to the living room where I spot a fuzzy blanket and promptly get comfortable on the sofa.

Sitting on either end of the large sofa, Tate and I start chatting about our childhood and I find myself laughing more than I ever have as Tate describes what it was like growing up with Eeva. I can't help but feel more drawn to him as we slowly get to know each other, the mate bond making it easy for us to open up to one another. Before I know it, I am comfortably curled up against him as we cuddle. The lighting in the room coming from the small fire crackling away in the large fireplace..

"You should go to sleep." Tate whispers, his hand drawing soft circles on my back as I yawn for the eighth time in the last three minutes.

"I don't want to." I whisper back, looking up at him and staring into his eyes. He chuckles and lowers his forehead to mine, rubbing our noses together.

"Then how about we get ready for bed and you cuddle with me in my room while we watch something on T.V.? This way, if you fall asleep, you'll be comfortable." He reasons, planting a kiss on my forehead. I want to protest, want to continue talking and learning about the man that was made for me, but reason wins and I nod.

"Okay. Just so you know, I like cuddling." I agree, getting a deep chuckle from Tate.

"I have noticed you like cuddling." He muses, playfully tugging on my hair. With a grin, we head upstairs where I promptly make my way to my room in search of pajamas and find all the new clothes bought today put away neatly in the closet. Smiling, I send a thank-you text to Eeva before picking out a pair of baggy pajama pants and a soft cotton T-shirt for bed then head to the bathroom to clean up and change. When done, I make my way down the dark hallway towards the only room with light filtering through the door.

The first thing I notice when I walk into the room is Tate's scent as I look everywhere for him. It clings to everything, soothing me and making me want to curl up and sleep even more. A door to my right opens and out walks Tate from what I realize is the bathroom with a pair of pajama pants slung low around his waist, and his chiselled torso bare for me to enjoy. He climbs into bed before inviting me to join and promptly pulls me to his side as soon as I climb into the king-size bed under the warm blankets. I watch as he pulls out a remote for the T.V. from under his pillow and roll my eyes at this, deciding that we will need to make a rule that the remote must be on the bedside table as Tate flicks through the channels looking for something to watch, finally landing on Finding Nemo.

"Really?" I ask, laughing at his choice of movie.

"What? It's a classic, babe." He states with a roll of his eyes, and I giggle again.

"Okay, okay, we can watch it." I concede as I snuggle closer to Tate. I smile when his hand continues to rub circles on my back, his head leaning towards my direction every now and then to kiss the top of my head. Sometime during the first few minutes of the movie, my eyelids grow heavy, and I find myself falling asleep.

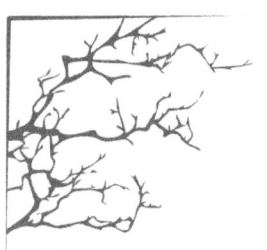

Chapter 10

The first week of being with Tate flies by as he and I get used to the routine of living together. I had slowly moved my clothing and other items into Tate's room, smiling when I learned that he had kept half of his walk in closet open for when he found his mate. The vanity I fell in love with in the guestroom was moved the day after our first time in bed, Tate making sure to place it in front of the large bay window that faces the backyard stating I deserve the best lighting when getting ready. The best part about this week is the time I spent exploring the house as much as I wanted, learning there is a basement with a large workout room on the fourth day of living here. I couldn't help but squeal with glee when I saw all of the workout equipment, going as far as doing some light workout with a worried and panicking Tate frantically trying to keep the heavier weights away from me much to my protest. It seems he has accepted me being pregnant and has slowly warmed up to calling the twins our pups.

There were times when walking around the forest with my mate when we would pass by his pack members, and his possessive side would show. The first time I convinced him to go for a walk with me, a Warrior got too close thinking a rogue was attacking his Alpha. I had to pull Tate's black wolf form by the scruff of his neck off of the Warrior while screaming and yelling at him to calm down and back up. I could tell with just my touch alone he visibly relaxed and soon became worried he might accidentally harm me. With me distracting Tate, the Warrior was able to run free to a safe distance and Tate wrapped his huge furry body around me, his black fur warming me up as his scent rubbed into me. I introduced myself as Tate's mate, my hands scratching my mate's ear as the Warrior stared back. With a respectful bow, he left us alone to continue our walk in the forest that day. I guess that Warrior warned the rest of the wolves as a way to stop them from accidentally attacking me since we rarely saw anyone else. Even when we did see another wolf, they would stay a respectful distance away from Tate and I, greeting us with a respectful bow.

I can't help but relish the sight of the calm forest as I sit on a fallen log. Tate is running around being chased by small children in his wolf form as Eeva and I watch on. Eeva's mate is Tate's Beta, and due to pack business, he is on a mission to make a treaty with a new smaller pack and will return later tonight. For the last few days, the four of them have joined us for meals and outings around the territory until Last night her mate left for the new pack.

"How is Tate now with you being pregnant?" Eeva asks as her youngest, Jonathan, manages to jump onto Tate's back, getting a cheer from his two brothers while the pup clings to his uncle's fur. I chuckle at the young pups with their uncle. It makes me excited for when the twins are born, and Tate could play with them like this.

"He still has some issues with it, but he has come around. Honestly, if you had seen him when I was designing my office, you would have thought they were his pups, he even calls the twins ours." I answer, rolling my eyes as I think back to when I found the perfect room for my office.

"He is such a worrywart and wouldn't allow me to paint or move any furniture. Don't get me started with even doing a small workout. I'm positive the only weights I'm allowed to touch are the one- and two-pound weights." I rant, feeling annoyed by how my mate acts. Two days ago, the paint and furniture, as well as the laptop and electronics for my office arrived. I tried my best to carry the lighter objects up the stairs, but Tate would take them from my hands and make me wait inside the room. When he stepped out to take a call, I had decided to start painting, nearly spilling the can of paint when he came in to lecture me about resting while he does all the work. It took the whole day, but I managed to get the room decorated while barely having to move a muscle and being very annoyed by Tate's attitude around me doing any form of work. But it does make me smile knowing how caring he is towards me and my pregnant state. I know deep down that he will make a wonderful father to the twins.

"Speaking of that office of yours, how is it going for you?" Eeva asks. I had started my college courses back up again three days ago. It felt nice having something to do when left alone at home while Tate was working. Tate had gone out and surprised me the day my office was completed by buying all the art materials I would want plus more that I stored in the closet reminding me that he is proud of me for not giving up my career path and that the pack could use an interior designer even if I will soon have Luna duties to perform.

"It's going really well. I love having a space of my own. I somehow managed to get caught up with all the work I missed out on." I answer, leaning back on the tree behind me and taking a deep breath. I haven't become a member of the pack just yet, and neither have I taken on the role of Luna yet. Tate and Eeva suggest I wait until after giving birth as the ritual may cause harm to the twins. Instead, I spend my free time when not with Tate or Eeva doing my schoolwork or learning about the pack and my duties as a Luna. Some things I do now with Bloodsvain are look over the businesses and go through the members' list to see who needs to be given a role in the pack. Tate had asked me to redesign a few of the buildings they own, and I happily took on the challenge when he said there will be an unlimited budget.

"Well, that's good. Finish your schooling so you can start redesigning the pack house. Goddess only knows it needs an update." My friend chuckles. I feel a wet nose sniffing at my hand and turn to see Tate looking at me, a bemused expression on his wolf face.

"Is it time to head home?" I ask, my hand reaching out to scratch under his chin as the three boys slowly trudge over.

"Mom, can we play with Uncle Tate again later tomorrow?" Vinny asks. The eldest of the three has his brother Jonathan sleeping on his back as the second pup comes up behind him. I open my eyes for Andy to come in for a hug as he sleepily rubs his eyes, the pup letting out a yawn. I hear the sound of Tate shifting into his human form and putting on clothes before picking up the pup, taking him from my arms and wrapping an arm around my shoulders.

"They are all tuckered out and need their bed now. Let's get Eeva and the boys home, then we can have a quiet night." Tate says as Andy falls asleep against his uncle's shoulder. The sight of Tate holding a pup causes me to smile. I can't wait for the next few weeks to fly by so we can raise the twins. Eeva takes Jonathan from Vinny as the six of us walk through the forest towards Eeva's house. I decide that walking is now done as I sink into the comfortable rocking chair on Eeva's front porch that I jokingly state will be rehomed with me soon while Tate rolls his eyes and takes Andy inside with Eeva chuckling behind him before taking Johnathan in as well. Vinny gives me a hug, saying good night before he sleepy trudges into the house. I have a feeling Tate will find him on the couch in the living room and have to carry him to bed as well.

While I wait for my mate, I watch the leaves on the oak tree fall to the ground. Fall is my favourite time of year with beautiful colours and the chance to wear cozy warm sweaters, there is nothing much to hate about it other than the cold rainy days. When the weather is as nice as it is today, I would I find myself missing running in wolf form. I know that in this slightly chilly weather I would be able to enjoy a run without dying from the heat of the glaring sun on my thick fur like I do in the summer. But my favourite part is being able to dress up for Halloween, the only time I am very childish.

"Comfortable?" I look up to see Tate smiling down at me from his spot as he leans against the door frame. I smile at my mate and hold my hand out for him, watching him take it and lean forward to leave a kiss on the back of it making my skin shiver from the sparks that come with the mate bond

"Can we get a rocking chair for our porch?" I ask as Tate helps me to my feet and holds me close in a gentle hug.

"Sure. We can get two if you want, one for each of us." He suggests, causing me to grin. The idea of having a comfortable rocking chair on the porch makes me sigh contentedly as I can just picture spending my mornings with my laptop and a cup of tea as I do school work. We say our farewells to Eeva before getting into Tate's Jeep and driving home.

Tate decides to order us a pizza for dinner, picking it up on our way home from a mom and pop shop. As soon as pull into the driveway, I waddle towards the porch and instantly make my way onto the sofa while Tate grabs us drinks and plates from the kitchen before curling up beside me while we agree to watch Say Yes to the Dress. Tate won't admit it, but I got him into the show. Yesterday, I caught him secretly watching it in his study, so I took a quick video to send to Eeva. Apparently, she couldn't stop laughing when she saw the serious look on Tate's face as he commented that some girl should have chosen the Lazaro dress that flattered her figure and stated that if I had not come along as his mate, she would have sworn he was gay and using his exes as cover ups.

"Have you decided on baby names yet, Laina?" Tate asks as I take a large bite of the meat lover's pizza.

"Not yet. I have a few names in mind right now, but we can decide when they are born." I answer once my mouth isn't full of food, smiling sheepishly at Tate. I watch his reaction closely, catching a slight smile playing on his lips.

"I agree, we can decide when they are born." He agrees instantly leaning over to kiss my cheek. With dinner done and the show over, we decide to head to bed early as our nephews tired us out. I love the feeling of falling asleep in his arms with his scent wrapping around me. Soon we will be able to complete the mating ritual. I just have to wait another three months for when the babies are born for us to be together forever.

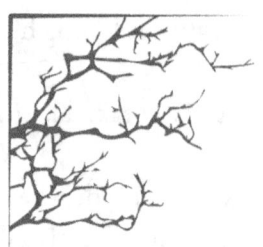

Chapter 11

Pain!

It is all I can feel with it gripping my body in terror as I wake up, clutching at my sides. I let out a scream as a spasm rocks through my body, causing me to curl up as best as I can to try and alleviate the stabbing sensation in my abdomen. Something inside me tells me that something is wrong, that something is happening to my babies as tears stream down my face.

"Tate!" I scream out, praying that the sleeping wolf beside me wakes up quickly. I don't know how much of this pain I can endure. Feeling my mate jump out of bed, I catch his green orbs glowing, searching for danger. His bright eyes soon land on my curled-up form and panic settles inside me while I whimper as another wave of pain shoots through me, the tears continuing to flow.

"What's wrong, baby?" I see his own panic-stricken look on his face as Tate rushes around the bed and to my side. His hands brush away the hair that sticks to my face, his eyes searching my body for any clue that could be causing this pain. My body shivers from the cold sweat now coating my skin as I cry out in pain once again when another stabbing sensation shoots through me.

"I... I don't know." I cry out, fear lacing my voice as I answer his question. I close my eyes as yet another spasm rocks through me and do my best not to scream myself hoars. All I know is I need help, and I need it now. Suddenly, a light flashes across my closed eyes and I find myself involuntarily opening them to see Tate turning on the lights in our room and bringing a cellphone to his ear.

"Doc, have a bed ready at the hospital now!" He orders without hesitation, ending the call just as swiftly as he started it. He stuffs the device into his pocket before gently picking me up. With me now securely in his arms, he pauses as something catches his eyes and does his best to shield me.

"Fuck." He curses, panic radiating off of him. I turn to look down at the spot I was just laying only to see a large spot of dark read blood and the feeling of something wet and sticky on my legs alerts me that something is wrong with my babies. Fear once again grips my heart as I clutch at my pregnant belly. I pray to all the Gods and Goddesses who may listen that my babies will be okay.

Tate rushes out the house as fast as he can and places me gently into the passenger side of his Jeep, strapping me in and shutting the door in one practically seamless motion. I watch my frantic mate rush around the vehicle with panic in his eyes before he settles into the driver's seat, not bothering to put on his seatbelt before he speeds out of the driveway.

"Hang on, Laina." He pleads through gritted teeth as I scream with pain yet again. I am grateful for being safely strapped in as Tate increases the car's speed with each and every scream and moan of pain that escapes my lips. Somehow he manages to quickly avoid wolves that cross the road, all while screaming at them to get out of the way. Fear and despair lace his voice while he assures me that everything will be okay and to just stay awake. His eyes flicker between my body that is curled in on itself and the road, his knuckles white from tightly gripping the steering wheel as he talks to me, trying to keep my mind off of the pain. The drive feels like an eternity has passed until the Jeep finally screeches to a halt in front of the building I remember to be the pack hospital. Wolves rush out to greet Tate while he rushes to my side and gingerly takes me out of the passenger seat, the smell of blood lingering in the air.

"Let's get her to an ultrasound, stat." A man orders, pushing a bed towards Tate and allowing my mate to settle me onto the surface. The group of doctors and nurses rush us inside as my eyes glaze over from the pain. All I can do is weakly hold onto Tate's hand.

The next thing I know, I find myself in a large, white room, a cold gel being squirted onto my stomach while Tate holds me down. Tears escape from my eyes when I notice the nurse readying an ultrasound machine and a sinking feeling of dread weighs down my chest.

"Alpha, you need to stay calm and listen to what my team says." The man states plainly, his eyes looking sternly at Tate while a nurse does her job. My eyes wander over to a screen, the ultrasound image showing a picture of what I know to be my babies even with my blurry, tear-filled eyes.

"She is going to have to go for emergency surgery now if we are to save their lives." I hear the nurse state grimly. The scent of blood continues to grow as I feel something pierce my arm, noticing an I.V. dripping fluid into me. Soon, the medicine takes effect, and drowsiness begins to set in.

"Baby, listen to me! Everything will be fine, and when you wake up, I will be right here waiting for you." I hear Tate's voice as his fingers wipe away my tears. He kisses my lips gently and nuzzles his face into the crook of my neck. Finally, darkness takes me, and the pain disappears. I just hope that my babies are okay.

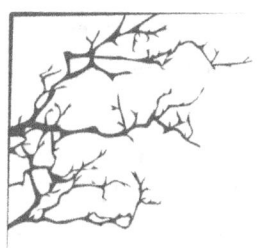

Chapter 12

Beep

A soft beeping fills the room, causing annoyance to bubble inside me. The pain from earlier is finally gone and all I want is sleep.

Beep

There it goes again. I sigh, exasperated, realizing that this sound isn't going to stop until someone turns off the stupid machine making said noise.

Beep

Groaning, I open my heavy eyes and see a spotless white ceiling above me. The room is dimly lit, making the otherwise sterile room comfortable for me to open my tired eyes without flinching.

Beep

My eyes search the room for where the sound comes from until finally, I notice a scattering of strange machines only for my gaze to land on the one machine causing that awful noise. A stupid heartbeat monitor glares and blares back at me, the steady beeping monitoring my heart beat. I wish that someone would shut it off so that I can return to peace and quiet.

"How are you feeling, beautiful?" My head turns to a hoarse voice as I catch Tate smiling at me with relief. He looks haggard and tired with dark circles under his eyes. He scoots over on the chair he's sitting on to come closer to the bed where I lay, taking my hand in his as he places a soft kiss on the back of my hand.

"I feel numb and not as bloated. Why do I feel normal again?" I answer, a frown on my lips. My limbs refuse to move for me to rest my hand on my stomach, to feel the twins inside me, my ritual at this point. I go to turn my head, but Tate stops me, forcing me to look into his eyes as he gives me a sad smile.

"Before you look, listen to me." He says in a sad tone, his green eyes tearing up as a weak smile plays at his lips. A bad omen tugs at my heart as he kisses my forehead and takes a deep breath inhaling my scent.

"The doctor tried to do everything he could. Only one of them made it." His words are soft and slow, and silence follows as what he just said begins to sink in. With eyes widening and tears blurring my vision before they cascade down my face, my heart begins to break when everything settles.

I lost one.

My babies... and I lost one.

"Hush, Laina, it's going to be okay." Tate consoles climbing into the bed with me and wrapping me in his arms. I clutch at his shirt as I bury my face into his chest, letting out heart-wrenching sobs. All the praying I did to save my twins did nothing. One had died on me and now I feel like a failure of a mother. But that is because I am, I failed my babied in keeping them safe.

"W-What h-happened?" I hiccup out through my sobs pleadingly. I need to know how one of the twins died.

"The umbilical cord choked her to death. Somehow, she managed to get it wrapped around her neck, and her sister tried to help free her on instinct. That's why you bled so much." I couldn't help but feel pride for the sisterly love the two had built inside my womb, but my sobs grow knowing that the two would never grow up together. The daydreams I pictured of two little pups chasing each other around the home Tate and I built in the last few days shatter as sadness takes hold of me.

Knowing they will never grow up together breaks everything inside me, that they will never celebrate their birthday, or gossip about boys. That they will never plan on what path in life to take. Pure sorrow fills my heart and mind and I let the pain take over as I cry my broken heart out.

Suddenly, the sound of a tiny wail breaks my sorrowful state and brings me back to my senses. Tate sighs, brushing away the stray tears on my face and kissing my eyelids before getting up and making his way to the end of the bed. The sound of wailing comes from a wooden bassinet I hadn't noticed before, a bassinet that Tate reaches over and rises with a pink bundle in his arms, a soft smile on his face. He slightly bounces the fluffy bundle while making his way back to me.

"Hush, little one. Mommy just woke up and is hurting too. You'll be in her arms soon." He coos as the tiny bundle quiets slightly but continues its little sobs.

"Is she...?" I ask hopefully, my eyes following the tiny, crying baby in his arms.

"Yes. She is your - I mean – she is our little girl, our daughter." He answers with a loving smile as he passes the bundled-up baby into my waiting arms. I find myself enamoured as I stare down at the little pup, her cries silencing as she settles into my embrace. I smile at her, wiping tears off of her tiny little face and watching her doze off once again now that she is safe in my embrace.

"Hi, sweetie. Welcome to the world." I whisper, gently kissing her face while Tate climbs into the bed with us. He wraps his arms around me, letting me lean into his chest as we just sit in the quiet room. Well, an almost quiet room. That stupid heartbeat monitor needs to be destroyed.

"Hello, Alpha I- oh- Luna, you're awake." A nurse greets as she approaches the room with a bottle suited for a newborn in her hand. She stops at the door, smiling at the three of us as her eyes glaze over. I have a feeling she is linking someone before her focus returns to the three of us in the bed.

"I was going to come to feed the little princess, but would you like to?" She asked, coming to my side of the bed and extending the bottle towards me.

"Actually, I wanted to breastfeed her if that's okay." I state, wanting to refuse the formula-filled bottle. I watch as the nurse sends a sympathetic smile my way as she takes one of my hands gently and places the bottle into it before backing away a respectful distance.

"Unfortunately Luna, because of the drugs used during the operation, you will be unable to breastfeed. I'm sorry to ruin your plans." She says quietly. I nod dejectedly at her, knowing that some medications can affect the breastmilk of a nursing mother and decide that arguing with her will bring nothing. I move the bottle to a more comfortable position in my hand, bringing the rubber nipple to my baby's lips and coax her into accepting it, smiling happily as she proceeds to drink knowing that she will need the nutrients to grow.

"You're a natural!" The nurse states, and I smile at her enthusiasm.

"I used to babysit and help out at the pack hospital at my old Pack. I learned how to care for pups and how to coax newborns into drinking from a bottle." I answer my eyes, never leaving the pup in my arms. I watch as the nurse visibly relax with my words and guess that she probably knows I'm sixteen and most likely thought I wouldn't know how to raise my own child with me being so young.

"That's good to know. The doctor will be in tomorrow morning, and another nurse will come to bring the next bottle when you need it. I'll leave the three of you now to enjoy the rest of your evening. Have a good night, Alpha Tate and Luna Laina." The nurse gives a respectful bow before exiting the room. Tate and I stay silent, both of us enjoying the calm night as our baby sips at her bottle. Soon, with the bottle empty and the little pup burped, Tate takes her away to have her diaper changed before placing her back into her bassinet.

He crawls back into bed with me after moving the bassinet to my side of the bed, both of us needing sleep after the last few days we've had. Snuggling into my mate's embrace, I close my eyes and let my exhausted body have the rest it needs. Between the traumatic birth of my pup and learning the loss of the other, I need to let my body and mind settle if I am to be a good mother to the little one sleeping soundly beside me.

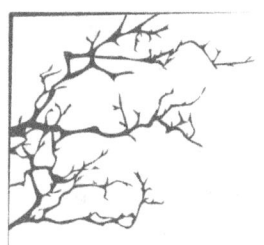

Chapter 13

My eyes once again open to the annoying sound of the heartbeat monitor and all I can think is how much I hate that machine with a passion as it continues to beep with my every heartbeat. Glaring at the monitor, I slowly sit up only to feel my body being pulled back down and held captive against a muscular chest.

"Where do you think you're going?" Tate mumbles, his voice husky with sleep as he nuzzles against my hair. I grin and relax against my mate, deciding to leave the grudge against the machine connected to my body for now as I enjoy the sparks that ignite by the connection of our bodies.

"I was going to smash the stupid machines connected to me." I admit with the heart monitor once again beeping to punctuate my statement. I can't wait to get rid of these machines, especially the one with its annoying beeping. I just want to be home with Tate and our baby girl and mourn the death of my other child quietly. As if connected to my thought of her, a tiny cry of protest rings out from the bassinet. Tate groans before releasing me from his arms. He proceeds to stand from the hospital bed to gently lift the small pup from her bed, cooing softly to her as he cries settle down.

A light knock is rapt on the door before the nurse from last night walks in, giving us a quick greeting and checking over our pup before handing me a warm bottle. Taking this as our cue to feed, the little baby, Tate hands her to me with her still wrapped in her pink blanket and I get to work with placing the rubber nipple to her lips and watching her latch onto it. The sound of my pup feeding fills my heart with warmth, and I take the time to just stare at her innocent little face.

"So, do you have any names for her?" Tate asks as I feed our baby girl. I have a few, but there were two names I would want for her first and middle name.

"Julia Chris Randall-Silvermoon," I answer absentmindedly, turning my head just far enough to see the shock on my mate's face when I say his last name.

"Why my last name?" He asks, unsure. I grin before I turn back to Julia. Seeing that her eyes were wide awake, staring back at me as she releases the now empty bottle, her face content at being filled. I hand the bottle to Tate and proceeded to burp her, smiling when she lets out the smallest burp before she settles into me.

"You may not have sired her, but as far as she will ever know, you are her father through and through. I will not allow anyone else to raise her but my mate, and that is you." I answer honestly, seeing the beaming smile grow radiantly as Tate comes to sit beside me and pulls me into his arms, his lips kissing my temple gently as we look down at Julia.

"I plan to name her sister Kelly Lynn Randall-Silvermoon. She needs a name to be buried with." My throat clenches with pain as a whimper escapes. I could still feel the shattering pain that comes with Kelly dying before even having a chance to live. I would give anything to turn back time and have the girls born just a day earlier to prevent this tragedy, but I know I can't. I would have to live knowing that I now have a little angel living with my parents in the Goddess' court. Calloused hands wipe away stray tears that fall from my eyes and I take in Tate's scent, calming myself as I lean closer into his embrace. I am glad I found Tate when I did, I don't think I would have survived that night my pups were birthed if I hadn't.

"May I ask why Kelly?" Tate questions gently, his hands drawing soothing circles on my arms.

"She is named after my great grandmother. I remember her being kind and caring when I was a pup, and I hope that she can take care of her namesake with my parents where ever their souls are." I answer. I feel my arms slowly growing tired in their position of holding Julia, watching her little eyes slowly close. She is adorable when sleepy, and I wish I could take a picture and send it to Chris.

"Let me see our little Julia." Tate whispers, his hands moving from around me to in front as he lifts our now sleeping baby from my arms.

"Hey!" I protest, trying to reach out and take her back from Tate, only for my mate to elude my reaching hands and gently rock Julia in his arms.

"Hush, babe, Julia is sleeping." He scolds me with a playful frown on his face. I watch as he takes her to a table, seeing his quick hands change her diaper before shaking my head helplessly and lean back in the pillows. I watch silently as Tate cleans up Julia without waking her before returning her to her bassinet and joining me in bed. As he settles in and wraps me once more in his embrace, a knock on the door sounds before opening. A man in a lab coat appears in the entryway with a friendly smile on his face.

"How are my patients today?" The man asks, walking towards my bed and nodding respectfully at Tate and me. A clipboard is held in his left hand while he fumbles in his right pocket before procuring a pen and clicking it open.

"Well, Julia is fast asleep, and Laina here is comfortable. I think the machines have her annoyed." Tate answers, causing the man I now know as my Doctor to look quizzically at us just as the stupid heart monitor beeps once more, causing me to growl at it.

"That's our pup. Yes, I am comfortable, and yes, I am ready to destroy the machines hooked up to me, especially this stupid heart monitor." I answer the Doctor, turning my head to glare at the heart monitor as it makes an especially loud beep. The doctor chuckles for a moment at my statement and writes notes in my file. I could see the amusement in his eyes before he turns to quickly scan Julia. I swear if I didn't place my hand on Tate's leg, he would have growled and bared his claws at the doctor, who is only doing his job.

"Both of you seem to be doing well, and my estimation right now before I do a check-up is that you will be able to go home tomorrow at the latest." I smile at the Doctor's words, excitement filling me at the prospect of going. I want to leave this hospital with its sterile smell. I want to be at home with the scent of Tate wrapping around me in our comfortable bed and the smell of breakfast as we sit in our breakfast nook.

"I am Altrex, the pack's Doctor, but everyone calls me Doctor Rex." Doctor Rex introduces himself as he comes to stand on the other side of my bed, away from Tate. I could tell my mate's protective side is taking over as his arms tighten slightly around me, and he constantly glances at our sleeping pup.

"I can't wait to get you two home safe." He grumbles into my ear, causing a bemused smile to spread across my face while he nuzzles my neck. Men, they could be jealous monsters at the most random of times.

"Now I have to check your cuts and stitches and do a few more tests to make sure you are healing fine. Tate, if you don't mind, I need you to let Laina go so that we can see how well she is healing." Doctor Rex states with his own bemused expression. I can tell right away these two are friends as Tate grumbles incoherent words, which I believe are curses towards the Doctor, before he gives me a kiss on my cheek and releases me. I watch Tate stand only to hover close to the edge of the bed causing me to roll my eyes while I slowly sit up.

Doctor Rex performs the usual checks from listening to my lungs and heart – although the stupid heart monitor is still beating at a steady rhythm – to taking my temperature and blood pressure. After going through the motion, I am told to lie down and raise my shirt just enough for him to see my incisions from the emergency surgery. I turn my head, looking away and into Tate's eyes, not wanting to look at my flat stomach right now while Doctor Rex skims over the stitches and takes note of what he sees in my file.

"I have some good news. After checking everything over, I believe you can head home tonight." Doctor Rex announces before mentioning I can fix my shirt and sit up once again. Tate helps me straighten out clothes and supports my upper body as I slowly sit up before my mate joins me in bed and pulls me into his arms.

"Your incisions are healing faster than I thought, but for the next two weeks at least, you are to be on bed rest. This means no running, shifting, exercising or heavy lifting. Just relax with little Julia and laze about all day." Doctor Rex continues with a smile. The thought of being in my own bed tonight brings a smile to my face while I take a deep breath.

"Okay, Doc, I'll behave." I agree, snuggling into Tate and yawning.

"Only if you take this Goddess awful machine out of this room!" I add after the heart monitor beeps again. Goddess I wish I could smash it right now.

"I will prescribe you some medication to help with the pain. In about two weeks, you should be back to normal." With that, Doctor Rex leaves and I smile, getting closer to Tate. A nurse comes in and unhooks my body from the multiple machines but the I.V. drip. Finally, the stupid beeping from the heart monitor is gone, and exhaustion claims me once again.

"Why don't you take a nap, beautiful. Tonight, we will be home and sleeping." Tate suggests, kissing my cheek gently and running his fingers through my hair.

"Okay," I yawn out, closing my eyes. Doctor Rex did put me on bed rest, and I plan to get as much sleep as I can while tending to Julia.

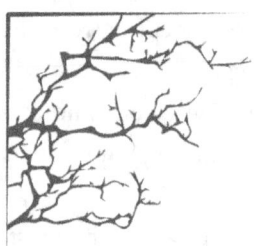

Chapter 14

"For Goddess' sake, give me the car seat Tate!" I growl out in frustration, throwing my hands in the air. We have just pulled into our driveway after Julia and I were released from the hospital about an hour ago and Tate decided to leave any form of lifting to him. The pack hospital sent us home with many bags full of newborn equipment from bottles and formulas to a blanket that my nurse – Abigail – had bought as a gift to us, her Alpha and Luna. I knew the car seat would be alright for me to carry as it practically weighs nothing with my werewolf strength, but my protective mate refused to let me carry it into our home.

"Its fine, Laina. I have everything handled." Tate assures through clenched teeth as he strains to carry everything in his left hand while the car seat is held in his right. I roll my eyes as I hover around the car seat with Julia inside, oblivious to her parent's arguments as she sleeps happily.

"Clearly you don't with how you are gritting your teeth." I retort with, rolling my eyes and placing my hands on my hip. He pauses to glare at me slightly for a moment, and I glare back, neither of us refusing to back down.

"Don't sass me, Laina. Get the door for me instead." He growls out, motioning with his head towards our front door. I scurry around him as quickly as I could and rush to turn the door knob to our house before holding it open for Tate to somehow manage to squeeze into the frame with a smug grin. Stupid male ego.

"I told you I could do it." My mate gloats with smugness tinting his voice. I once again roll my eyes at his childish behaviour while I close the door and Tate places the bags down gently before settling the car seat on the floor. I walk into his open arms for a hug and take a deep breath. It feels good to be home again. Pulling away from me and placing a chaste kiss on my lips, Tate turns to unstrap Julia from the car seat, a smile on his face as he holds the sleeping newborn gently in his arms.

"Come on, princess, let's get you to bed." He coos, turning to give me a quick peck on the cheek before making his way towards the stairs. Confused by his words, I follow Tate up the stairs wondering where his destination is.

"Tate, we haven't created a nursery yet." I call out furrowing my brows. How could we put Julia to bed when we have yet to finish the preparation for our pup? Tate just looks at me with eyes that suggest he is hiding something from me as he winks playfully, not bothering to answer my concerns as we continue towards the second floor and past my office coming to a stop in front of a closed door situated directly across from our own room. I know this room well, considering this is where we had placed all the furniture and nursery items inside intending to use this room for our twins – for Julia now that we only have her left.

"Care to open the door for us?" Tate asks cheerily, a grin spreading across his face. I roll my eyes and step forwards to turn the handle and push the wooden door. My eyes widen when I take in the scene before me, confused at how a bare white room could change so drastically in the last two days. The walls are decorated with many soft colours designed to be a fairy tale forest scene in the light of the setting sun. The furniture chosen during my shopping trip with Eeva is built and set up around the room with only one bassinet set up and ready to be used. The diaper changing station holds a basket with each needed item ready and in reach. My favourite item, the rocking chair, is placed beside yet another bay window where I can rock Julia asleep and sip an herbal tea. I can't help but look on in awe. This is my dream nursery.

"I told you that you left the design for this room to me, Laina would love it Tate." A familiar voice says bemusedly. I turn to face the direction the voice came from only to see my cousin Chris leaning against the wall behind me, a grinning Tate standing off to the side as he looks on happily. Without a second thought, I rush into the arms of Chris, burying my face into his chest as his arms wrap around me.

"Hey, Lainy. I missed you." Chris whispers, his shoulders shaking and voice cracking. I nod in reply as sobs wrack my body. It's been over four - almost five - months since I had last seen Chris. I could remember the tears on his face as the car drove away when being designated a Breeder. Now I could finally be reunited with my best friend, the person I confide in. I am finally reunited with my cousin. Slowly, my tears come to an end, and I am left gasping for breath, finding myself on the ground with my cousin holding me.

"Better?" Chris asks, wiping tears from my cheek. I only manage a nod while my emotions stabilize, unable to voice anything right now. I had missed Chris so much, our brief phone calls and texts being the only small communication we had since I met Tate, neither of us wanting to alert Sam to my situation. I held in so much that I wanted to say, so much has happened since I ran away that I wanted Chris to know but couldn't tell him. Now I can.

"I am so proud of you, Laina. You stayed strong and managed to free yourself." Chris whispers, kissing my forehead and giving me one last hug. I crawl out of his lap to allow Chris to stand before taking his outstretched hand and letting my cousin help me to my feet.

"How are you here?" I question once I feel confident to speak without crying again.

"Tate called me. News had spread in the old pack that you had run into this territory beforehand. When he called, I was terrified, but I felt so relieved when he told me that you are his mate. After that, Jack and I packed up the house and everything in it and moved here. I knew you would be safe by your mate's side and I could finally find you. When we arrived at the house, Jack and I met Eeva. She told us about what happened, and the three of us decided to clean the house and prepare the nursery with how you had designed it in your sketchbook." He explains, a smile on his face as Chris turns to look into the nursery. I follow his gaze to catch Tate rocking our pup in his arms, giving Chris and I some space with our reunion.

"Thank you for this." I smile, turning to thank my cousin. I needed this surprise seeing a room designed the way I had sketched out years ago. Chris nods with a soft smile, motioning me to go to my mate, who settles a sleeping Julia into her bassinet with a tender smile on his face as he gazes down at the pup before him. My legs carry me until my arms wrap around Tate from behind, allowing the love I feel for this man to seep into our bond. Hopefully soon we can link each other.

"Thank you for allowing my cousin here." I whisper, burying my face into his back and taking in his scent.

"You're welcome beautiful. I figured having your family here would help." He says, pulling me to his side. For a moment, we take in the silence of the house while gazing at Julia. It felt right having her home asleep in her bed safe and sound.

"I hope I am not interrupting anything, but dinner is ready." Jack's familiar voice has me turning in time to catch Jack wrap his arms around Chris and give my cousin a loving kiss. It feels like the old days when I would be deep into my design homework for the two to interrupt me and force me to take a rest and eat.

"That's good because I am starving." I laugh out loud, pulling Tate along with me to where Chris and Jack stand. Its nice knowing I would be able to taste Jack's cooking again, that we can be a family in Bloodsvain. The four of us leave Julia to sleep and make our way down the stairs towards the kitchen where sounds of a ruckus can be heard, making me grimace for a moment.

"Sit down. Your Aunt and Uncle are coming down to eat now." I hear the distinct tone of Eeva's voice when rounding the corner of the hall and walking into a lively scene of Eeva and a man trying to corral the pups Jonathan, Andy, and Vinny into the breakfast nook. I chuckle at the two chasing the three boys around while threatening to take away their games and toys.

"Laina, hi!" Eeva stops her pursuit of her pups to rush over and pull me into a hug. Her hands pat my shoulders gently with a grin plastered on her face.

"Oh, thank the Goddess that you're alright." She rushes to say with relief, her eyes scanning me from head to toe before stealing me from Tate and settling me into a chair at the breakfast nook.

"We thought to make some comfort food after the last few days you've had, so Jack suggested bacon mac n' cheese." This unknown man states when he manages to settle the three rambunctious boys down.

"I am Loren, by the way. Eeva's mate." Loren introduces himself holding his hand out for me to shake. Smiling, I take his hand and shake it, watching Eeva curl into his side with a childish grin on her face.

"I'm Laina, Ta-"

"Tate's mate and my new Luna, we all know who you are now." He states with a playful wink. I could tell right away that I am going to like having Loren around.

"Welcome to the family."

"Thanks, Loren." I chuckle out. Soon everyone is seated with a plate full of the carb-tastic concoction that Jack whipped up, the house feeling warm and lively with my family sitting around me. It reminds me of when mine and Chris' parents were alive, how the nights would be filled with laughter and warmth and to feel the same way again brings small tears to my eyes. In the end, we spend the meal sharing stories of our childhood laughing.

"She didn't?" Eeva asks in disbelief.

"She did. She walked up to the kid and smashed her cupcake in the poor kid's face all because he called her adorable." Jack says, and I glare at him. He is talking about the time I met one of Chris's friends from another pack as that friend's younger brother proceeded to treat me like a damsel in distress when he realized he would have to be in a girl's presence for the next few days.

"In my defence, I was training to be a deadly fighter." I say matter-of-factly as I take an angry bite of the gooey, cheesy dish. I was thirteen when this happened, and I remember wanting to be a Warrior at the time, to fight and protect the pack. What a joke my loyalty turned out to be in the end.

"The best part is she then proceeds to cry because she no longer had a cupcake." Chris finishes the story causing everyone around the table to roar with laughter. I grumble into the remaining food on my plate before getting up to clear the table now that everyone is done eating.

"Nu-uh Laina, you're on bed rest, so I have this." Eeva says, shooing me to my seat once again. Her pups have already finished eating fifteen minutes ago, Jack leading them into the living room to set up a Disney movie for the three to watch before returning to join us in our conversation. I watch as Loren and Eeva clear the table, Tate gently pulling me down to sit back and relax. Jack helps to clean the table with a wet rag before Loren and Eeva return with pastry boxes that I recognize from her diner in hand.

"Since everyone is finished eating, it's time for dessert." Eeva states, taking the lid off the boxes to reveal a box full of Danishes and a box full of jumbo Cupcakes. I reach for a vanilla cupcake loaded with sprinkles in and on the frosting, sinking my teeth into the delicious treat. We continue to tell stories about how Eeva and Loren found out about the two of them being mates and some about Tate as a child courtesy of Eeva. We plan to take our conversation to the living room when the tiny cries of Julia interrupt us.

"Let me go get my little niece." Eeva volunteers before disappearing from our sight. Loren chuckles and looks at Tate and me apologetically.

"She wants to try for a daughter soon. Because of Laina, she has baby fever bad right now." He explains, causing Tate to groan. Moments later, Eeva appears with Julia in her arms.

"She is adorable!" My sister-in-law gushes, her eyes never leaving Julia's tiny face.

"What is her name?" Loren asks, going to stand by his mate to peer down at my pup.

"Julia Chris Randall-Silvermoon," Tate answers, and I smile.

"Julia as in your mother's name?" Chris asks, looking at me with a grin.

"Yes, and Chris as in you." I answer my cousin, watching his eyes widen for a brief moment before he stretches out his arms expectantly at Eeva.

"Give me my new cousin." He says to Eeva only for the latter to turn away from Chris and hold Julia closer to her body.

"Get a bottle ready, and you can feed her." She states, and I smirk as my cousin gets up, fumbles around the kitchen to find the needed items that Eeva cleaned and put away and prepares a bottle. With a warm bottle now ready, Chris takes my pup from Eeva before sitting back down beside Jack. I watch the two men become captivated by my little girl, their eyes never leaving her face. It would be nice if they could adopt a pup of their own soon. The two men take turns feeding and burping Julia, giving Tate and I a chance to cuddle while our family showers our pup with love and affection. My smile grows watching everyone realizing that Julia will definitely be spoiled as she grows.

"We bury Kelly, her twin sister, tomorrow," I announce quietly as I now hold a sleeping baby in my arms. The room grows silent with this information.

"We will be there." Loren speaks up, giving me a small smile as everyone else in the room agrees. I nod and smile sadly as I snuggle into Tate, yawning.

"I think it's time for everyone to sleep." Tate chuckles, rubbing my back gently and causing my eyes to grow heavy.

"Yeah, we should get these children to bed now. Good night." Eeva agrees as Loren heads into the living room to gather the boys. When they leave, Chris and Jack head into the guest room that I once occupied, bidding us good night and offering to help with feeding Julia throughout the night. I just think that the two have baby fever and plan to talk to Tate to see if the pack has a small orphanage.

With the house settling in silence and Julia once again fast asleep in her own room, I settle into bed with Tate curling into his arms and quickly falling asleep. I missed being home.

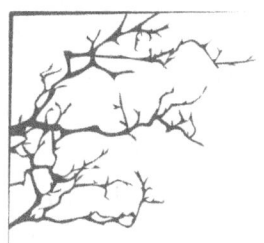

Chapter 15

"You ready?" Tate's voice floats across the room towards me, the melancholy inside its depth reminding me what we are about to do. I sigh, taking a last look at myself in the mirror with my blue eyes holding unshed tears in them once again as sorrow fills me. I stand wearing a long-sleeved black lace dress with my hair in a high bun. Today will be a long and depressing day, one the I am not truly ready to face. Strong arms turn me away from my pale reflection and press my head into a sturdy chest and with shaky breaths I take in Tate's scent to calm myself down and stop the tears the threaten to spill.

"You don't have to go if it's too hard, Laina. Everyone would understand." He whispers, placing light kisses on my forehead as he rubs my back gently. He knows I am close to breaking again, heck, any mother would be close to breaking on the day they burry their baby.

"I have to, Tate. She deserves to know how much I love her and will miss her." I whisper out with a whimper into his chest. Taking another deep breath to steady my emotions. Once I feel ready, I take Tate's hand and the two of us make our way down the stairs where Jack and Chris fawn over Julia, a soft smile on my lips as I watch the three of them.

"Who is a fabulous little baby? You are, yes, you are little Julia. And your big cousins here are going to make sure you stay fabulous with clothes fit for this little princess." Chris coos as he taps gently on Julia's tiny nose. Sadly, I have a feeling that what he is saying will come true and that, like myself, Julia will be showered with clothing growing up. I feel Tate stiffen beside me as Chris bounces Julia in his arms while he talks about all the things she will get growing up and what she might become in the future, causing my mate to growl lowly where only I can hear it. Tate has grown is extremely possessive ever since rushing me to the hospital and I guess with Chris acting this way my mate must feel that his position of being Julia's father is being threatened.

"Behave, Tate. Chris and Jack are always like this, especially Chris. He means no harm." I sigh out, wrapping my arm around Tate's waist and trying to calm my mate down as best as I can. Instead of calming down, Tate rolls his eyes and continues to glare at Chris, pulling away from me. Hurt fills my already bruised heart at my mate's reaction. Trying to calm myself down, I turn away from Tate and shy away from his touch when he reaches for me, the realization at what he has just done settling into his face as I walk towards Chris and Jack taking Julia from Chris's arms and cradle her as I breathe in her baby scent.

"Julia and I are riding in your car, Chris." I decide, hearing Tate give a low, possessive growl. I turn to glare at my mate. Today is already a hard-enough day for me, and I will not allow his attitude to take over and hurt me even more emotionally.

"Wouldn't you rather be with Tate?" Jack asks cautiously, his eyes darting between Tate and me.

"No. I would rather ride with family than be stuck in a car with a possessive ass that can't control his attitude today." I answer honestly, bending down to place Julia in her car seat before Jack carefully picks it up. Chris grabs Julia's diaper bag getting ready to leave with worried filled eyes directed to me.

"Why are you being so difficult? A moment ago, you were ready to cry, and now you're acting like a class-A bitch!" Tate growls, directing his anger towards me. My heart cracks slightly as a few tears slip out from the corner of my eyes, and I shake my head at Tate.

"I'm only acting like this because of you." I snap back at Tate, watching as his eyes widen in shock.

"Chris is being not only a cousin but also an uncle to Julia, and you get jealous of him. He's gay and has a mate, but just because you feel slightly threatened, you start growling and being an asshole. Today is not the day to do this, Tate. I am burying one of my pups. Do you understand the pain I am in?" I continue, more tears streaming down my face as Chris holds his arm out, preventing me from going to where I left Tate and slapping some sense into him.

"Chris is my best friend. When my parents died, he raised me. So, excuse me for taking my family's side when my mate starts acting like a grade-A douchebag." I finish my rant and turn on my heels before proceeding to drag Chris to his car. I need to be away from Tate for a moment. Jack follows suit and helps me secure Julia and her car seat in the back seat before the three of us settle into the car ourselves.

"Just drive, Chris." I sigh, seeing the hesitation in my cousin's eyes for leaving Tate in the house alone. When my mate smartens up, then I will talk to him. But today is not the day to act the way he is. The engine starts, and Chris proceeds to back out of the driveway. My eyes stay focused on Julia beside me as I wipe away the wetness on my face. The drive to the church is short as we pass through the forest roads. The trees shake, and leaves break off, falling to the ground. I take the time and try my best to compose myself as Chris parks in front of a gorgeous, white brick church that Eeva told me was built over one hundred years ago with the cloudless blue sky providing a lovely scene. For such a sad day, it is beautiful out. Maybe the Moon Goddess felt sorry for me losing my pup Kelly and provided a beautiful scene to send her off.

Chris comes to the side Julia's car seat is secured in and offers to carry her inside. I reach for the diaper bag, but Jack grabs it before I can, giving me a side hug and a kiss on my forehead. It makes me happy having these two here, to support me when I need it the most. I am not sure I could handle dealing with Tate and his ego alone on a day that is so hard for me. We make our way into the church's opened double doors when a wolf in a long robe steps forward from the dais and gives me a warm smile.

"Luna, so nice to meet you, but I am sad that it had to be under these circumstances." The minister greets, offering his hand for me to shake. I smile sadly and look around the room, my eyes searching for Kelly's body.

"I-is she?" I couldn't help but let a few more tears fall as I ask, my question trailing off as the words I want to say get stuck in my throat. I wanted to see her for the first and last time, to know what my darling pup looks like before I have to lay her to rest.

"She is in the other room; would you like some time with her?" The minister asks with a sympathetic gaze. I nod slowly, motioning for him to lead the way while Jack and Chris smile reassuringly at me and takes Julia to the front pew to entertain the newborn. I am led to a room to the left of the stage where a wooden table with a black satin table cloth stands. On top of the table is a small wooden casket with white satin that cradles the body of a tiny newborn, who is a carbon copy of Julia. The minister leaves, closing the door behind him while I slowly walk forward until I stand before Kelly, my fingers grazing her small cheeks gently. She is so, so cold, her little body stiff from the embalming. I never thought that I would be here, looking down at a little pup with pale skin and chestnut coloured hair like Julia and me.

"Hi, Kelly." I choke out as tears once again flow down my face. Something compels me to gently lift her lifeless body in my arms as sobs begin to take hold of me. I fall to my knees while staring at the still face of my baby girl, here eyes closed as if she is only sleeping, but there is no life to her little body. The sweet little pup who used to kick inside me just days ago, would make me smile just thinking of what she and her sister will look like, and I would never get to watch her grow up. She will never feel my touch or be comforted in my arms. She'll never grow up with Julia.

"I love you, baby girl." I whisper, kissing her sweet little face, my tears falling onto her pale little cheeks. I sit in the small, quiet room, just holding onto Kelly and slightly rocking back and forth. I wish I could turn back time so this day never happens. Wish that we had made it to the hospital faster to save her and her sister, but nothing can change that day and there is no one to blame.

"Laina?" Eeva calls out to me gently. I turn my head to look at my friend, watching her take slow steps to stand before me, a sad smile on her face as she holds out her hands.

"It's time. May I take her?" She informs, asking me gently about Kelly. I hesitate for a moment before nodding, allowing Eeva to take Kelly from my arms. Eeva gently places Kelly into her coffin and rearranges her pink dress so that it sits elegantly on my pup's body as more sobs come from me.

"Ssshh, it'll be okay." Eeva whispers, taking a seat beside me on the ground and wrapping her arms around me. I bury my face into my friend's shoulder and allow myself to grieve for my pup, the notion that I will never watch grow up, who will never run around with her sister, running through my mind over and over again. For a while, the two of us stay in this position as Eeva allows me to cry, my sobs slowing down until I am able to catch my breath. She takes out cleansing wipes from her purse and helps me clean my face, squeezing my hands gently before helping me to my feet. I turn to look at Kelly one last time, rearranging her dress and taking a small headband I had made last week. It was a black band with fall flowers and a colourful butterfly. Julia is already wearing the matching headband, and it feels right to let Kelly wear her own headband today.

"Goodbye, sweet girl," I whisper, giving her a final kiss on her tiny forehead before Eeva leads me out of the room gently. Walking back into the central part of the church, I catch Tate in the back talking to the minister but ignore him. Instead, I join Chris and Jack in the front, taking Julia from Jack's arms and holding my baby close to me. We all take a seat on the benches as the minister starts his speech about the balance of life and the blessing from the Goddess, Loren and Jack carrying the tiny coffin to the front where everyone I know could see her. I already had my moment, so I just stare at Julia, not wanting to see the small coffin. Someone slides into the spot next to me and strong arms wrap around me, pulling me close as Tate's scent wraps around my body like a warm blanket.

"Laina, I...I'm sorry. I was an ass this morning." Tate apologizes and those few words are all I need to turn into his chest and cry silently, careful not to wake our sleeping pup in my arms. The rest of the funeral is a blur. The only thing I remember is the coffin being lowered and buried in the tomb where Tate's family is buried. She will forever be a Randall-Silvermoon and Tate's pup no matter what.

I don't remember how I ended up in bed curled under the covers, but I know that Tate allowed Chris and Jack to care for Julia for the night while giving me some space. I needed some time alone after the long, heart-wrenching day I've had. Tate is in his office, using the time to organize the pack for the next few days so he can be with me, but ever so often he comes into the room to check on me and bring me small meals, making sure I eat to continue healing. After the last time he checked in on me, my body feels zapped of all energy and I decide to close my heavy eyelids and let sleep welcome me. Tomorrow I will wake up and get into a routine as a new mother but for now I need to find some peace in the loss I am facing.

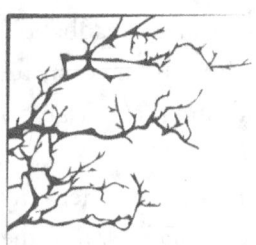

Chapter 16

Light slowly drifts in through the sheer curtains, falling across my eyelids and causing me to wake up. Strong arms are wrapped around me with my back against a sturdy chest. The tingles against my skin tell me that it's Tate as he snuggles closer to me. I need to get my mind off of yesterday and move forward. I will always love Kelly, but Julia needed her mother to raise her. Today is a new day, and slowly my grief will settle down with time.

Tate gently pulls away from me and kisses my forehead before his presence leaves the bed. Ten minutes pass by till I decide that I did not want to stay here in bed forever and I throw the covers back to stand. Stretching, I make my way towards the bathroom for a shower, letting the warm water cleanse away the smell of grief from yesterday off of my body. I feel more refreshed as I shut off the water and wrap my body in a fluffy towel and frown when I realize just how over sized the towel is. I am still learning to get used to my small stomach once again and one thing is for sure, I will need some towels that fit me later. I step away from the master en-suite and pad towards the closet while towel drying my hair. Something about a morning shower always makes me feel lighter and energetic. Dressing in a short fall dress, I braid my hair and make my way downstairs towards the smell of breakfast cooking in the kitchen.

"Come here, princess!" I hear Tate's voice before seeing him and everyone else as I round the corner to the kitchen entrance just in time to watch Jack pass Julia to my mate.

"Good morning." I say, smiling as I walk towards them, kissing my mate on the cheek before taking Julia from him.

"Hey, we were having daddy-daughter time!" He exclaims while I sit down on a chair with her in my arms across from my mate.

"And now she is having some cuddles from her mommy." I retort with a giggle.

"New-born babies are cute but boring." Jack says with a sigh as he smiles at my daughter. I fake gasp at him, shielding Julia from Jack's sight and shaking my head at my cousin-in-law.

"Shame on you. She is busy being adorable." I say in mock scolding before kissing my pup gently on her little nose.

"Yes, she is, and you need to be busy eating," Tate adds in with a chuckle. I smile when my mate places a plateful of food in front of me and a glass of orange juice to accompany my meal. But I protest when he takes Julia away from me.

"Hey, I had her!" I exclaim, reaching out to take our pup away from him again.

"And now you are eating." He smirks making me glare at him as he takes Julia back to his seat.

"She may not be my flesh and blood, but the moment I saw her, I knew she would be my little girl." He says with a soft smile on his face. I smile at his declaration as I give in and begin to eat, letting him cuddle our pup. The four of us enjoy the quiet morning, taking turns passing Julia around and taking pictures with her. I smile when Chris and Jack announce that they are looking at adopting their own pup soon once they settle into their own house here in Bloodsvain. It finally feels like life is set on the right track for my family and me.

Suddenly, everything turns into chaos as wolves in uniforms worn by the Council of Elders storm into the kitchen, the sounds of glass shattering from the windows breaking open. Julia is placed into my arms with Tate backing me into a wall, taking a protective stance in front of us, a threatening growl rolling over the crowd.

"Laina Starcrest, you are under arrest for kidnapping!" A man states as he steps forward, weary of Tate. I could tell he did not want to go against my mate, and I had a feeling he would lose if Tate attacked.

"Tate Randall-Silvermoon, step down. This she-wolf stole a pup from Samuel from Pine-" I growl loudly, cutting the man off as I send a vicious glare his way.

"I did no such thing. This is my pup, and she was born a few days ago along with her twin, whom we just buried yesterday." I snap, holding my baby closer to my chest, protecting her. I hated these men who decided it would be a smart idea to invade my house and threatened to take my pup away from me.

"Alpha Sam said you would say that, but he has documents for a baby boy born two weeks ago." The man states, taking out what looks to be a copy of fake documents. Sam must have been prepared to fight for these pups, but too bad for him. He will never hold a claim to Julia.

"Look closely, idiot, my mate is holding a baby girl!" Tate roars, and everyone freezes, the men sniffing the air. The man in front of Tate looks at him in confusion before peering over his shoulder towards me.

"It seems that you are speaking the truth. What were the elders thinking?" The man I now assume is the leader states as he catches a glimpse of Julia. I turn my body so that my back faces the men, guarding my pup from their gazes and sending a glare in their direction.

"I'll tell you what they were thinking. They weren't!" I growl out in anger. The leader looks at us again, but I keep his curious gaze off of Julia. He has no right to see her.

"How about we talk this out at the head office? My crew will fix up your house. Sorry, by the way." The man concedes with a shrug, getting ready to turn away.

"Sorry! YOU'RE SAYING SORRY WHEN YOU CAME IN TO TAKE MY MATE AND PUP BECAUSE SOME WELP SAID SO!" Tate roars as he charges the man, pinning him to a wall with his hands around his neck, his face set in rage as he chokes the man. Some of the wolves rush to Tate's side, working hard to loosen my mate's grip around their leader's neck only to be elbowed or headbutted out of the way by a very pissed-off, protective Alpha. They fucked with the wrong wolf today. I sigh and hand Julia to Jack before walking over and placing a hand on Tate's cheek, seeing his eyes turn to me as he releases a growl.

"Tate, calm down," I say calmly, trying to ease his hands away from the wolf's neck.

"NO, I WILL N'-"

"You can, and you will." I let authority into my voice while my blood simmers with the power I rarely use. He blinks a couple of times, probably surprised at my command before staring at me.

"Tate, please." I sigh out. He growls once more and finally lets go with a huff of breath before throwing the leader of the guards to the ground with a loud, sickening thud, causing me to wonder if the leader broke a couple of bones in the process. Tate glares at the man before backing away and heading towards Julia, carefully taking our pup from Jack and holding our baby in his arms. I watch as he visibly relaxes and smiles gently. Tate fully accepts Julia as his pup and it makes me so happy. Knowing my mate will be fine, I turn on my heel and glare at the man, who is now gasping for air as I walk towards him and lean down so that my face is an inch away from him, letting the power of my blood wash over his frame. I watch him stiffen with fear as I look into his eyes, my own anger radiating off of me.

"Now, you will get the Elders to come HERE, or I will call the Alpha King and have HIM deal with this issue. Do I make myself clear?" I emphasize a few words, and the man nods, getting his phone out and dialling a number quickly. My eyes never leave him, and I watch him visibly shudder. If he thought Tate is scary to deal with, he has never faced a pissed-off mother werewolf who is willing to kill anyone who threatens her pups.

"Elder Ross, it seems like the information given to us was incorrect, and because of the way we handled things, they want you and the others to come here... Of course... Got it, see you then." He hangs up and leans against the wall breathing heavily as sweat drips down his forehead

"Two hours. They will be here in two hours." He answers, and I stand, letting the pressure ease off of him.

"Good, your men can fix my house now while we wait for their arrival. I expect the Council to pay for everything." I order, giving each of them a glare. No one protests knowing this mistake is their fault, as every wolf readies themselves to repair the damages they have done. I need to talk to Tate about added security to our home to protect Julia and any other pups we will have as well as find out what idiot allowed them to cross our pack line and beat the ever loving fear of the Goddess into them. I sigh and turn towards Tate, seeing that he has one arm open while looking at me. I smile and take the few steps into his embrace as he holds Julia and me.

"Now you can tell them what happened to you." I nod at his words and press my face into his chest while taking in his scent.

"Well, Jack and I will make sure the house gets fixed properly. You two go relax with Julia and wait for the Elders to arrive." Chris volunteers giving us an exasperated sigh as he looks around at the mess. I know my cousin will make these wolves work like slaves for what they did. Chris could be sadistic when pissed off, and I can see the rage simmering behind his eyes. After thanking Chris and Jack, Tate leads me away from the kitchen and out the sliding door onto our deck. Thinking we are stopping here, I get ready to rest on a patio chair, only for Tate to grab my wrist and lead me away from the house.

"Where are we going?" I ask, curiosity filling my voice. Today is unusually warm for an early October morning, and part of me worries that Julia will get cold if she is out here for too long.

"It's a surprise." He answers with a mischievous grin. We walk hand-in-hand for a few minutes into the forest, just past our house, when the sounds of waves reach me. Suddenly, Tate stops and blocks my view, smiling at me with a now sleeping Julia resting in the crook of his right arm.

"Ready?" He asks, and I giggle. I could tell he has planned this surprise for a while, and I couldn't wait to see it.

"Yes!" I answer, getting a wink before he moves aside. I gasp as I see a beautiful white gazebo resting on a huge pond as if it were floating on the water. Water lilies float across the water and large, smooth, circular stones big enough to fit two people at a time create a pathway to the gazebo. My feet carry me from stone to stone until I find myself at the entrance to the beautiful place. A small fireplace radiates heat around the area, causing me to smile at the coziness while taking a seat on one of the comfortable chairs. Tate places our sleeping pup in a bassinet, covering her with a blanket, before taking a seat next to me and we gaze out across the pond.

"And now, we wait for the Elders to arrive." Tate whispers as a few ducks swim by.

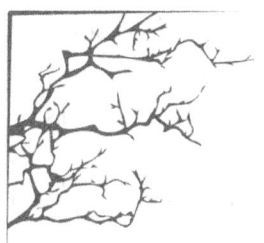

Chapter 17

"It's been two hours. Where are they?" Tate growls out as he paces around the gazebo. I sigh, deciding to focus on feeding Julia while my mate stews in his frustration. It's been two hours since our house was infiltrated by the Council Guards and Tate and I have grown tired of waiting for the Elders to arrive. They were the ones who ordered to take me and my pup into custody, there were the ones that were wrong so they should be the ones rushing to come and apologize.

[Laina, repairs are almost done.] Chris' voice calls out through our link, making me smile. Judging by his tone, he is having a blast ordering around our very unwelcomed guests.

[Good, make sure the money for repairs come from the Council.] I remind my cousin, getting a chuckle from him.

[Trust me, I already have a bill made and ready to go. I will be bringing it to the pack Lawyer later to have it notarized once the repairs are done before we bring it to the Council.] Smiling, I reiterate what Chris told me to Tate, getting a nod of approval from my mate as he takes out his phone and sends a text.

"I texted Adam, the pack Lawyer. He is on his way with his laptop to work with Chris." Tate states with a grin, looking out at the water. I relay this to Chris before shutting the link down to focus on Julia. By now her bottle is gone and her eyes lids are starting to close. I can tell that my little one is trying hard to fight the urge to sleep and I chuckle, gently patting her back to help her fall asleep.

"Alpha, Luna." A voice calls out from the shore, making me jump slightly from the sudden appearance of a wolf who carefully steps across the stone pathway before coming to stand at the entrance of the gazebo.

"I was told to inform you that the Elders are here. Do you want them to be led to the gazebo?" The man asks. I take in his appearance and notice our pack insignia on the shoulder of his shirt, my curiosity of this man being piqued.

"Nice to meet you Luna Laina, I am Mateo, the Head Warrior here." Mateo greets me, giving me a friendly smile that I return with my own. Before I can say anything, Tate lets out a possessive growl, moving to block my line of sight.

"Is there a need for you to be staring at my mate, Mateo?" Tate asks, his body shaking. I roll my eyes and place Julia in her bassinet before standing and making my way to Tate's side where I promptly smack his shoulder and watch as my mate winces and backs up, giving me a look that reminds me of an injured puppy.

"Tate behave. Mateo isn't a threat." I growl out, giving my mate a warning look. I can feel Mateo visible relax now that I am here to tame Tate and prevent him from attacking a member of our pack.

"Thank you, Luna. I am only introducing myself since you will be running our pack with the Alpha." Mateo agrees, backing up two steps most likely to avoid Tate and his possessiveness.

"Well thank you, Mateo. Is there anything else we need to know?"

"Yes, we've also doubled security patrols since this morning's incident and Beta Louren is currently entertaining the Elders. Should I bring them here or would you like to meet them at the pack house?" Mateo answers, updating us on the situation at hand. I look to Tate, wanting to hear his input but he shrugs before wrapping his arms around me.

"They caused this mess because they wanted to detain you, so you decide." Tate states, placing a gentle kiss on my forehead.

"Then bring the Elders here and inform someone to bring refreshments and snacks as well." I order, pressing myself closer to Tate as I feel him shudder. This situation must be hard on him.

"I understand Luna. With his agreement, Mateo bows before leaving, his six-foot-something frame crossing over the stones nimbly once again.

"I hate it when males look at you. You're mine." He growls to himself, holding me tighter.

"And I hate when females look at you. But Mateo is a high ranked warrior, his concern is of my safety, not what I look like without clothes." I state with a chuckle, Tate rolling his eyes as he takes in my scent.

"I know, but I can't help how protective I am over you." He grumbles into my hair.

"I know Baby. How about we sit and wait for Mateo to bring the Elders over." I suggest, pulling away to take his hand in mine. He nods, leading me back to our seats as we listen to the soft waves crashing below us.

"When they come, let me talk. It's my story to tell and I need them to know that I am a Luna and an Alpha wolf, that they can't intimidate me nor get away with placing a hit on me or anyone without knowing the full truth." I watch Tate's face as I voice my need to speak. My life was torn apart because of a law that the Elders got rid of and did not maintain. Had they done their jobs and traveled to each and every pack over the years to make sure Breeders were abolished, I would not have been in this situation.

"Fine, but if I feel that your life and Julia's is in danger, then I step in." He agrees after a few minutes pass. I can tell that allowing me to take the lead is hard on him, but he also knows that I am right and that I have to be the one to confront the Elders.

"Okay, deal!" I smile and kiss Tate happily. With this topic settled, we quietly wait for our guests to arrive. Another hour of waiting passes with a few Omega's bringing snacks, coffee and tea for us to enjoy. Chris came once with the baby bag and a few bottles in tow for Julia before leaving to resume managing the Council Guards. Finally, Mateo returns with Louren beside him, the two wolves leading a group of elderly looking wolves through the trees and towards us. I recognize the Council of Elder's insignia on their jacket immediately. Louren and Mike stand on either side of the pathway leading to the gazebo, motioning for the elders to cross first. I watch the interaction, spying an Elder that protests at first before Louren says something that causes the Elder to shrink into himself in defeat before crossing the stones with the others.

With all the elders crossing the stones, Louren follows before Mateo does, the two large wolves making sure that they cant turn around. With everyone now here, the Elders join Tate and I at the table, sitting down without shaking our hands or giving us a simple greeting. It takes everything in me not to growl at them, the disrespect they are showing rubbing me the wrong way.

"Two more Omega's are on their way with more refreshments." Louren states as he takes a seat beside Tate, glaring at the elders before us. Sure enough, as soon as Louren sits, two Omegas accompanied by two Warriors appear. The Warriors help to bring the refreshments to the gazebo, placing trays before us before they cross the stones and stand guard, preventing anyone from disturbing us once the Omegas leave. Mateo stands at the entrance of the gazebo, waiting for orders and scanning his eyes over the surroundings for any threats.

"Mike, we need another witness other than Louren to stay here while we converse with the Elders." Tate says through gritted teeth, his eyes glaring at the wolves that sit before us. I reach for his hand under the table and squeeze gently, knowing exactly how he feels. This is our territory, and their disrespect has us on edge more than the incident of their lackeys crashing into our kitchen.

"Yes, Alpha. It's why I have all of the appropriate equipment ready." His eyes glaze over for a moment before two more wolves appear in our line of sight. They carry what looks to be a camera set as they too enter the crowded gazebo and begin to set up the electronics, including a voice recorder, around the gazebo with precise movement. With a bow of respect to us, the wolves turn and leave the vicinity. Mateo double-checks everything before sitting beside Louren, his own gaze a glare directed to the Elders.

"Now, let's get this started." I say with everything settled, folding my hands neatly on the table while staring at the Elders.

"Didn't your parents tell you it's rude to stare, little girl?" The man in the middle - the Elder that tried to argue with Louren- scoffs, his distain clear as day on their face.

"My parents couldn't teach me much because rogues killed them." With my snappy retort, the Elders stare at me with open mouths, and I have a feeling the Three men to my right are trying so hard to keep their composure and not burst out laughing.

"Now, why was there an arrest warrant on me?" I ask, the Elders growling at my direct questioning and disrespect towards them.

"What gives you the right to demand answers?" A she-wolf visibly bristles at my questioning. I simply send a glare her way, holding my hand out to stop Tate from doing something that he might regret.

"Because Samuel Lightran forced me to be a Breeder as well as other females in my old pack." I snap back just as quick, shutting that woman up.

"Not only that, he raped me to have an heir." I add with a growl. Before I can continue what I want to say, the Elder in the middle stands up, slamming his hands on the table and glares at me.

"My great-great-nephew would do no such thing!" He yells, quickly to defend Samuel. My eyes carefully observe this wolf and I soon see similarities between the man that raped me and the elder before me.

"Really, do you want proof that I got pregnant just a little over four months ago by your great-great-nephew?" I ask, allowing the power in my blood to boil over and watch as this man shrink into his seat.

"I ran away, wanting to protect my pups -yes, pups as in two- from that vile man because what he did, raping me for a week, is wrong and I refused to allow my babies to be raised by a man like him. Unfortunately, a few days ago I had to have emergency surgery due to complications, and only one pup survived. We just buried her sister yesterday only for this bullshit to happen this morning." To prove my point, a small cry is heard after my words and Tate swiftly rises to pick up Julia and soothe her. The Elderly she-wolf who questioned me earlier takes a long look at me, her eyes holding sympathy and curiosity s something inside her mind clicks.

"You are Laina. Eeva said she had found a wolf who was a forced Breeder. She didn't say which pack she had run away from." She states, and I smile at her. It seems like I have found an ally in this group of Elders and decide to treat her with a little more respect. Thank you, Eeva, for reporting this through the proper channels.

"Yes, I am Laina, the she-wolf who was raped and bred illegally. Now I suggest you see the Pinepaw Pack unannounced, with me, Tate and Chris – my cousin and technical guardian as I am only sixteen – present so that you can see where I was kept and where other Breeders are kept." I answer, stating what needs to be done as I turn my gaze to the Elder that is related to Sam. I glare at him as he glares at me, letting out a warning growl. I have a feeling this Elder is in ca-hoots with his great-great nephew and I refuse to allow him near me any longer.

"He stays out of the conversation since he could warn Sam, and then you will never know the truth. Keep him under strict observation so as not to alert Pine Paw." I add at the end. The man's face starts to turn red with rage, his fists slamming into the table, shattering it as the sound of glass breaks and everything else on the table falls to the ground. I am grateful that Tate is holding Julia away from the table as I let out a low growl of warning. He is walking on thin ice right now.

"You cannot make me do anything! If I want to be here for all the details, I will!" He roars at me, the disrespect evident in his eyes. I stand, my hand reaching out to grab the collar of his shirt as I pull him closer, my face inches from his as my canines start to grow.

"I can and I will since you are related to the man that raped me. Now, sit down, shut up, and behave. You also owe me a new table." The Elder and I had a stare down as we glared at each other. I refuse to release him, relishing in the fact that he is a foot shorter than me and a lot weaker as well. I am done being the weak pushover from a few months ago when Samuel decided to make me a breeder. I am a soon-to-be Luna and a mother. I will do whatever it takes to get justice and protect my pup.

"Ross, shut the hell up. We already decided to leave you out of this." The female Elder commands as Ross turns his gaze from me to the elder that spoke.

"You can't do that, Dian." He states as he too glares at her. I have a feeling he see's she-wolves as lesser beings and I pray he gives me a reason to end his life.

"As the head Elder, I can and I will." The woman, Dian, says. I smirk in triumph, releasing Ross and sitting back down beside Tate, who informs me Julia is asleep once again. We watch as the elders have another conversation through their link before Ross growls in frustration and stalks away.

"Sorry about that, Laina." Dian apologizes with a sigh, and I smile at her.

"So, can we have a civil conversation now?" Tate asks, looking down at the table frame.

"Of course. We will also have a new table sent your way soon. We already received the bill from your pack Lawyer so the funds will be in your accounts by tomorrow night the latest." A man to Dian's right answers, his friendly smile reminding me of a doting grandfather. With everyone settled, we decide to allow Omegas to clean the gazebo before we continue our conversation.

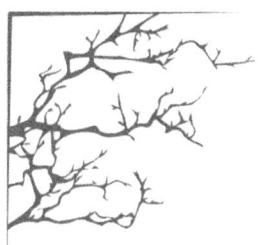

Chapter 18

"Good night, sweetheart." I whisper as I lower Julia into her bed for the night. The sounds of running water can be heard from across the hall from Tate and my bedroom. I smile, watching my pup for a moment before heading towards my room and stretch my sore muscles.

"Time for a bit of R and R?" I groan to myself, rubbing my shoulder.

"Yes, and we are having one together tonight." Tate says, wrapping me in his embrace and kissing my forehead.

"But-" I begin, ready to protest.

"No buts, beautiful, we need some time to ourselves." Tate cuts me off, poking my nose playfully. I smile gently and nod, stepping out of his arms and undressing.

"I will only do this if you give me a massage," I state, dropping my pants and underwear onto the ground.

"Okay, deal." His voice is a whisper as he hugs me from behind once again, his body pressed to my own and just as naked as I am. Without warning, I am scooped into his arms as Tate carries me into our large bathroom, placing me gently into the large tub filled with a bubble bath. He climbs in behind me, gently pulling me closer to his body before his hands knead my shoulders and back, making quick work of the sore muscles I have and releasing the tension that has built up over the last few days.

"I know you're still healing from your surgery, so we will only have a bath tonight. But I can't wait to make you mine forever." He says with longing, his voice husky with need. My heart flutters and I think about how we have yet to complete the mating ritual. Everyone in the pack I have met has called me Luna but I have yet to be initiated into the pack nor marked and claimed by Tate. Some days I feel like an imposter but I remind myself that we are just waiting for me to be healed and healthy enough for both.

"When will I become a member of the pack?" I ask as I lay back against his chest and enjoy the sparks from our skin touching as the warm water relaxes muscles Tate could not get.

"Whenever you feel like you're ready." He answers, kissing my forehead.

"What about this Saturday? It's a full moon, and it would be a perfect time." I suggest, getting a breathtaking smile from him.

"Deal. We will do it at the pack house, and it's a week before we go to Pine Paw, so that gives you time to explore the pack territory as their Luna." He agrees instantly. The water soon grows cold and Tate is the first to leave the water. Before I can climb to my feet, he bends down and scoops me into his arms once more, the water dripping off of us and onto the floor that thankfully has towels placed on it.

"I would love to make out with you like a bunch of hormonal pups, but you need your sleep." He groans out, peppering my face with kisses as he gently places me on my feet and wraps a towel around my shoulders.

"So, grab one of my shirts to wear to bed while I shave." He adds. I smile standing on my tip toes to place a soft kiss on his cheek then rush to the walk in closet and right to his dresser, going through the neatly stacked shirts and finding a V-neck t-shirt that matches his eye colour. Hastily putting it on with a pair of plain black boy shorts and towel-drying my hair all before slipping under the covers. Soon, Tate comes out with a towel around his waist and heads into the closet, his face neatly shaven. He returns minutes later with pyjama pants slung over his hips loosely and shirtless, stalking towards the bed and pulling me into his arms as he crawls into his side of the bed.

"Goodnight, beautiful" he whispers, kissing me gently.

"Goodnight." I whisper back, yawning as I snuggle closer to him, sleep taking over. He chuckled at how fast I am falling asleep, and I smile, opening my eyes to sneak one last look at him before I journey into dreamland.

"I love you." His voice is quieter than a whisper, but I hear those words clearly, and they stay with me as darkness fades in and I fall asleep feeling safe and sound.

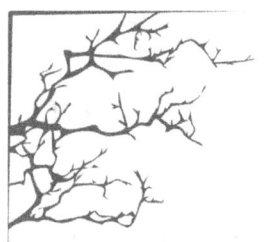

Chapter 19

"You look beautiful, Laina. Everyone is going to love you." Eeva praises me as I turn around in a circle looking at myself in the mirror. Today is the day I will officially become a member of Bloodsvain, the day I will take my place as Luna. I have already considered this pack home since meeting Tate and Eeva, already considered the wolves my pack mates and now I will officially become one of them. Nerves flutter inside me as I smooth out the strapless, cream, figure-skating dress I was told to wear by Eeva. The front half of the dress falls down to mid-calf while the back half of the dress ends in a two-foot train that trails behind me. The material is light and flowing, leaving the dress to flutter in the wind when I move.

My long, chestnut hair is styled in curls away from my face, and a crown of wildflowers rests on top of my head. White gold bangles adorn my wrists, and white gold armlets wrap around my forearms and upper arms, adding to the majestic feeling that I emit. Eeva took the time to paint the pack insignia on the center of my chest in dark, blood-red body paint, with golden paw prints scattered on the visible skin all over my body, as per the tradition of a new Luna. ensuring everything is in place before turning to face Eeva. With Eeva's house being so close to the pack house and the lake where ceremonies have taken place for hundreds of years, it became her duty as Beta Female to protect the lake and when she mated Loren, it became his as well. This also makes it the perfect place to prepare for the ceremony.

"Are you sure? I'm sixteen. What if they don't want someone young and inexperienced for their Luna?" I ask, pacing the length of her bedroom. Part of me worries that the pack will resent me for being so young. Tate and I have a ten-year age gap but I also know that some mates could have an age gap as large as one hundred years between one another thanks to our long life span.

"News has already spread about you. People can't wait to meet you and get to know you. They want you as their Luna." My friend explains with a grin on her face. I know Eeva had started spreading the news about Tate finding his mate the day we met. I also have a feeling that the warriors Tate and I have talked with on our walks have said a few things to other pack members. Even the ones I have met and talked with personally have called me Luna and gave me their full respect.

Sighing, I return to the full-length mirror and gaze at my reflection. My pale skin has turned to a healthy glow with more rest and healing. Tate made sure I rarely did any heavy lifting and even locked the workout room so I couldn't try and sneak in a quick workout. Here, I feel loved and happy. I feel safe. And its because of these feelings that I worry I wont be a good Luna to them.

"Besides, you're not the only one getting accepted into the pack." Eeva continues, and I smile. Eeva is right that I wouldn't be the only one joining Bloodsvain. Chris and Jack are joining the pack tonight, and so is Julia as soon as I am accepted. I couldn't wait to watch my baby girl grow up in a strong pack that stands together and not have to fear about becoming a Breeder. She will have endless possibilities when she shifts, and it makes my heart swell with pride thinking about it.

"Okay then." I mumble, taking a deep breath to steady my nerves.

"I can do this." I whisper to myself, staring into my reflection as my blue eyes twinkle. A wolf howls in the distance, causing me to jump from the sudden noise. I glare when I catch Eeva clutching at her side with laughter at my reaction. Excuse me for being jittery today.

"Are you afraid of the big bad wolf?" Eeva jokes at my expense. I just roll my eyes and walk to the table that holds a pot of tea that Eeva and I have been sipping throughout the day, lifting my glass and taking a needed drink of chamomile tea.

"Not one bit, considering that the big bad wolf is my mate." I retort, with Eeva fake-gagging at my cheeky response. She sighs before getting to her feet and handing me a shoebox.

"Well, that was the signal for the ceremony to start. Put these on, and we can go." She explains. I slip on the white Egyptian sandals before we head downstairs and out the back door, taking a dark path into the woods. The fallen leaves crunch under my feet, and I smile at the warm fall night and the fresh, clean air in this forest. Fall is my favourite season, and as I look up at the full moon, I can't help but smile. My life is full now. I have a mate I wanted to be with, a pack I know I will love, and a beautiful pup who will hopefully have siblings in a year or two. Today will mark my beginning of forever with Tate as his Luna of the Bloodsvain wolves, and I can't wait. It feels right being here.

Eeva and I converse about upcoming events the pack holds for October, my favourite being the pumpkin carving that pups and their mothers do the day before Halloween. It felt nice knowing the pack comes together as a community for fun holiday events. The dark forest soon brightens up with lanterns hung every so often on trees until the lake comes into view. The pack is already congratulating the regular wolves who have just finished being accepted into the pack. As the Luna, it is customary for me to join the pack last during a joining ceremony, as I can connect to every current member in the pack. But part of me believes Tate just wants to say he saved the best for last.

Noticing our presence, the pack turns to greet Eeva and me as they separate into two sides, opening a large path for me to walk through. As I walk past the wolves, each one bows to me respectfully. I smile at them feeling their acceptance in the air until my eyes face forwards just as the path opens up to reveal the edge of the lake illuminated by the full moon with Tate standing inside. He smiles at me, and I smile back, taking the last few steps towards him until I stood directly across from my mate in the chilly water, the moon making the water appear silvery below us.

"Today, we welcome Laina Starcrest as a new member to our pack, as my mate and as our Luna!" Tate begins, his voice loud and carrying past the group of wolves. Cheers of excitement follow his words, causing a blush to crawl along my skin. Waiting for the crowd to settle down, Tate takes the time to look into my eyes, mouthing the words 'You look beautiful' to me. When silence settles over the lake once again, he takes a deep breath.

"Laina, do you promise to uphold the laws of the pack and perform the duties of your role as a just and true Luna?" Tate continues, asking me the one question every Luna is faced with answering. I see the love and devotion behind his gaze, causing the nerves I felt earlier to turn into giddy butterflies. I have an amazing mate.

"I do." I answer confidently, conviction filling my voice. I felt whole answering Tate back, knowing that my role will always keep me beside him as we lead as equals.

"Then we welcome you to Bloodsvain as a member of our pack and our Luna." He raises his left hand, a blade in his right as he slowly cuts a line before turning the handle for me to take. I copy his movements, cutting a line into my left palm and wincing from the pain of the blade. Taking my bleeding hand, Tate grasps mine, and our blood mingles with one another. All at once, pack magic flows into me, causing my knees to buckle with its force and Tate reaching out to grasp my waist to keep me from falling. I close my eyes as the power opens up the link to the pack, many voices filling my head. I needed to wait for the magic to settle before I could close each channel off and be able to have silence once again. Taking a deep breath, with our bleeding hands still clasped, I feel Tate shift until I am leaning against him. My body shivers as the magic runs its course and settles down, allowing me to turn off the pack link and tune out the voices of the wolves I will be leading. Finally, silence resumes once again, and I open my eyes, seeing my reflection and noticing the neon blue glow. I am finally a member of Bloodsvain. Cheers erupt around me, and I jump from the sudden noise. Shaking my head helplessly at the celebrating wolves, I turn to catch Tate glaring at our pack as Loren walks forward and hands us each a towel to clean our hands. The pack continues to cheer loudly for a few seconds until a loud wail sounds to the left, quieting the pack while Chris steps forward to hand me an upset Julia whose eyes still glow like mine. She and I were now members of the pack, and I was happy that as her mother, I would be the only one who has to go through the initiation since she is still a newborn.

"We're home here in Bloodsvain." I tell her as she quiets in my arms and I walk out of the water. I watch the glow fade from her eyes, finally noticing that she has my blue eye colour. Tate finishes speaking with Mateo and Loren then joins us on the shore, wrapping me in his embrace and kissing me passionately in front of everyone. I feel the promise in his kiss that soon we will be fully mated, and I couldn't wait for that day to come.

Flames catch my attention when I pull away breathlessly from my mate. Bonfires were lit up just a few feet away in the clearing beside the lake, and the smell of food wafts towards everyone in the wind. Taking my hand, Tate and I lead the pack to celebrate. I smile and laugh as I get to know my new pack mates while Tate finds excuses to fill my plate with food. Julia is carried away by Eeva, Chris and Jack as the three, thick as thieves, explain that she needs to learn about her territory as Tate and my pup. Every now and then, Tate would bring her back only for one of them to steal her again, but I know she is safe. She is surrounded by her family, and each member probably fears what would happen to them if something happened to Julia. They know how vicious and blood-thirsty Tate could be, but they would soon learn what I could do if my pup is harmed. Hours pass as we party and I watch as my cousin and his mate make friends. The moon is high in the sky, and by now Julia sleeps in a baby carriage making Tate and I decide to end the celebration now and allow everyone to go home to sleep. We were saying our farewells for the night, exhaustion settling in when loud threatening howls sound in the night. I freeze with fear as I know those howls all too well.

"Is that rogues?" Someone asked, and I shake my head, turning to look at Tate with fear.

"Pine Paw," I whisper, picking Julia up and clutching her to my body, careful not to wake her.

"CHRIS! JACK!" He yells as I feel two pairs of hands grab me, with my cousin and his mate on either side, ready to protect Julia and me.

"All pregnant wolves, pups and mothers to the shelter. Ten warriors go to protect them and my mate and pup. Chris and Jack stay with her. Any able-bodied wolf ready to fight, follow me. Anyone who cannot fight is expected to head into the shelters as well. Stay safe, everyone." My mate orders before taking my face in his hands and kissing me. This one is different than before. It is needy and filled with emotion, but it ended too quickly before I am whisked away by my family while Tate and other wolves rushing towards the sounds of the howls.

[I love you!] His voice fills my head, the first time we have linked since meeting before it is cut short. He cut the pack link from me no matter how many times I reached out to him, I could not hear his voice. He is in Alpha mode, and only the battle to protect his pack and family matters right now.

Before I know it, I find myself in the pack house being led into the kitchen where the large pantry is wide open. A section of the back wall is pulled away, revealing a secret passage that many wolves rush down. Warriors guide the pack down carefully, mothers carrying pups and holding onto the hands of their older children. Chris and Jack stay next to me with Eeva and her boys behind us. I feel the tension in the air as we are led into a large room with couches and mattresses scattered around. Everyone finds a place to sit comfortably, my family and friends taking two large mattresses and pressing them together to huddle on. Finally, the last she-wolf with a small toddler in her arms enters the large room with the last of the Warriors filing in. The Warriors shut the large doors that can only be opened from inside this room. We were trapped but we were safe.

"Everything will be fine. We will all be safe, so please stay calm." Eeva states from our spot in the farthest corner of the room. The wolves who were either family or close with one another form small groups and converse. A bassinet is placed beside me, courtesy of one of the Warriors, and I thank him as I place Julia inside and wrapping a warm blanket around her. I feel a blanket being draped over my shoulders as Eeva smiles at me.

"It can get cold in here. Tate will kill me if you get sick." She jokes, nudging my shoulders as her boys go off to find their friends.

"Thank you," I whisper, leaning into my friend. The two of us talk for a bit, my tired body now alert and waiting for news on Tate and the warriors.

"Luna?" I look up to see a group of pups walking over tentatively - their wide eyes staring at me with hopeful gazes. I quickly mask my emotions, putting on a brave face in front of these pups. It would be bad to show my own fear during my first crisis as Luna.

"Yes?" I ask with a friendly smile, feeling Eeva squeeze my hand reassuringly.

"Will you tell us a story?" A little girl about ten years old asks, and I smile a little more genuinely.

"Of course, that's not a problem. How about I tell you a legend my own mother taught me?" They all jump with excitement before taking a seat in front of me. More blankets are passed around to the children as other young pups come to hear the story.

"Long ago, before Werewolves and Vampires lived, Gods and Goddesses ruled the earth. They walked like us, talked like us, and ruled the humans. Some could change into animals, some lived in the forest, and others held dark secrets. There was this one goddess who was called Luna Dea, the moon goddess." I paused as their eyes twinkle.

"Luna Dea was happy. She was one with wolves that walked with her. The people loved her, and the Gods adored her, but she wanted something. She wanted a child. For years, she walked the earth, watching humans raise their young and wishing for her own, but she knew that she needed a soulmate. One day, she came across a house in the woods. A man was cutting down fallen logs with wolves by his side. She was intrigued, and for days she stayed by his side. Little did Luna Dea know that Sat Dei, the Sun God, had been following her, wishing that she knew just how much he loved her-"

"What a stalker." Jack cuts me off, and I glare at him, watching as Chris smacks him upside the head and causing everyone to laugh. I roll my eyes at my cousin-in-law, enjoying this relaxed moment before turning to look back at the kids.

"-But Luna Dea was already in love. Sat Dei had an idea, and he left to the heavens to find a gift that Luna Dea would love, but it took years. When he returned, he found Luna Dea in the human man's arms, her belly round with children that would come any day.

"Furious, Sat Dei attacked, turning his gift of the stars into silver. For fear of her soulmate, Luna Dea bit the human, transferring her wolf power to him, a future Alpha, while the silver was stabbed through her heart."

"This stopped Sat Dei in his tracks. He looked on in horror at what he had done to his true love, who was now in the arms of the human. She turned to the father of her children, begging him to cut them out before she died, and he did. As she laid with her three children in her arms, the first werewolves born, she turned to Sat Dei and said with conviction, 'Your Children will be slaves of the night, your beautiful Sun their curse, while mine will know the loving embrace of the Moon." With those last sounds of her soft voice, she turns to her love, her soulmate, and says, 'May our children find their true half and know a love as strong as ours.' And at the highest peak of the full moon, her soul became one with her place in the sky. Stricken with grief, Sat Dei went to the nearest village and found a woman. For nights, he used her until she stood her belly round with child."

"He was overjoyed, his memory of Luna Dea and her last words a haze."

"Soon, the day came when three children were placed in his arms, and with joy, he took them out to see his sun. But they screamed as their skin burned. Quickly, he rushes inside, holding his babies as their mother came to help, picking one up only to scream in pain as the infant bites into her, draining her of blood. Sat Dei didn't know what to do other than to lure young women to his house to feed his babies. They aged faster than usual, and as they reached a month old, they were already the height of a four-year-old and could venture out at night."

"On a full moon night, Sat Dei looked up at the starry sky to see the moon looking down. He cried. It was Luna Dea, and he remembered her last words, realizing his children were slaves to the sun because of his actions."

"Grief coming into his soul faster than the day he killed Luna Dea, he did something no one thought would happen. He took a branch with a sharp end from an oak tree and stabbed his arms, legs, and stomach. Drawn by the blood, his children rush over to where he lays bleeding in their small house, and they began feeding on their father's body. As the sun rose, he took his place in the sky, forever chasing after Luna Dea. Today, we call their Children werewolves and vampires. When Luna Dea was stabbed with silver, it caused our weakness to the substance, and when Sat Dei stabbed himself with wood, he caused vampires to be weak to wooden stakes." I finish the story explaining our origins. It is a historical tale I memorized that my mother would tell me on long cold nights in front of our fireplace. The children clap and thank me for taking the time to tell this story as the older ones process my words. I could see some inquisitive minds that stayed behind to ask me about the legend, and I answer as best as I could. Some mothers nod at me in respect, admiration in their eyes while they usher their pups to comfortable spots trying to get them to sleep.

Once all the pups fell asleep, the adults huddle together too anxious to sleep. The thoughts of what is happening outside swirl inside my mind. Is Tate safe? I wonder, looking at Julia, who sleeps peacefully.

"What does Pine Paw want with us?"

"Why are they here?"

"Will our pack be alright?" The other wolves voice their questions, causing a small pit of guilt to seep into my heart. I know why Pine Paw was here. I turn my head to see Jack looking at me, sending me a reassuring smile while Chris leans against him, eyes closed.

'Open the link for me and Chris.' Jack mouths, and I nod, letting my mind focus on the two men I trusted.

[Are you okay?] Jack asks as soon as our link is opened. I sigh and send a weary smile his way.

[No, I want this to be over, and I want Tate.] I could feel tears forming in my eyes, and I shake my head. I couldn't cry right now when these wolves rely on me as their Luna to be strong for them.

[The only explanation is that they want you and Julia, Ross must have told them.] Chris speculates. I felt that something was off the moment Ross left the table when the Elders came to my house. It made sense that Pinepaw would attack now, but it is a suicide mission doing so. Bloodsvain is feared by many packs in the country.

[Get some rest. If something happens, we will wake you.] Jack suggests, pulling Chris closer to him. I know he is right and that I need sleep, but as I lay down, sleep decides to evade me as worry gnaws at my mind. I just hoped that Tate is safe.

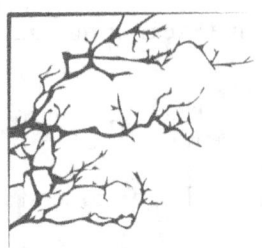

Chapter 20

"The poor Luna. Not even fully mated yet, and the Alpha is already on his death bed." A voice says loudly as growls sound afterwards with these disrespectful words.

"Shut up! What if she hears you? Besides, Doctor Rex said there is a chance he will survive." I jolt awake from these words, my eyes scanning for the source when I spot two she-wolves huddled together, their eyes darting about. I don't see any sympathy for the situation in their eyes and irritation floods me. It is wolves like these that cause disharmony in the pack. Getting up and slowly walking towards the girls. I feel the others' eyes on me while they wait for a good show. The doors to the shelter are once again open and everyone could have left, but something tells me the pack kept these gossiping bitches here so that I can deal with them. Good. At least the pack has loyalty to Tate and me.

Standing behind the two she-wolves, I let out a warning growl and watch as they stand straighter, fear coursing through them. They can sense me, sense that they have just angered their Luna.

"I suggest you both shut up. Talking about your leaders behind their back, especially with one of them in the room, is grounds for punishment." I grind out, letting the power of a Luna suppress them. I let the two girls sweat for a moment as they realize their mistake before turning on my heels and walking away, letting the pressure ease off the two.

"Send them for extra training for the next two weeks." I order to one of the Warriors, watching as his glare flickers to the two she-wolves as he scoffs at them.

"Yes, Luna. I will personally see to their training." He answers, motioning for another Warrior to help escort these she-wolves out. With this settled, I return to taking a peek at my daughter and see how she is doing, smiling when I realize Chris has her in his arms, feeding her.

"Your parents would be proud of you, Luna." Chris grins, using my new title. I roll my eyes at my cousin before a frown takes over. Were those girls speaking the truth, and is Tate injured? As if answering my question, a familiar face in the crowd makes their way out of the shelter. Mateo approaches me, and it is then that I realize Eeva and her boys are gone.

"Luna, Doc told me to come to get you." His face holds a grim look, one that holds sympathy that is directed at me. I feel my heart drop as dread fills me. Tate is okay, right? I think, taking a shaky breath. Chris hands me Julia as Jack comes to stand behind me, giving me a shaky smile as the two men support me for a moment.

"Okay, Mateo. Lead the way." I motion towards the door, letting my Head Warrior guide me towards the exit as we climb the stairs and exit the pantry. Chris and Jack stay behind me, making sure no wolf can rush ahead of me. I could tell what Mateo and Doctor Rex have to say is serious. Instead of taking me to the front door to drive to the hospital, I am lead to another room - one that is guarded heavily. I notice the elevator first, Mateo pressing a button that allows our group entry as it ascends. Time feels like it is ticking by slowly, growing my anxiety. The elevator holds a sombre atmosphere as we pass each floor until landing on the fifth floor. Rushing out as soon as the elevators open, Mateo leads us to a set of closed doors, his hands shaking as he opens them. What greets me first is that annoying sound of beeping from the heart monitor. This sound causes my heart to stop momentarily as the scent of blood, and of my mate, reaches my nose.

"Laina." Eeva's strained voice reaches me when I slowly pad into the room, taking note of the sterile environment. I turn my head to see my sister-in-law walk towards me, a strained smile on her face.

"We won and drove them away with no deaths, but-" Her voice cracks as she falls to the ground, hugging herself. I stand there, tears falling down my face as someone takes Julia out of my arms. I notice Jack giving me a sad smile as he adjusts Julia in his arms.

"Go to him, Laina. Chris and I can take care of Julia." Jack's voice reaches me as he steps away. I give a slight nod, turning to look at the figure on the bed, barely breathing, where the sound of the heart monitor beeps away. I hated that noise from my own time in the pack hospital, but right now, I was grateful for this annoyance. It meant that Tate is still alive. Taking a few hesitant steps before rushing to the side of the bed, I collapse beside Tate, clutching at the blankets that cover him.

"You...can't...leave...me!" I cry out, hiccupping between each word.

"Please...Tate, wake up." I plead, burying my face into his side and crying harder. I had already lost a child; I couldn't lose my mate as well. I cried like I did at Kelly's funeral, praying that the Moon Goddess will not take him away from me. Julia needed her father, and I needed my mate as well.

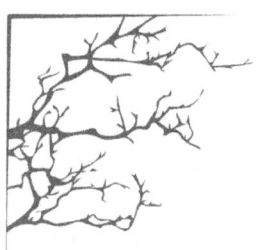

Chapter 21

Beep

That sound is starting to get on my nerves, but it means that he is still alive. Tate is alive. I still have hope to hang on to.

B*eep*

"Hi, Tate." I whimper out, watching the rise and fall of his chest.

"The Elders and I postponed the attack on Pine Paw until you wake up." My words sound hoarse as I try my best not to cry. Slowly, I put Julia on his stomach, watching her move slightly towards his face. It's been two weeks since Tate went into a coma. Two weeks since he was injured protecting us and because of that, I refused to return home without him. A room next door was set up for Julia and me to live in while we wait for Tate to wake up and since then I have been helping run the pack, making sure businesses continued as usual, having hunting days planned to refill the pack freezers before winter and preparing for a Halloween party for the pups.

"Julia is getting bigger. She misses her Daddy." This time my voice is a whisper, and I carefully move Julia so that she is by his side, moving his arm so that it wraps around her. I hate knowing his life still hangs n the unknown. Hate seeing our pup without her father doting on her. We haven't even mated and I may lose him forever.

"Please, Tate, it's been two weeks. We need you." I cry out, my head lowering to the bed as tears flow again for the umpteenth time. My body shakes from my quiet sobs as the stress between being strong for the pack and the pain of being without my mate takes its toll on me. I needed Tate more than ever to open his eyes, to reach out to me and let me know that things will be okay. I don't know how long I can last without him.

"Laina?" I straighten in my seat and turn to see Doctor Rex standing at the door. His face is grim as his lips are set in a firm line.

"What is it?" I ask, trying to sound strong, although my tear-stained face says otherwise.

"We need to talk. It has been two weeks, and he is still on life support. The coma he is in is getting worse." More tears flow, and I try to wipe them away as quickly as I can, but I couldn't help it, and in seconds I feel Rex wrapping his arms around me and letting me cry. Finally, my sobs came to an end, and Rex hands me a handkerchief to wipe my tears.

"I'm glad someone can sleep through this." He states, and I turn to find Julia snuggled up to the man who stepped up to be her father. The man that looked into her eyes the day she was born and decided that she was his pup no matter what.

"Just continue, please." I whisper, Rex letting out a long, sad sigh. I hate long-winded stories, and these past two weeks my higher ups have learned to either get right to the point in their reports or wait an hour for wasting my time when I have a pack to run with my mate in a coma.

"We need an answer by next week, wolves can't survive on life support forever. And his time is almost up." Rex states as empathetically as he can, his hand squeezing my shoulder comfortingly.

"I'm sorry you have to go through this, but as his mate you decide whether to take him off of it or not." I can feel his eyes on me, feel the sympathy in his gaze as he lets silence settle between us. I nod, unable to voice anything as a lump in my throat forms and I do my best to hold myself together. Rex sighs again, apologizes to me before he walks away and the door clicks shut. I am left alone with my mate and our daughter. His life is in my hands now, and only I could decide if he will stay on life support or if I let him go and join the other side with Kelly and our loved ones.

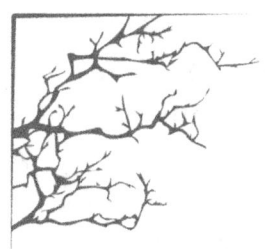

Chapter 22

Beep

"Are you sure, Laina?" The sound of the heart monitor's steady beeping follows Eeva's question as I look at Tate's still form.

Beep

The sound continues on as everyone looks at me with worry in their gaze.

"I'm sure. It's better than letting my mate suffer." I whisper out. Eeva nods, knowing that the decision for her younger brother to be taken off life support lies in my hand.

Beep

Rex slowly walks over to the life support machine and lets out a long, sad sigh. I see the pain in his eyes as he stares at Tate with a sad smile, pain that we all feel as we watch the slow rise and fall of his chest. I couldn't let him continue to suffer no matter how painful this all is.

"Goodbye, friend." Rex whispers sadly before flicking the machine off. Slowly everything comes to a stop as the machines shut down. The room grows quiet now, reminding me that the last memory I have of my ate is of him rushing off to fight and defend our pack from Pine Paw. The only thing working is the heart monitor for now but even that will slowly stop.

Eeva takes Julia from my arms and motions for me to go to Tate, she already said her good byes to her brother, promising me that she will take charge of the pack while I grieve. With tears in my eyes, I move towards his bedside, staring down at the man I fell head over heals in love with. The man that saved and protected me from Pine Paw. I swear that I will get my revenge and kill the bastard that injured my mate.

Beep

My heart breaks at his still form, and with one last try, I open the link just between us, bending down and kissing his lips gently.

[I love you.] I confess with tears flowing down my face and onto his as I stand straight. I wipe away the wetness on his cheeks as I try my best to give a wobbly smile. Just over a month with Tate and I know that my life will never be the same without him. The sound of the heart monitor slows down, with each beep taking longer to sound. My heart cracks just a bit. It takes everything in me not to break down now. I need to be strong with so many eyes watching, need to be the Luna Bloodsvain needs before Eeva can take the position of Alpha. But all I want is to break down, to fling myself across his body and cry.

Beep

The final beep sounds, and the room goes silent. With tears streaming down my face once more and sobs ready to wrack my body, I turn away from the bed, ready to walk away as my broken heart shatters even further. My mate, the one the Moon Goddess blessed me with, is gone.

BEEP

The machine starts up as I take a step away. I think nothing of it, Rex already prepping me that this might happen. Something to do with an electric current in our bodies.

BEEP

BEEP

BEEP

My steps falter briefly. The machine is going off as the heart beats grow steadily, each one coming faster than the last. I turn with wide-eyed at the heart monitor that made a comeback stronger than I thought it ever would. That annoying sound from the machine I truly and utterly want to destroy is something I relish with joy as it can only mean one thing.

[La....] it was weak, but it was Tate's voice reaching into the void that has been our link for the last few weeks.

[I'm here, baby, please wake up.] I link him, rushing to his side and clasping his hand. I can hear Eeva asking Rex what the hell is happening, but he shushes her and I thank him for that as I focus on Tate, focus on the sparks that brush against me where our skin touch.

[Laina....] His voice is louder, and my tears turn from ones of pain to ones of joy. He is there, I can feel his presence in my mind.

"Whatever you did, Luna, it worked. He is waking up." Mateo's mate Ashlyn, a nurse assigned to help take care of Tate, says from the door. Rex shushes her, the room returning to silence once again as the heart monitor continues to beep louder. No one else dares to come near as I clutched his hand tighter fearing that they might end what ever miracle is happening.

[Laina, where...] I hear his question loud and clear even if he can't finish it.

[I'm here. All you need to do is wake up.] I reply as I looked to the sky outside the big window, staring at the moon that shines down on us. Please Goddess, don't take him from me too.

[Just open your eyes baby.] I plead, turning my head to find myself staring into forest green eyes that I haven't seen in two weeks.

"I...did." His voice is hoarse from not being used in so long, and I can't help but laugh as he states the obvious. Letting go of his hand to fall into his chest and cry, I clutch his shirt as relief fills me. I feel a warm hand pet my head as fingers run through my hair gently, and I look to see that it is Tate doing this with what little strength he has, his face looking guilty.

"Sorry...you...waited," Tate whispers, and I laugh again.

"I'll always wait for you baby, I love you." I reply before moving to kiss all over his face, ending at his lips. His lips move with mine in a heated, passion-filled kiss, feeling his hand clutch my hair.

"Um, can you guys save that until after he gets better and you are in your own home?" Eeva says awkwardly, coming to stand with Julia in her arms. I pull away from Tate with a blushing face forgetting that others were standing with us when joy overcame me from Tate finally waking up.

"Can....I?" He looks at our daughter, and I smile, taking her from Eeva and putting her beside him with his arm around our little girl. His face is one of joy as he snuggles our baby close to him, relief filling me.

'Thank you Goddess.' I pray, closing my eyes. Everyone stays for a few more minutes before Rex, with tears in his eyes, orders them to leave before having a bassinet and other baby equipment rolled into the room for Julia. I refused to leave Tate's side now that he is awake, refuse to step away for one second only to find him laying there motionlessly again. I need to be beside him to know that this is not a dream, that my mate is safe and sound. With everyone gone and Julia asleep, I let Tate snuggle into me, his head on the crook of my neck with arms wrapped tightly around me. My hands play with his hair gently, feeling his body relax as his eyes droop with exhaustion.

"I love you." He whispers, and I kiss his cheek.

"I love you too." I reply back, smiling when he falls asleep with a happy grin on his face. I stay awake a little longer watching the man I love. He did everything he could to protect Julia and I when Pine Paw attacked, and I had almost lost him. I am happy I have a second chance. Yawning, I snuggle closer to Tate, hugging his body to mine as tightly as I can without hurting him.

"Get better soon, my love," I whisper before falling asleep wrapped up in his warm embrace and addictive scent.

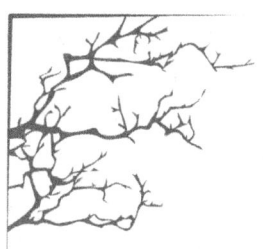

Chapter 23

"Laina, I am fine!" Tate sighs as I fluff his pillow for the umpteenth time today. It has been three days since he woke from his coma. Three days that I spent hovering over him when not taking care of Julia. Eeva announced to the pack that due to Tate waking up, I would be focusing my energy on his recovery and thankfully her and Loren took over our duties for us.

"No, you're not, so stop complaining and let me pamper you." I argue back, hearing Tate mutter something about me being a worrywart. How the tides have turned. When I ended up in the pack hospital due to the twins, he hovered over me until I was released, then hovered some more when I finally returned home. Now it is my turn to take care of him. Thankfully, Chris and Jack have Julia for the day, allowing me and Tate some time alone.

"If you want to pamper me, there is a great way that I can think of." Tate says, catching me off guard as he grasps my wrist and pulls me on top of his body. I feel him wince when my knee hits the wound on his thigh, and I try my best to get free and off of him, only to be held tighter by my mate.

"Tate you need to be careful." I scold lightly, looking into his eyes as I stop struggling, realizing I might cause more harm to his wounds.

"Cuddle with me, please. We haven't spent much time alone, and I just want to feel you close." His voice is a low, hoarse whisper sending shivers down my spine. I relent to his request and rest my head on his shoulder, snuggling in close. The room is silent as his hands slowly moved from my back, under my shirt to run up and down my sides slow and gentle, sending tingles of pleasure through me where his hands touch my skin. I sigh in contentment, gently kissing Tate's jawline and relishing in the fact that he is alive and healing. That soon we can return home with our daughter and focus on his recovery before we destroy Pin Paw for that they did.

"I love you, Laina." He whispers, turning his head to kiss my forehead. I giggle, relishing in his affection and thanking the Goddess once more for not taking this man from me. I have never felt so happy then I do with him and I am grateful that this happiness isn't going to end any time soon.

"I love you too Tate." I whisper back, moving my head and connecting our lips together. His hands stop moving, pulling me impossibly closer to his body wile my hands snake up his chest and around his neck, bringing his head closer to mine as our kiss deepens. I squeak in surprise when Tate manages to flip us so that my back is pressed against the bed and Tate on top. My legs wrap around his waist as our lips continue to collide with our passionate kiss. Tate slowly grinds against me, sending more pleasure travelling inside me, causing me to gasp and moan. Taking this opportunity to plunge his tongue into my mouth as one hand slowly explores along my stomach to rest on my breast, Tate lets out a possessive growl sending shives along my body once more. Another moan escapes my lips, and I flick my tongue across his, gaining a feral moan from him as he presses his bulge against me, and I curse the jeans I decided to wear today. Slowly we pull apart, panting from the kiss. His eyes are dark and filled with lust, and I have a feeling my eyes matched his as he leans his forehead on mine and takes a deep breath.

"God, you're so beautiful." He groans out before claiming my mouth in another passionate kiss, one arm supporting him above me, while his free hand explores under my shirt, my own hands feeling every muscle, every scar and every movement of his body. I wanted him. I wanted him above me, below me and inside me. I wanted to completely mate with him. The kiss ends prematurely as the door opens, causing both of us to growl and glare at the intruder.

"Hey, this is a room for patients. If the two of you want to make love, then go home, for crying out loud!" Rex exclaims, holding his hands up in surrender and rolling his eyes. It takes a while for my hormones to settle down before Rex's words settle in, and happiness fills me.

"Wait, I can go home?" Tate asks with hope lacing his voice. I smile and push Tate off of me gently, making him sit on the bed before I push myself up to sit cross-legged on the bed, my hand reaching out to hold onto Tate's.

"Yes, you've healed nicely over the last few days, and your scans show that your brain is surprisingly functioning normally, although that's still medically debatable with you." Rex answers, chuckling at Tate's enthusiasm.

"Just take it easy at home and rest, and no rough sex. I get you two haven't completed the mating process yet, but I don't need to see any of you as a patient again for a while." I blush as Rex continues his instructions of what Tate needs to do when we return home. Part of me understands that he still needed time to rest, but another part wants to fully be mated to him as quick as possible. Rex stays for a moment to do a quick check-up on Tate before allowing Ashlyn to come in and remove the I.V. from his arm. After getting the final go-ahead to leave, Rex and his team remove the medical equipment to be stored away in the pack house for emergency use leaving Tate and I alone.

"Now, where were we?" He asks, his voice husky as he leans his head towards mine and kisses me passionately once again.

"How about we go home first, go for a relaxing bath-" I start to say the moment we pull away to catch our breath.

"And continue where we left off before being so rudely interrupted." Tate finishes my sentence twirling a lock of my air around his fingers. I smile and nod, climbing off the bed and holding my hand out for him to take. I watch my mate slowly stands to his feet wincing from the almost healed injuries before taking my hand and pulling me in for a hug.

"I'm driving." I state sternly, looking up to catch Tate's frown at me.

"No, I am." He counters, rolling his eyes at me. I sigh in exasperation and push him playfully onto the bed, watching my mate wince and groan for a moment I smile apologetically at him before taking the keys to his jeep out before offering my hand out to him once more.

"You are in no shape to drive Tate, so I will. No arguments." I rebut with, watching him slowly stand and try to take the keys from me, growling when I jump back out of his reach. For a few minutes, he tries to take the keys away, and I focus on staying just out of his reach. Every time he would swipe left, I would doge right. If he tried to grab me, I jump pack. I watch as frustration builds inside my mate, his body slowing with each move he makes.

"Fine, you can drive." He relents frowning at me and pouting like a child. I chuckle at his behaviour and make my way into his arms, standing on my toes to plant a kiss on his cheek. From there, I take his hand and the two of us walk into the hallway and take the elevator down to the main floor. On our way out of the pack house, the two of us pass by pack members that congratulate Tate on getting better. It feels like a huge weight has been lifted off the pack now that their Alpha is better.

After chatting with a few of the wolves, Tate and I manage to finally find solace in the Jeep. I catch Tate sighing, taking a deep breath of air that doesn't smell like the pack hospital and reach out to squeeze his hand. No more hospital trips for us for a while. Turning the Jeep on, I put the vehicle into drive and head in the direction of home.

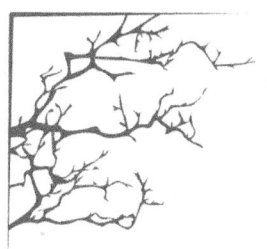

Chapter 24

Pulling into the driveway, I shut off the Jeep with silence filling the interior. It feels good being home after spending over two weeks at the pack house Jack informed me that Eeva took Julia from them while driving home, making me chuckle. I think Eeva is secretly happy to have a little girl over for the night as she has told me many times she is trying to have a daughter with Loren. A soft snore beside me catches my attention. When I turn to look at Tate I giggle, a soft smile blooming on my face as I watch my mate doze off with his head back against the seat. He looks so peaceful with the fall light streaming in through the window.

Carefully I lean over, making sure not to wake Tate and place a gentle kiss on his lips. When I end the kiss ready to pull away, strong hands pull me close and I find my chest pressed against Tate's. Warm lips press against mine as we move in a slow rhythm, his lips sending shivers down my body making me let out a small moan when he nips at my bottom lip before his tongue pries open my mouth and delves inside. Our tongues dance around for dominance until I give in, letting him take control of our kiss and relish in the pleasure he brings forth in me. His hands snake around to my ass, groping me and somehow bringing me onto his lap to straddle him where I feel his large bulge press against me.

Slowly I grind against the bulge in his pants, causing not only a moan to escape my lips but a feral groan from him. His hands guide my hips down onto him, moving me in a way that causes me to pull away as a cry of pleasure escapes my lips. Both of us are gasping for breath, our eyes glazed with raw pleasure as we stare at each other, the need to mate so strong that I am ready to give in, ready to be his.

"Bedroom, now!" Tate orders in a husky growl, his voice barely a whisper as his lips attack the sensitive part of my neck that leaves me wet and needy. I am too horny to argue with Tate about his possessive attitude. I needed him.

Needed to feel his body pressed into mine. Needed to feel him deep inside me with how I craved his touch. Needed the release only Tate could bring to me and I to him.

Leaving my neck to kiss me once more, Tate pulls away to rest his forehead on mine, needing to catch his breath. I smile lustfully at him, my own lips moving to attack his neck leaving hickeys in my wake and getting a lust-filled growl out of Tate. Opening the passenger door, I slowly climb out, releasing my assault on his neck ready to go unlock the front door only to find myself pressed against the Jeep with every inch of Tate pressed against me. His hard bulge presses against my stomach while he caresses my exposed skin. I shiver from both the pleasure caused by Tate groping my sensitive breasts and the cold air prickling at my heated skin, the combined sensual overload making me release another loud moan.

"Let's go inside, Laina." He says against my mouth before deepening the kiss once more and forcing me to walk backwards to the front door, pulling away long enough to unlock and open it. Once inside, the door is slammed shut and fingers pinch and pull at my nipples, eliciting loud moans from my mouth that get swallowed by Tate's kisses. A hand leaves its assault on my breasts to weave its way into my hair, pulling my head back as Tate bites and sucks on the sensitive skin on my neck.

"I want you, Laina. I want you underneath me as I make love to you." Tate groans against the base of my neck, his hot breath making me shiver.

"Then take me." I consent, giving a soft smile as an astonished look fills Tate's eyes. I squeal in surprise when his hands leave my body, only to lift me bridal style into his arms causing me to worry about his remaining injuries.

"Be careful, baby!" I exclaim with concern, placing my hand against his cheek gently and looking at his body, checking to see if his wounds were aggravated.

"I'm fine. The only medicine I need is you." He retorts with rolling his eyes and silencing any protest I have with yet another passionate kiss, his tongue forcing its way into my mouth once again. Distracted by my mate, I soon find myself being lowered onto our bed with Tate between my legs. He slowly grinds into me and I meet his movements with my own as our hands frantically undress each other. Hovering above me, Tate's eyes take in my naked body, his right hand caressing my cheek and I turn my face to kiss his palm keeping my gaze on his.

"You're so beautiful." He whispers, his eyes unable to hide the love he has for me behind the gloss of lust. I blush at his words looking away, knowing I still had a small amount of pregnancy weight and scars from the surgery on me that have not fully healed. For the first time, I feel a slight bubble of insecurity rise inside me.

"What's the matter?" Tate asks, tilting my head so that I am once again looking at him.

"I'm not beautiful." I whisper, hoping to hide the insecurities inside me. He smiles, leaning forward and placing soft kisses all over my face, making me giggle and relish in the feel of his adoration.

"You're right." He mumbles after placing a kiss on my cheek.

"You are gorgeous, smart, strong, and brave." He continues, kissing me in between each word before pulling away to stare at me.

"Most of all, you're mine and I love you." My heart flutters at his confession, tears filling them as I state at the man I love with all my heart. In Tate's eyes I am perfect, and I feel his love pour through our bond. Wrapping my arms around his shoulders, I pull Tate forward and kiss him passionately, tears of happiness spilling and falling along my cheeks.

"I love you too." I whisper, pulling away to catch my breath, getting the most dazzling and affectionate smile from my loving mate.

"I want to do this right, Laina. I want to make love to you slowly when I make you mine forever." Tate confesses, running the hand that caresses my face down my chin, over my breast and past my stomach lighting a path of sparks that sets my body ablaze and moans to escape me. I gasp when his hand finds their destination and he slips a finger inside me, moving gently against my wet puss and causing me to cry out. He doesn't stop there when his lips descend onto one of my nipples and his free hand pulls at the other one making me into nothing but a moaning, lustful mess.

"Does it feel good?" He asks, adding another finger inside me as I clench at his arm, shouting his name while an orgasm causes my body to twitch with extreme pleasure.

"I'll take that as a yes." He whispers, bringing his lips to mine and kissing me. My lips open to allow his tongue inside, claiming my mouth as his once more while his fingers continue to bring me close to the brink once again. His lips leave mine only to trail down my body, kissing and biting as his fingers are pulled out of me, leaving me whimpering with the need for more. But I don't have to wait long.

His warm tongue sweeps across my clit, licking up my juices from my orgasm and causing another gasp to exit my lips. One hand clutches at his hair and the other the bedsheets while he licks and nips at my soaking wet pussy. As I reach my second climax, Tate pulls away before I could orgasm, causing a noise of protest to leave my mouth. He kisses his way back up my body until his lips wet with my cum press against my own in a heated kiss. Spreading my legs further, he positions his hard cock against me, rubbing the tip against the entrance to my soaking pussy and making me move my hips in hopes of gaining release.

"You okay, Laina?" Tate asks with a smirk, one hand pressing against my stomach to stop me from moving as he slowly teases me, torturing me in waiting for him to finally claim what is rightfully his.

"No, I want more." I whimper, pressing against the tip of his throbbing cock and moaning from the pleasure it brought while smirking as he lets out a feral growl. It seems I am not the only one ready for more.

"I know, but I am going slow." He groans out as I move against him again, wrapping my legs around his waist. His hands stop my movement once more as he holds me in place so that he can lean forward and claim my lips once again. His cock enters me inch by inch, my wet walls helping him move smoothly until I felt his body pressed firmly against mine and his length is buried deep inside. Pausing inside me, Tate's body shivers with the pleasure of us beginning the mating process, the bond throbbing like his cock inside me, making me whimper. His lips move from mine to nip at the skin on my neck as he begins to thrust in and out, each thrust causing my cum to leak out of me and drip down my legs. I cry out in pleasure, moaning Tate's name like a prayer and moving my hips in sync with his. His thrusts increase in speed, and our bodies grow sweaty from our mating until the pleasure builds inside me. My eyes glaze over for a moment with lust as I call out to Tate, feeling his canines extend. With a final thrust, I find my release, my juices coating Tate's and my thighs when he releases his hot seed inside me. His canines pierce my skin, marking me as his. When he pulls away, my head moves on instinct and lips find the crook of his neck, my own canines piercing him. Tate leans his forehead against mine when my canines retract, the two of us basking in the fulfillment completing the mate bond brings and grinning like children in a candy store while we look into each other's eyes.

"I love you, beautiful." He whispers, nuzzling our noses together.

"And I love you, sexy," I whisper back with giggling as he nuzzles my cheek. I feel him gently pull out causing a moan to leave my lips once more with how sensitive I am. He chuckles, his eyes clouding with lust as he looks down at my now sore body covered in his bites and hickies.

"Are you up for round two?" He asks, his eyes meeting mine. I quickly shake my head no knowing I could not handle another round just yet.

"Can we just snuggle and fall asleep?" I ask with a yaw, my body feeling drained of energy. Tate chuckles again, flopping onto his side of the bed and reaching out to pull me to his side. The blanket is wrapped around us as I snuggle closer to him, a content smile on my face as our scents mixed with the smell of sex wraps around us..

"Sleep then. I will be here with you, my beautiful little mate." I yawn at Tate's words and smile, resting my head on his warm shoulder and drift off to sleep.

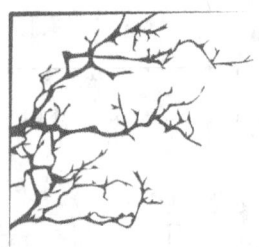

Chapter 25

The warm body underneath me shifts, making me groan as my sleep is interrupted. A deep chuckle rumbled underneath me, disturbing me even more and making me open my eyes in frustration. Glaring at Tate for waking me, I notice the soft morning light illuminating my mate as his soft lips press against my temple. My body is sore and a slight tinge of pain coming from my neck brings the memories of last night to mind and I blush, feeling a little embarrassed. Tate and I have mated and marked each other. A grin spreads across my face as I nuzzle against Tate's neck, catching sight of the mark I left on him and the feeling of being whole fills me with Tate being completely mine and me being completely his.

"Good morning, beautiful." Tate whispers, his hand running through my hair gently. I close my eyes, relishing in his pampering as a yawn escapes my lips. I could use a few more hours of sleep.

"Good morning, handsome." I reply, my voice laced with sleep as I mumble out my greeting. For a few minutes we just lay in bed enjoying each other's silent company and taking in the first morning as a mated pair. I missed lying in our bed together away from the sounds of a hospital room and being home alone with Tate is just the perfect thing we needed after nearly losing him. Home is the best place to be with no one to bother us and no nurses to walk in and disturb our rest every so often throughout the day. It's a place I feel safe and secured, a place I call my own without any fear.

"Hey, Laina." Tate whispers, his fingers drawing slow circles on my shoulder.

"Yes, baby?" I ask, tilting my head to look into his dark green eyes. I love his eyes.

"When was the last time you shifted?" I could hear the concern in his voice. Wolves have an urge to shift and release their primal side; it keeps us healthy and sane. The only exception for this is if we are pregnant or seriously wounded.

"Two weeks after I found out I was pregnant. Sam and his Warriors were hunting me down and if I hadn't shifted, I would have been caught." I answer honestly, shuddering as I think about that day. I remember how terrified I felt that day. I thought I had found a nice town to hide in, renting out a small one-bedroom cottage while I figured out what to do. At first I kept my guard up, waking every night at the slightest sound fearing that it was Pine Paw coming to get me. But soon I began to relax, thinking that I could settle down raise what I thought to be just one pup in.

After a couple of days of feeling safe away from Pine Paw, I grown accustomed to a routine until Sam and his Warriors barged into town looking for me. My landlady called the cottage phone and informed me about these men looking for me, and the best excuse I could give to the nice elderly human is that he was an abusive ex trying to drag me back home. She bought me some time to pack and leave. That day, I shifted once again and ran for my life, with only my bags on me. I decided to stay in wolf form for a week until I made good time and was days away from Sam. It took a few for the Pine Paw wolves to find me after that. At the time I was heavily pregnant and shifting could have killed us. But I got smart. I had a warned the people I met that I had an abusive ex after me and when a friend from the diner I had found work at came into contact with Sam, She called the house we shared and warned me about him. I took off once again to find myself in Bloodsvain territory.

"If Rex gave you the okay to shift, we could go outside in the backyard, and you can let loose." Tate suggests, and I grin. This would be the first time my mate would see my wolf form, and I can't wait to show him.

"Actually, he gave me the a-okay last week!" I answer instantly. Bouncing off the bed, I rush into the closet, hearing Tate chuckle behind me and take one of his shirts that covers me like a dress before bringing him a set of clothes as well.

"Excited to shift?" Tate asks with a laugh as I help him dress into a pair of baggy track pants and a V-neck t-shirt. I sigh when I spy the extent of his still-healing wounds, my heart clenching as I think about how long it might take for him to heal. I had a feeling last night took a toll on his body, but the need to mate with each other and be linked together forever was too intense to fight any longer. I'm proud our primal instincts took over but made a small vow to not do anything else until Tate is healed completely.

"Yes, I miss running so much and really need to stretch my legs, especially in wolf form." I answer as Tate stands. He takes my hand, and the two of us make our way slowly down the stairs and into the kitchen where we slip out the back door. Tate takes a seat on one of the padded lounge chairs while I run back inside to grab a blanket to wrap around him. Once I am satisfied that Tate is warm and comfortable, I quickly remove the shirt from my body, hearing a lustful growl from my mate, feeling the heat of his gaze skimming down my back and ass, causing a blush to crawl on my cheeks. Rolling my eyes, I stretch my body and prepare myself mentally to shift. With a leap off the deck, I shift midair landing gracefully on my paws and shaking out my fur. Stretching my limbs, I turn my blue-white fur with black-tipped paws body to look at Tate, his eyes in awe.

"You're a beautiful wolf." Tate whispers while I pad up the deck stairs to come site beside him, my tail thumping against the wooden deck happily. His hand reaches out to run his fingers through my fur, and I let out a soft whimper of pleasure, closing my eyes happily.

"Why don't you run for a bit around the area? I'll be fine." My ears perk up with this suggestion, and I look to Tate with a wolfish grin.

[You sure, baby?] I ask into our link with uncertainty. Part of me wants to stay close to Tate, but another part of me needs a good run.

"Positive. Link me where you are ever so often." Tate assures, poking my nose playfully. I agree, licking his fingertips before taking off.

My paws carry me through the forest around our house first, leading me to the lake with the floating gazebo where I take a drink of the crisp and clean-tasting water. My eyes scan the area, watching ducks and geese swim across the crystal-clear water and I think about how good their tender flesh would feel between my canines before taking off again. I explore as far as I feel comfortable with, linking Tate every now and then of the areas I pass and which pack members I cross paths with. The wind rushes through my fur, and the scents of our territory bring a sense of belonging through me, causing my heart to swell with pride and happiness. Each pine tree holds a unique scent that brings a touch of never-ending life, while the oak, maple, and birch trees slowly have their leaves falling and decaying onto the cold forest floor below.

Another hour passes by while I push my body as far as I can, leaping over fallen logs and splashing through puddles and small streams, but I know I have to head back soon. With a sigh, I loop back towards home as two hours have passed with the run in wolf form, leaving me feeling refreshed and renewed with all that has weighed my mind and body down the last few weeks. Taking a shortcut Tate and I would normally take on our walks I reach home in about thirty minutes, seeing Tate with his phone out just in time to snap a picture of me.

"Did you enjoy yourself?" Tate asks as I shift and put the large shirt back on, crawling into his lap to snuggle with him on the lounge chair.

"Yes. When you're better, let's go for a run together." I reply, kissing his jaw and resting my head on his shoulder.

"Sounds like a plan. Eeva texted me just a few minutes ago. She is bringing Julia home and should be here soon." I groan slightly at this information. Part of me is enjoying have Tate to myself, and I didn't want anyone coming over today. But I missed my pup too much and wanted Julia safe and sound at home.

"Does this mean our quiet time is over?" I ask, getting a chuckle from my mate. He tilts my head back gently to plant a long kiss on my lips, pulling away with a smirk and leaving me breathless after a few minutes.

"We can have quiet time to ourselves later tonight, so don't worry." He promises causing a blush on my cheeks once again. I have a feeling it would be hard to not make love to my mate so that he can heal properly over these next few days. With a sigh, I climb off Tate and stretch before helping him to his feet. Once he is steadily standing, we walk back into our house and Tate goes to sit in the living room while I make my way upstairs to put on a pair of leggings, keeping Tate's shirt on. Heading back downstairs, I catch Tate holding the front door open while Eeva pushes a stroller inside.

"Hey, Eev-" I start to greet my sister-in-law and friend.

"Shh, my niece is sleeping." Eeva scolds, parking the stroller beside the bench in our entranceway to take off her shoes. I roll my eyes at her and quietly walk over to peer inside to see the angelic face of Julia deep in her sleep. I missed my little girl so much and couldn't help but run a finger gently across her chubby cheeks.

"I'll bring her to her room." Tate whispers as I straighten up, letting him pull the stroller closer to where he stands. Carefully he bends down to unstrap Julia from her stroller and cradle her in his arms. I feel grateful that I can watch him pick up our pup inside our home again, no longer confined to a hospital bed and unable to do anything with our daughter.

"Do you need help?" I ask, stepping closer to plant a soft kiss on Julia's forehead and getting ready to assist Tate up the stairs.

"No, I'll just take my time." He reassures his eyes focused on the sleeping baby in his arms. A soft smile plays on my lips, and I step back to give Tate room to turn around.

"Okay then. Call out if you need help." I agree. He smiles at me and kisses my forehead before making his way upstairs. I know better than to wait for him and hurt his Alpha pride, so I turn to Eeva, who has a smile on her lips and a knowing glint in her eyes.

"So, how does it feel to be completely his?" I blush at her words, my face becoming a heated crimson.

"I don't know what you mean?" I feign ignorance and turn, heading towards the kitchen with my growling stomach protest because of the lack of food.

"Please, I can smell my brother all over you and inside you. Plus, the house reeks of... you know what." She practically laughs out as she follows after me.

"Did you guys do it in the hallway or something?" I feel my cheeks heat up even more as I busy myself with turning on the oven, grabbing a box of Delissio frozen pizza from the fridge and popping the pepperoni party size into the hot oven. I just ignore my friend and turn on the kettle to make some tea to sip on.

"C'mon, I know you're fully mated to him now. I can see the mark peeking out from under the collar of that shirt you're wearing." I didn't know how red my face is, but I smile, my hand reaching for the sensitive spot on my neck. I turn to face my friend, finally conceding to spill the details.

"It feels amazing, and it was amazing, and Eeva, I can't wait to fee-"

"Okay, too many details." I laugh at her reaction, a look of horror on her face as I was about to spill all the details of how amazing sex with Tate was last night.

"Well, you asked." I come back with, smirking at the look of horror still plastered on her face.

"But that's my brother!" She practically yells, running her hand through her hair.

"You still asked." I shrug, pouring a cup of tea for us. She sighs in defeat and sits down at the table and after checking the pizza, I join her, bringing the mugs over.

"So, when do you want to go shopping for some new clothes?" I laugh at the random question - at Eeva's attempt to change the subject - when the sounds of the front door opening and closing reach us. Seconds later, Chris and Jack walk into the kitchen carrying take-out boxes.

"Oh, you're up. We went and got some take-out, but I smell pizza." I laugh at Jack's words and watch as he and Chris set the food on the table. Taking a whiff of the Chinese food wafting from the containers, my stomach growls - protesting its need for food as soon as possible.

"By the way, Laina, was that your wolf I saw earlier today?" Chris asks, going to the cupboard to grab some plates. I smile happily, making my way to check on the pizza and nod.

"Yes it was, I needed a good run and haven't shifted in months. I needed to let loose." I respond. The smell of the pepperoni pizza spills out into the kitchen with the golden crust signalling it being cooked. Taking the pizza out of the oven, I rummage through a drawer for a pizza cutter coming out victorious. While I cut the pizza, Chris and Jack set the table. The sounds of footsteps on the stairs signal Tate joining us, and just as I put the pizza on the table with the Chinese food. I smile when Tate places a kiss on top of my head before greeting our family. He carefully slides into the bench, wincing for a moment before getting comfortable before I slide in beside him. Chris and Jack sit across from us while Eeva takes the seat at the end.

"This is what I needed. My family, pizza, and some take-out." Tate exclaims as he squeezes me closer to his side and planting a kiss on my cheek. I smile resting my head against his shoulder as I take in the quiet calm. It's been a hectic month since Tate and I first met and just being able to appreciate the small things together made the everything we went through worth is.

"So Eeva, where are the rugrats and your mate at today?" Chris asks, piling Chinese food onto his plate. I quickly snatch the spring rolls just in time to place a couple onto Tate and my plates before passing the appetizer around. Jack has a habit of eating all the spring rolls, which Chris and I hate.

"They went to the cabin about two hours away from here with their dad for the weekend. They want to soak up the last few rays of sun before snow kicks in so I have the house to myself." Eeva answers happily, stuffing a slice of pizza into her mouth. I smile at the normality, filling mine and Tate's plate and enjoying this night. The five of us talk for a while until Chris disappeared for a moment to get a crying Julia who is cradled in her father's arms as Tate feeds her.

Sometime around seven Eeva left, wanting to enjoy the alone time she rarely has. I laugh at her enthusiasm as she talks about the things she is going to do without having to deal with children this weekend – one of them being sleeping in tomorrow. After Eeva left, Jack and Chris went to bed. They have been slowly renovating a house they found abandoned and had slept at the pack house last night to give Tate and I some privacy. I think we all can't wait for them to move out and into their own place soon.

With a quiet house and Julia once again in her room asleep for the night, Tate and I find ourselves snuggling in front of the fireplace. His hands draw small circles on my back as we lay on the sofa held in each other's embrace.

"Have I ever told you how much you mean to me?" Tate asks quietly, turning my head so that we are looking into each other's eyes.

"Yes, whenever you get the chance to." I answer, my voice barely above a whisper.

"Well, I don't say it enough." He adds, bending his head forward and gently kissing me. My hands cling to his shirt as our lips move in sync, a small moan leaving my lips when he flips us over so that Tate lies on top of me. Pulling away breathless, he kisses the tip of my nose before resting his forehead on top of mine.

"Laina, you are the most beautiful, talented, amazing person I have ever known. You are my queen, my best friend and my true love, and I will always be here for you. If I make you mad, I will fight for you to smile and love me again. You make me happy, and you bring the sunshine back into my life." He smiles shyly at me before he kisses my lips once again – this time the kiss is filled with passion, one that ends way too soon. We find ourselves panting, foreheads pressed together once again and tears well in my eyes.

"Why are you crying? Are you hurt?" I can feel Tate tense above me as he frantically asks his questions, his face filled with worry and his eyes scanning for any signs of injury. I giggle at his reaction and wrap my arms around his neck, pulling Tate closer to me and burying my face into the crook of his neck where my mark sits on him.

"They are happy tears." I answer with a giggle, kissing his mark gently. Tate sighs with relief, turning us until I am lying on top of him again. His fingers wrap around my hair, playing with the chestnut locks and lulling me to sleep.

"I love you, Tate. I love you so much it hurts when I am not with you." I whisper, feeling the tears of joy slip down my cheeks. Tate gently moves so that the two of us are sitting, his arms wrapped around me, keeping me on his lap and hugging me tightly to his body.

"And I love you, Laina. You're my world, and I will do everything I can to protect you." He whispers, nuzzling my own mark that he left on me last night. One I will have for the rest of my life. I nod against his shoulder with his words, pulling back from the hug to slam my lips into his, feeling his arms hold me tighter against him. His hands move to my hips, and he lifts me up as he stands, my legs wrapping around his waist as the kiss turns passionate once again. His noticeable erection is pressed to my thigh and a moan escapes my lips. This seems to be the undoing for us as I find myself being carried up the stairs, Tate bringing me to our bed.

Passion ignites within us, my body sizzling with the pleasure every touch of his brings. His lips find every sensitive area, sucking and kissing my skin, causing a flood of wetness to form between my legs. Our clothes are torn off in a rush, the two of us just wanting to be close with only skin touching and no barriers to come between us until his hard cock is nestled deep inside me.

We spend the night lost in each other's touch, crying with pleasure and each release giving a silent vow to always protect and love each other as our primal urges take over.

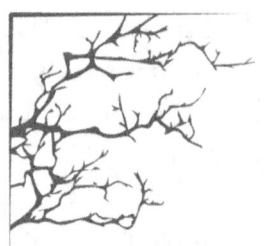

Chapter 26

Bright light fills the bedroom, forcing me to awake and making me crave the darkness under a pillow to fall back asleep. My body is sore from the last two nights making love to Tate, causing me to wonder if Tate is fully healed or not. No man should be this energetic when on bed rest nor should he be this eager to fuck with such primal urge.

As my consciousness settles in, I realize that I am pressed under Tate, his hand removing the pillow from my head and the realization that his hard cock is still deep inside me, reminding me that I passed out last night after being filled by my mate. The memories of last night flash through my head, causing me to blush as I think how my body bent to Tate's will. I can feel myself grow wet once again and slowly grind into Tate, moaning when his cock twitches inside me.

"Someone having issues?" Tate's husky voice fills my ears as he slowly moves inside me, massaging my sore, sensitive walls. I moan again, arching my back to feel even more, gaining a chuckle at my wanton reaction from my mate.

"I'll take this as a yes then, baby." He whispers, his lips finding my mark and nipping at the sensitive skin. He picks up speed, the sounds of moaning and grunting filling the early morning air as I give in to the pleasure mating with Tate brings.

ॐ

The smell of bacon and lavender tea forces my groggy eyes opening to see a tray set on my bedside table, a single purple tulip in a small glass mixing with the fragrance of breakfast. A gentle smile spreads across my face at the sight of Tate's handwriting and a shirt of his placed beside the tray. Sitting up in bed, I stretch my sore body, noticing the bruises and love bites from my mate and I chuckle at his possessiveness in always finding a way to leave marks on me while reach for the large shirt, tugging it on.

Tate walks in just as I reach for the tea with a squirming Julia in one arm and a bottle in his free hand. He settles in beside me on the bed as I eat, feeding Julia while we enjoy the comfortable silence. I reach for my phone, taking a chance to snap a picture of my little family and catching Tate off guard. He informs me that Chris and Jack went to their house to continue their renovations, leaving the three of us home alone.

"So, I was thinking we could have a movie night." Tate says out of nowhere a smile on his face as he lays a fed and changed Julia on our bed between us.

"We can go to the mall, find some movies to watch and get some snacks to have a night in. I think your cousin and his mate will be staying in their house for the night since it's almost ready for them to move in." He continues, helping Julia onto her stomach for some tummy time. I smile at the suggestion, happy to know that Chris and Jack will be leaving our house soon. It will make having time alone with Tate easier when they are fully moved into their own place.

"Okay, sounds like fun." I reply after thinking about it, finishing the last of my food. I place the tray onto the side table beside me once again and carefully move closer to Tate, wrapping my arms around him and nuzzling his neck. Part of me did not want to move from our comfortable bed, but the idea of a date night with my mate has excitement and giddiness taking over me.

Deciding to get dressed, I leave Julia in Tate's care and quickly make my way into the closet grabbing a light fall dress to put on after I take a much needed shower. Each step I take has me wincing slightly, the slight pain reminding me I will that I need to remind Tate to calm down. Before I head inside the bathroom, I catch Tate smirking at my discomfort and glare at him. Asshole. He knows I am sore from him and must be feeling so proud of himself.

Closing and locking the bathroom door, I place the dress on the hooks attached to the door and turn on the shower. The baggy shirt is thrown to the side before I comb my hair out and step into the shower. The running water eases the slight pain from my body, making moving and walking a lot easier by the time I turn off the shower and step out to get ready to leave. I towel dry my hair and body slipping into some undergarments before pulling the dress on and piling my semi-damp hair into a messy bun on top of my head. Heading out of the bathroom, I Tate is no longer in the room as I pop back into the closet grabbing a pair of flats from the shoe rack and after grabbing my purse from my vanity I make my way down stairs to find Tate with Julia in her car seat and the baby bag strapped over his shoulder.

"Are you ready to go?" Tate asks, lifting the car seat into his arms.

"Yes, I am. No sex tonight, please. I need a break." I answer, stating my need to skip on our nightly exercise. My mate smirks at me, planting a quick kiss on my lips and agreeing as we leave the house and into the jeep. He secures Julia's car seat in the back behind the driver's seat before placing the baby bag on the floor of the jeep. I smile, thinking I am one lucky she-wolf to find such an accepting and caring mate as I climb into the passenger seat.

The drive to the mall is filled with us talking about our favourite childhood movies. Tate was shocked that I grew up seeing almost all Disney movies but once I pointed out that with a gay cousin and his mate raising me and that I was raised differently from other werewolves he instantly understood and chuckled. I reminded him that Julia will be spoiled and subjected to romance movies and Disney marathons and the motivational message of "she can do anything if she just put my mind to it" like they did with me. They built my confidence and gave me the freedom to learn who I was growing up, allowing me to be the she-wolf I am today. The was well received by Tate as he realized that with Chris and Jack taking Julia for the night meant more alone time for us to create siblings for her, making me roll my eyes at my mate and his enthusiasm to keep me in our bed locked in constant mating.

The mall thankfully came into view soon and after pulling into the mall parking lot, the two of us make quick work of getting Julia's car seat connected to the stroller. With her safe and secured, Tate takes the lead in pushing the stroller into the mall entrance.

"So where to first?" I ask, hooking my arms around Tate's bicep, feeling him flex with my touch. I catch sight of people doing double-takes at us as we walk by and have to do my best to hold in my laughter. I guess seeing a six-foot-seven-inch man built like a bodybuilder pushing a baby-pink stroller and a short girlfriend beside him is a sight to see.

"We could head to Wal-Mart and look in the electronic section and grab snacks all in one go." He suggests, and I nod. Wal-Mart is located on the other side of the mall, and we take the time to window shopping and enjoy the stroll. Before we reach Wal-Mart, I come to a stop in front of Build-A-Bear, practically dragging Tate into the store to create three wolf stuffies for each of us. He has a bemused look the whole time we spend in the shop as I childishly run around searching for the right outfits to dress the wolf stuffie in clothes suited to Tate and my style finishing with a baby wolf that once paid for I place beside Julia in her car seat.

"Was that fun?" Tate asks, chuckling, the boxes housing each stuffed animal in the basket at the bottom of the stroller.

"Yes. I've always wanted to go there and do that as a child. Just never had the chance too, and now we each have a Build-A-Bear." I giggle out the answer, my eyes sparkling with joy. We finally make our way to Wal-Mart, the blue entrance greeting us. I nod respectfully to the greeter at the front while grabbing a flyer from the rack to see what's on sale. Reluctantly I release Tate's arm to go and take a shopping cart from the corner before returning to my mate and pup. The two of us walk around the grocery section first heading in the direction of the snack aisle and standing in front of the products on display.

"What should we get?" He asks with slight confusion, and I laugh, nuzzling his neck gently.

"How about we get some popcorn, chips, chocolate and ice cream?" I list out snack ideas, making it easier to narrow down what we will snack on for the night.

"Okay, baby girl, pick out what you think would be good for tonight then." Tate laughs. I nod and kiss his jaw before turning towards the chips and grabbing two bags of ruffles plain chips and some sour cream and onion dip. I grab three cans of Pringles - two original flavours and one pizza flavour – as an afterthought before we walk further down the aisle to look at chocolate bars.

"What's your favourite chocolate?" I ask, grabbing a bunch of Smarties and Kit Kats.

"I like the dairy milk ones." He answers, his face focusing on Julia as he takes pictures of her with her stuffed wolf. I nod, grabbing the milk chocolate and cookies and cream before turning to him with a coy smile.

"Maybe we can see what flavours chocolate enhances our nightly activity." I whisper coyly. His eyes slowly darken with my word while his arm snakes around my waist, pulling me closer to his solid body.

"It sounds like we will need more chocolate then." Is his comeback, his voice low and husky when it enters my ear. I giggle and step away from him, grabbing more milk chocolate and cookies and cream bars, my mind racing on what we could do with the sweet substance. With a childish grin on my face, we head over to my favourite aisle, the ice-cream aisle. I select a tub of Chapman's French Vanilla and Mint Chocolate Chip laughing when Tate places a Neapolitan ice cream into the cart, commenting that mixing the three flavours together is 'The bomb dot com babe.'

"Do we have all the snacks we need?" I ask Tate while aimlessly grabbing a bottle of Wal-Mart white wine off the shelf.

"Yes, we do. All we need now are the movies." Tate answers before steering the stroller towards the electronic aisle. We come to a stop in front of the large 'New Release' display. Tate questions which movies I have seen since they came out in theatres, and I answer that I haven't seen any new movies since May. It was hard going to a theatre when running for mine and my babies' lives and freedom. This prompted Tate to start picking each and every last movie off the display and putting them into the cart with the snacks, a smile on his face.

"Guess we will be having movie night for a while." He chuckles, coming to kiss me chastely. I couldn't help the bubble of happiness swelling inside me with how pampering Tate is to me. I am happy to be mated to him with how he's protected me and accepted Julia as his.

We make our way to the self-checkout, where Tate informs us that he will get the car and bring it to the front entrance of Wal-Mart to make it easier for us, handing me his credit card and telling me the pin before running off in the direction we came from. With a silly grin on my face, I take my time scanning the items, my eyes scanning over two of the movies: Onwards and Maleficent: Mistress of Evil. These would be the two we watch tonight.

A Wal-Mart employee offers to push the cart outside for me as I finish paying, and I thank her while the two of us exit the automatic doors. Tate comes to a stop just as we reach the edge of the sidewalk and opens the trunk of the jeep, thanking the teen for her help while he puts the bag away, I settle Julia into the car and climb back into the jeep as Tate takes the cart to the cart coral inside the Wal-Mart before returning to the Jeep.

It is mid-afternoon by now, and my stomach started protesting with the need for food, causing my mate to chuckle at me. Deciding to grab lunch, Tate parks the Jeep in the parking lot, and the two of us decide to walk over to the Tim Horton's to grab a quick lunch. There I feed Julia as a couple of elderly ladies comment on how beautiful she is and – adding to Tate's already sky-high ego – saying how she resembles Tate. This must have helped solidify Tate forever being her father, as his eyes beam with pride. Only a few of us would know the truth of how Julia was conceived. Finally finishing our food, we make our way home where I take Julia who is snuggled in her car seat with her wolf plushie and place her into her swing the moment we enter our house. After making sure she is secured and still fast asleep, I help Tate unload the car and put the ice cream in the freezer right away to keep it from melting.

"So which one do we watch first?" He asks, picking up his coffee as I sip on my white hot chocolate.

"Let's watch Onwards first. Since Julia will be with us while we start our movie day, it's only right to do the child-friendly movies first." I answer, walking into the living room where Tate is organizing the movies on the shelf below our T.V.

"Okay, baby, Onwards it is." He chuckles out, taking my left hand and kissing it gently.

"We'll watch it on one condition." He smirks, and I tilt my head. Tate shifts from a sitting position to kneeling on one knee, his eyes finding mine. My heart stops for a moment as he stares into my eyes, with nothing but love displayed directly at me as he takes out a ring box from inside his back pocket.

"Laina, will you marry me?"

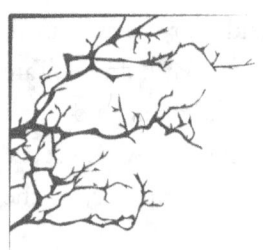

Chapter 27

I stand there in our living room, tears forming in my eyes. I know that, to some people, getting engaged within two months of meeting someone would be considered way too fast, but Tate is literally my soulmate, my other half, the person the Moon Goddess paired me with. I feel complete and whole when with him.

"Laina?" Tate's voice wavered slightly, his happy face slowly losing hope and I realize that I have stood there a few minutes without answering because his proposal has left me speechless. Quickly, I nod my head yes, feeling my tears flow as I jumped into his arms, causing the two of us to tumble to the floor as I kiss all over his face with joy.

"Yes! Always a yes!" I manage to answer once my shock has passed. He smiles, flipping us over so that I am underneath him as he smashes his lips to mine in a long and passionately, one that leaves me breathless and panting once we pull away. After a moment of basking in his love, Tate places a beautiful white gold ring with a heart-shaped diamond on my dainty ring finger, his smile beams so brightly as if he just won the lottery, a gold medal in the Olympics and the Prime Minister Seat of Canada all in one day.

Tate offers to order in some food for dinner as we climb to our feet, planting another kiss on my lips before he moves to the kitchen to search through our take out menus while I set about getting the Blue Ray player ready for our movie. My thoughts drifted to the ring as I stare at it, the plans for our wedding already in motion in my mind as I smiled happily. I want to wait for a bit for our wedding day wanting to settle the matters with Pine Paw first before saying 'I Do' to Tate.

"Penny for your thoughts?" Tate muses, bringing me out of my thoughts as I turned to look at his smiling profile.

"Pennies don't exist in Canada anymore, remember." I laugh, taking the offered wine glass from his hand and sipping on the sweetly-tart goodness.

"Well then, nickel for your thoughts?" He corrects himself, causing me to burst out laughing. I shake my head at my mate's childishness while he joins me to sit on the sofa, wrapping his arm around my shoulder and kissing the top of my head. If someone told me four months ago that the most-feared wolf next to the Alpha King is a goof ball, I would have laughed in their face and walked away. His reputation as a heartless wolf who slaughters all that appose him is one I have now learned is just for show. He is warm, kind and loving. He treats his pack as his family and respects those from the lowest rant to the highest in our pack. He is only ruthless when it comes to those that want to harm those he loves.

"So, what were you thinking about?" Tate asks, looking sideways at me. His hand gently playing with my hair and a blush creeps along my cheeks.

"Plans for our wedding," I confess, watching his smile grow wide with my words. Every girl has dreams for their wedding day, and I am no exception. I just want an amazing day filled with family and love. Something small and intimate and easy to sneak away from once the night ends.

"I know that even in a paper bag, you will be the most beautiful girl that day." He reassure me, taking my hand and kissing the ring. I giggle with his words, taking the time to snuggle into Tate's side with his arms wrapped around me. The fall sunlight filters into the room through the large windows, falling onto Julia, giving our child an ethereal glow. The quiet and cozy atmosphere warming my heart as I watch my little girl sleep soundly.

"I could stay here and watch her forever." I whisper, looking to Tate who nods and smiles at me before our attention return to our baby girl.

"I could too." He whispers back, kissing the top of my head, making my smile even wider. It feels perfect having my small family here with me.

Deciding to wait for Julia to wake up before we watch the first movie, Tate and I turn the T.V. on, surfing the channels until we decided on Murdoch Mysteries. Food shortly arrives, and Tate leaves me in the living room while collecting the delivery from the teen. I smell the scent of Indian cuisines as Tate rounds the corner with a large bag setting the contents out on the table as I run into the kitchen to bring out plates and silverware. We continue our show while eating. Something about the Victorian era always bringing out my love for interior design, especially with how Murdoch

Mysteries is set and designed. Some time into our second episode with the food eaten and dishes cleared away, Julia decides to voice her complaints.

"I got her." Tate says, getting up and walking to the swing where he lifts our child up, swaying side to side as he soothed her. He takes her upstairs for a diaper change while I make my way to the kitchen to prepare a bottle for our hungry baby. Making sure the bottle is at a perfect temperature, I walk into the living room just as Tate does, handing him the bottle to let my mate feed our daughter.

"Why don't you set up the snacks while I feed our little princess, and we can turn on the movie," Tate suggests. I agree, returning to the kitchen to grab the bag of snacks left on the counter and the Neapolitan and mint chocolate chip ice cream from the freezer. Setting the snacks out on the coffee table, Tate continues to feed Julia as I bustle about choosing the movie Onwards, placing it into the Blue Ray player before settling into the sofa beside Tate, who cradles a wide-awake Julia in his arms.

The movie slowly begins with some laughter coming from me with how the siblings act together, and Tate rolls his eyes.

"This movie is so basic." He grumbles, and I shush him, my eyes taking in everything.

"I like kid's movies; this includes Pixar and Disney films, so shush." I warn, pouting playfully as I snuggle closer. Movies like these always bring out the child inside everyone, leaving a lasting message that shapes children. I much preferred these types of movies to horror or thriller movies.

"Okay, okay." He says in surrender, wrapping his arms around my shoulder pulling me closer to his body. I smile and focus back on the movie, small noises from Julia every now and then coming from Tate's arms, causing us to laugh. As I watch the colourful memories float by, my own heart wrenching when they turn sad as life changed. It reminded me slightly of how mine had changed drastically from losing my parents to becoming an illegal Breeder, gaining a mate worth loving and becoming a mother to my babies, even if all I have is Julia to raise. I stop paying attention to the movie as I fell into my own thoughts, thinking about every last memory I made, all the pain I have been through, and all the happiness that found and lead me to where I am now.

"Baby? Babe? Baby girl?" I blink as I turn to stare at Tate, blushing slightly as I realize that the movie had finished.

"Sorry." I mumble, smiling sheepishly at my mate.

"It's okay. So where did you go?" He says, detangling himself from me to put a sleeping Julia in her swing, setting it on a gentle speed.

"I was thinking about my life. Watching the movie made me realize how much I have been through to get to where I am today." I say quietly, scooting over so that Tate could sit back down, having him pull me close so that our legs were spread out on the couch, his slightly wrapped around mine.

"Want to talk about it?" He asks, one hand playing with my hair, the other rubbing my back.

"I guess." I sigh out, taking a deep breath of his intoxicating scent.

"I never told you much about my parents." I whisper, clutching his shirt.

"No, but I knew you would in the end." He says, kissing the top of my head.

"I was six when they were murdered. My father was the Beta at the time, and a rogue pack attacked us when we were celebrating his birthday. I was still too young and hadn't shifted yet, so I was rushed into the panic room with the wolves who couldn't fight. When it was over, they were gone." I shudder as a few tears fell from my eyes, and I bury my face into his chest, taking deep breaths to calm myself.

"I'm sorry, baby." He whispers, kissing my head.

"So am I." I mumbled.

"I never got to say I was sorry to them. That morning I had fought with them about the dress I was wearing, wanting to be in jeans and a tank top so that I could play sports. But my dad argued, saying that the daughter of a Beta should be proper and look like a lady. I ended up saying I hated them, and those were the last words I said to them." I go on to talk about my parents, their strict rules but also their love for me. In the end I am left crying as I clutch Tate's shirt. No one knows that the last moments my parents and I had are the ones I regret.

"You wish you could take it all back." Tate states after explaining everything, his words making me look up to see his eyes full of understanding and regret as well.

"Every day of my life." I agree, resting my head in the crook between his shoulder and neck. He nods and hugs me tight as I sniffle, my tears now staining his shirt.

"The last time I saw my parents, I said the same thing, even told them their plane would crash." He admits, and I look up to see him watching me.

"They were on their way to make a treaty with a European pack, and they were missing my first soccer game in high school. They never missed anything when it came to Eeva, but they were busy every time something important to me came up. I felt neglected, and I grew to hate them. Truth is, I still do." I wait silently while Tate clutches me tighter to him, his eyes gaining a faraway look while I wait for him to continue.

"One day the Beta came to our house. Said the plane was shot down by an Asian pack, and there were no survivors. I vowed that day that I would never miss anything my children do. I want to make every day and every memory count." His eyes went cold as he talked about his parents but softened at the end as he looks to our sleeping daughter. I smile, wrapping my arms around his neck and pulling him close for a kiss.

"I love you." I whisper when we pull away smiling, our foreheads against each other's.

"And I love you too." He chuckles out, nuzzling our noses together. Tate later goes to explain that Eeva took over as temporary Alpha until he finished school. At the age of nineteen, he became the youngest Alpha ever. It explains why Tate is so ruthless when he needs to deal with other packs. We decided to continue our movie marathon in bed, Tate bringing the snacks into the room while I settle Julia in her bed. It feels like our relationship grew closer with our confessions about our parents. Both of us had the same vow to always be there for our pups and that thought brings a smile to my face.

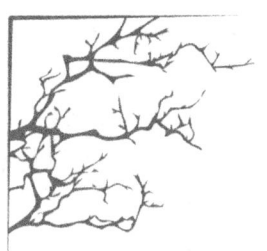

Chapter 28

Shivering slightly, my body slowly comes to consciousness and my eyes scan the room to see the sunshine falling in through the open window curtains. This morning the bed feels colder than usual, and my hands search for the warmth Tate always brings. Worried, I turn around to face Tate's side of the bed only to notice him gone and—judging by how cold his side of the bed is—he's been gone a while. Frowning, I slowly sit up, my body sore once again from spending the night with my mate and wonder where he might have went. Wrapping the blanket around my naked body, I search for any clue that my mate might have left indicating his whereabouts when I spy the note folded neatly on his pillow.

With a soft smile, I pick up the note and carefully unfold the paper to see Tate's neat handwriting on display. The note tells me that Tate decided to go to the pack house to take care of some business and catch Rex for a check-up. Chris and Jack took Julia for the day, wanting to give me some time to rest and sleep in. Warmth fills my heart with the wonderful family I have and my smile widens. I kiss the note, placing it on the nightstand stationed on my side of the bed before getting up for a quick shower and dressing in a warm baggy knit sweater, fleece-lined leggings and a grey scarf before heading downstairs. Entering the kitchen, I make a quick, light breakfast and take the time to scroll through my phone. I know I had projects due soon for my courses in college but those can wait. I wanted to do something fun for myself first as this is the first day to myself without the worry of Luna duties, raising a pup or having a loving yet overly protective mate hovering around me.

Taking a look at the calendar, I see that Tate has changed it from September to October, and an idea comes to me. Grinning like a Cheshire cat, I finish my breakfast and make my way to the garage. Texting Tate, I ask where he hides the decorations for Halloween. A quick reply comes, and I giggle first at the picture of him bored out of his mind during a phone call, and then with the information that the decorations are where I am heading.

Pressing the button on the side by the garage door, I watch the wind blow leaves across the yard. Deciding on my first chore, I get to work grabbing the rake from the wall and slowly raking the leaves into the middle of the yard on the house's left side. It took a lot longer than I thought it would, but eventually, all the leaves are piled high. Part of me wants to enclose the area around the pile of leaves, so I lean the rake against the sturdy oak tree and make my way into the large garage. After rummaging around, I find some large fences about a meter tall that can easily be hammered into the ground. I make a couple of trips going back and forth until all the temporary fences are laid out in a large enough area. Quickly I fence in the leaves only stoping to take a break once the fencing is done to make a sign with some old wooden boards, paint and nails that read 'Leaf Jumping Pile' that I have a feelign Eeeva's pups will love. I never knew how much of a handyman Tate was until now, and it makes me smile knowing that I had tools readily available for decorating and building.

Hammering the sign at the entrance of the fencing, I take a moment to admire my handiwork. I noted that the garden would need some work done. Obviously, the plants have been neglected since first arriving here, so I put myself up to the challenge. Not many people in Pine Paw liked gardening, but I find the rhythmic action to be soothing and relaxing. Searching through the garage, I find a few yard waste bags and some gardening gloves and set to work in the garden. I trim the bushes and prep the shrubbery for the winter that is fast approaching. My phone is blaring music from Spotify as I work outside, enjoying the easy exercise gardening brings. It feels nice moving my body again after having a baby and being cooped up healing or waiting for Tate to wake up from his coma. With a smile, I lean back to rest when my ringtone cuts my music short. Only a few people have my number. Rushing to pick my phone up, I throw my gardening gloves onto the ground and by pass looking at the caller I.D. to just swipe the answer icon.

"Laina here." I greet, heading onto the rocking chair that Tate and I had bought just after being released from my hospital trip.

"Hey, baby, how is your day going?" I smile at Tate's voice, closing my eyes and relaxing as the chair rocks.

"It's going well. I'm decorating the house for Halloween." I answer. My finger slowly moves to play with my engagement ring while Tate chuckles at my enthusiasm.

"There are more decorations in the basement and some in the shed behind the garage once you finish using the ones I keep year-round in the garage. If you need anything else, we can go shopping." I grin at the idea of shopping. I have a feeling that there will be more than enough decorations here at the house, but we could probably have the scariest house on the block if I find things I like.

"That sounds like fun. We can get some costumes too." I agree, giggling. I love Halloween and the idea of dressing up in costume just being carefree for the day. Part of me preferres going to haunted houses instead of trick or treating like most children would do growing up. It just feels more fun seeing what humans consider scary when to them werwolves are scary in and of themselves.

"And what would my baby girl want to be?" I blush at his words and think of Julia, him, and myself, an idea forming.

"Why don't we dress up as a King and Queen and Julia as a princess?" I suggest, hearing another chuckle.

"Okay, but we are not getting cheap Wal-Mart costumes. I have an idea of what we are going to get." He states. We talk for a few more minutes about dinner plans, how the pack business is going and if I need to head to the pack house to help – the answer being no . Unfortunately, his break comes to an end and with a promise to see each other soon, we hang up.

Placing my phone on the porch steps after resuming my music, I face two large yard waste bags filled to the brim after all that weeding and trimming. If I remembered correctly, tomorrow is garbage day, so doing the gardening today lined up perfectly. Hauling the two bags to the curb, I double-check the front yard before deciding that now will be a good time to start decorating and make my way inside the house bringing out each and every decoration box, starting from the basement and working towards the ones left in the garage.

It took another hour before I had each box in the garage, a total of ten lined up in a row. Rummaging through each box's contents and organizing the decorations, I find myself with many ideas and categories I can do to make the house the best one on the block. I notice that three boxes contain graveyard materials, and an idea comes to mind. A cemetery-themed haunted house will be perfect for children coming to the house for trick or treating.

Moving the headstones, from the box, I notice that they are made from styrofoam covered in concrete as I move them into place. Curiouse to see what is written on them, I take take the time to read each headstone when I notice they have a theme. Each headstone contains the name of a book character, some I recognize and others I did not and chuckle. I wonder who made these and if they are fan of classic literature. With the headstones in place, I return to the garage and find more temporary fences to create a path, zigzagging from the cemetery entrance of the cemetary to the exit that stops just before the front porch. At the end of this path, I set up an automatic coffin that opens with motion sensors to a zombie jumping out. The final touches are solar power lights that light the cemetery path in a red and orange glow. Taking a step back, I take a picture of the house and send it to Tate. I love how it came out and knew that Halloween this year will be the best one yet. Satisfied with my productive day, I make my way up the driveway, intending to go inside to start dinner.

Suddenly the street turns eerily quiet, and unease fills me.

[Intruders made it pass the border and are at my house!] I link the pack as soon as I smell the scent of wolves, getting ready to run into the house. Unfortunately I am too slow as I feel strong arms wrap around my midsection and another pair presses a cloth with some form of drug to my face, covering my mouth and nose. I try my best to hold my breath in order to not breathe in the drug that threatens to take me into unconsciousness. My hands claw at the ones binding me, trying my best to fight for freedom. I get a few curses of pain in response from the two men holding me captive. I need help and fast.

[We are on our way Luna!] Mateo links back with urgency in his voice. I want to respond, but my mind is focused on not breathing.

[Can you fight them?] Tate asks, his voice shaking.

[No, Tate help-] I start mind-linking my mate but everything soon turns black as I take a deep breath of air, my burning oxygen-deprived lungs unable to hold in my breath any longer. My body goes slack against the attackers, my arms falling to my side and tears forming in my eyes. I take one last look at the place I call home, my vission blurry and I send a prayer that my pack is able to reach me before I am taken away.

"Good girl." The attacker that holds me whispers in an all too familiar voice, caressing my hair and supporting my limp frame. The last thing I felt is his lips on my temple as my consciousness slips away, a burning pain searing into me from where his skin touches mine being the last thing I feel.

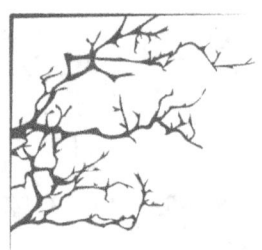

Chapter 29

My body floats in a state of numbness as I find myself consumed in darkness. I feel no emotions. No wave of energy from the pack link with Bloodsvain and barely a hum from the mate bond. I wonder just where I am as I try to piece together the hazy memories that led me to this state. My body is numb and it takes a while to realize that I had been kidnapped as I open my eyes and soon learn that I am tied down to a familiar bed that I thought I left behind months ago, my body naked once again ontop of the soft bedding.

"No!" I cry out in a despaired whimper, trying to free my limbs before anyone can walk in. I am back in the cottage I was once sentenced to as a Breeder over five months ago. This is the same cottage where my life was not my own because of Samuel Lightran and where the twins were forcefully concieved. I am trapped with nowhere to go and the bed is still as comfortable as I remember it. But it holds so many horrible memories that disgust rushes through me in waves.

"Well, look who's up." I bristle as a voice I could never forget floats to my ear, and let out a warning growl. I want to shift, need to shift to protect myself and I tried so hard to will my body to cooperate but nothing works. My body feels as weak as a human's.

[Tate?] I reached out through the bond, trying to reach my mate.

[Please, Tate. Answer me.] I beg, looking around to find some way of escape once again.

"It won't work, Laina." Sam's voice cuts through my attempt to link Tate to get help.

"There is currently a low dose of wolfsbane coursing through your veins." His voice is filled with humour as he steps into my line of sight. I see the triumphant smirk on his lips as his eyes glide over my naked form, lust and greed evident in his brown orbs. I hate this vile man.

"I am a Luna and leader of a pack. You have no right to treat me this way." My voice comes out strong and authoritative as I try to buy time to keep this man away from me. But my outburst only causes a chuckle of amusement from the wolf before me. He steps closer to my body, his hand running from my neck, over the swell of my breast where he plays with my nipple and lowers to trace the entrance of my womanhood, his touch leaving needles of pain in their wake. Fear washes over me, but I do my best to hide my emotions. I refuse to give him any satisfaction knowing I am afraid, that his touch causes excrutiating pain.

"I can do anything I want to you." He states, his eyes holding a touch of insanity to them.

"You're my Breeder, my property." He growls out possessively, his voice low and threatening as his head hovers above mine. He licks his lips as he hooks a finger just inside me, and it takes everything in me not to wince from the pain.

"I am a free person." I spat out, forcing my head to collide with his as I hear the satisfying crunch of bone. Watching Sam pull back and curse, I catch sight of blood starting to trickle down from his nose. He glares at me, his hand balled into a fist as he raises it into the air and I brace myself for the impact.

"You little-"

"Sam!" He stops as another voice fills the room, turning to snarl at the newest arrival.

"If you want her to produce pups, she needs to be uninjured." I recognize the voice, but I couldn't figure out where it came from. My mind is racing as I try to match this voice to a face.

"Now, go get Doc to look at that nose. We don't want it to heal crooked." The voice continues pacifying the angry Alpha male I have injured.

"Fine, but I get to punish her later, uncle." Sam says, then it hits me. The man is Ross, one of the elders that came to my house weeks ago.

"Fair enough, and when she gives you an heir I call being the next wolf that fucks her. It's been a while since I've been deep inside someone so tender." Ross agrees coming to stand beside Sam and trail his fingers over my breast with lust filling in own eyes. I growl at the two men, trying once again to break free, only to get amused chuckles from the both of them.

"Don't struggle, Laina. I want this perfect little body under my own, withering at my touch as I fuck you into submission." Sam orders, a glint in his eyes as he stares down at me in amusement. Soon the two leave me alone while Sam tends to his broken nose and Ross goes to Goddess only knows where. I am trapped once again but I need to get out, get to my family, and to safety.

I sigh and close my eyes trying to open the mate bond to reach Tate, but nothing is there. Tears finally formed in my eyes as I think about my mate and our little girl, feeling the ring on my left hand for comfort. At least Sam kept the engagement ring on my hand. My hair flows down my shoulders, covering my mark, and I wonder if this is so that no one sees I am mated. Breeders were supposed to be unmated females in the past. Taking any wolf who bears a mate mark is grounds for execution.

Realizing that I am back in this mess as a hostage now—as nothing more than a vessel to have pups—I let the tears fall. Hope that used to fill me to the brim from the freedom I gained with Tate starts to fade quickly. Unless a miracle happens, I will be trapped here for the rest of my life, never to see Tate, Julia, or anyone else I call family back in Bloodsvain ever again.

I must have dozed off in despair because the sound of the door opening causes me to wake with a start, the binds keeping me in place as I jump in fright.

"Hello, Laina, you look healthy." Doctor Freelan says as he stares at my naked body, his hand resting on my abdomen.

"What do you want?" I growl out, getting a chuckle from him.

"Nothing, just giving you a daily dose of wolfsbane and the special serum you have already been acquainted with before." He replies with a smirk, bringing a needle into view and jabbing it into my arm as he injects the liquid into me. I feel a slight sting from the wolfsbane, causing me to wince. Even in small quantities, this drug can cause harm to a werewolf. I was no exception as the pain from the injection causes me to whimper.

"Now, relax. You will be feeling good soon. I'll send Sam up in an hour when your body is at its horniest, and you are willing to participate in making our Alpha healthy pups again." With that, he flicks his finger across my breast. I feel nothing but disgust as he chuckles and gets up, walking towards the door and leaving me alone again. I lay here on this bed, feeling the wolfsbane make its way through my body, but nothing else. There is no intense heat like the first time the doctor injected me, no pain because my body craved to be touch, nothing. I smirk. This could work to my advantage.

Closing my eyes, I decide to rest a little longer, considering the intense heat I expected never came. If there is a way I can uncover my mate mark, maybe I could get free from this predicament quickly. I know Doctor Freelan respected mates and the mate bond, but that's about all that he respects next to the current Alpha. The door opens again, and I know that an hour has gone by as Sam's musk fills the room. He is undoubtedly horny and ready to take me by force this time.

"How do you feel?" His voice is husky as he tries to seduce me, moving in between my legs, rubbing his tip against my thigh. I don't answer him, my focus moving towards the door as it shuts, the Doctor coming into view.

"Don't worry, Laina, I am here to make sure he doesn't hurt you." Doctor Freelan reassures, taking a seat on the lounge chair beside the door.

"How about you let me go instead!" I say harshly, gasping as I feel Sam push inside me, the pain coursing through my body. It feels like knives are cutting through my insides as I scream, tears streaming from my eyes.

"That shouldn't have hurt." Doctor Freelan muses, confusedly, standing to his feet. Sam ignores my pleas for him to stop as blood flows out with each thrust inside me. I wanted this pain to end and prayed for death to take me first. Pushing harder into me, Sam grunts with pleasure as I try my best to thrash around, trying to get him away. I hear Doctor Freelan gasps the moment my hair falls away from my shoulder and onto the bed, revealing Tate's mate mark.

"Samuel, Stop!" Doctor Freelan yells out, rushing towards the end of the bed and dragging Sam away from me. I cry as Sam's length is pulled out of me, feeling the stickiness of blood coating my legs.

"Why did you stop me, Freelan!" Sam growls out, sending a punch across Doctor Freelan's face. I feel the rage simmering off of Sam watching as the doctor tries his best to stand up to Sam.

"Do you know how long I've waited to fuck this bitch? A week! She's been out cold for a week, and no one would let me touch her until she woke up." Sam continues to yell, his eyes turning red from rage. I do my best to make myself appear small, not wanting to catch either man's attention while the ripples of pain slowly die down. I do not want to go through that hell again.

"She is my woman, Freelan. I was there holding onto her body as she cried from her parents' death and knew right then and there I wanted her. On her twelfth birthday, I took her out in a dress that took everything in me not to fuck her in. My father and mother promised me that she would be mine and I would spend every moment with her as she grew up. I took her first kiss. I own her and her little body, and with the blood of Crestfur Alphas running through her, we would have created a stronger pack!" Same rants. It's true with what he said about taking my first kiss. Chris and Jack had decided that since I was safe with Sam, they took the day to themselves, allowing me to stay at Sam's house that night. I remember being shy since Alpha Blake and Luna Rose were out on pack business. Sam and I spent the night after returning to the pack in his room, with me wearing one of his large T-shirts as a nightshirt.

We were watching the Titanic when I felt his eyes on me, and as I turn to face him, his lips found mine. He went slowly at first, his hands wrapped around my waist until I found myself underneath him with his tongue swirling around my mouth and his hand groping my blooming chest. He promised not to go far as I was too young to be mated, but at the time, I remember him sticking my hand deep into his pants, showing me how to move as he continued to make out with me. Every now and then since that night, Sam would send me an outfit to wear—outfits that I now realize revealed too much skin for a young pup—and would take me out only for the night to end with us making out. It's why I always believed we were mates, that he knew from the beginning that I was his soulmate. Now I know that he was just grooming me to be his Breeder and sex toy to play with. This man is sick and used me as his own play toy, and I played right into his hands the day he made me a Breeder.

"I stopped you because she is mated. There is a reason why Breeders are un-mated females. If a mated female is touched in any sexual way, the action will kill her. That is why she is bleeding!" Doctor Freelan states, doing his best to hold Sam back from my body. Sam just scoffs at his words as his eyes rake over me once again, his reaction causing Doctor Freelan to gasp in a mix of horror and shock.

"But you knew that already." He gasps out, walking backwards to stand between Sam and me, shielding my body from the angry Alpha wolf before us.

"Who is her mate Samuel Lightran?" The Doctor demands just as the door shatters open.

"I am."

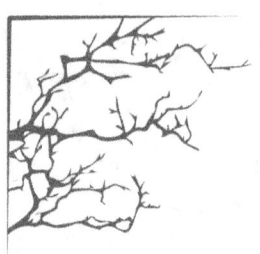

Chapter 30

"I am." I smile despite the pain as Tate's voice reaches my ear, my heart soaring at the fact that my mate is here to save me. I turn my head to look at Sam, his face a ghostly white as fear takes hold of this vile wolf. He is in a world of pain for pissing off my mate and kidnapping me. I'll be shocked if Pine Paw makes it out alive after today.

"Sam!" The Elder's heavy steps echo down the hallway carrying him towards the room I am kept.

"Bloodsvain has come!" His words are shouted to warn his nephew long before Ross bursts intot he room, fear and panic on his face as he abruptly stops when he realizes just who stands before him.

"Oh, Alpha Tate, how-" I hear a growl cutting off Ross' sweet, fake greeting before the sound of flesh tearing apart and the smell of blood other than my own fills the air. It seems there will be an Elders position to fill soon.

"Look, Tate, I was just taking back what is mine." Sam stutters out with fear lacing his voice. Holding his hands in surrender, Sam slowly backs away from the bed and away from me while Doctor Freelan continues his protective stance just in case Sam tries anything stupid. Tate slowly comes into view, his body splattered with blood but still so sexy. I've missed my mate so much.

"You okay, baby girl?" Tate asks, his eyes never leaving Sam's face. I feel the rage simmering around Tate's body, and I know wonder just how many have been slaughtered due to Sam's stupidity and greed.

"No, I'm not. I just want to be untied and go home." I answer. Tate gives Doctor Freelan a look, and the wolf soon busies himself by untying the knots that hold me tight. Even though I hate this wolf before me, I allow his touch as it brings me closer to freedom. Once all the ropes are untied, I slowly sit up with the help of Doctor Freelan, who backs away from me respectfully, his head bowed as he hands me a blanket from the side table. One I take and wrap around my body.

"I didn't know you are now mated. If I knew, I would have stepped in." Doctor Freelan says remorsefully. But his remorse could not save him as Tate reaches out and clutches his throat. I focus on massaging my sore wrists and ankles, now robbed raw from the ropes that were discarded in a heap. No sounds come from Doctor Freelan, but I know better than to look as the sounds of flesh once again tearing from another body resounds in the room. The loud sound of Freelan's dead body hitting the ground echoes, causing a panic-stricken look on Sam's face. His body is next, and I anticipate the moment when he takes his last breath.

Tate moves quickly like a fluid dancer. The sound of bones crunching brings to my attention that he has broken Sam's nose in the span of a second. My eyes watch each movement my mate makes as he lands punch after punch to Sam's face, seeing for once the blood-thirsty Alpha mothers use to scare their pups into behaving. Sam cries out in pain, falling to his knees and causing a swell of happiness inside me to see him suffer. He deserves it.

Attempting to stand, Sam lets out a fierce growl through his rearranged face. It is evident that his nose and jaw are broken allowing his blood to drip down his chin and onto the hardwood floor. I watch Sam rushing towards Tate like a wounded, rabid animal taking a final stand against an apex predator. But Tate just scoffs at Sam's measly attempt as he dodges the weaker wolf. Sam's movements become frantic while trying to claw at my mate, but his movements are slow, as if put into slow motion when faced against Tate. I can tell that Tate's focus is to draw Sam away from me as they near the window on the opposite side of the room.

With one last attempt at a successful attack, Sam lunges into the air only for Tate to use his own momentum and sending Sam crashing into the window as his body pauses in midair before falling two stories onto the waiting concrete below.

I blink, stunned at how Sam's fate has turned out. When I open my eyes, Tate is beside me, pulling me into his strong arms and kissing me passionately. Gone is the cold, distant man from before, reverting back into the loving mate I have gotten to know. His blood-covered body coats the sticky red substance onto my naked one while our lips smash together for a few more seconds before we pull away, panting.

"Baby, I've missed you." He whimpers, tears now flowing from his eyes. The once cold-hearted, murdering Alpha eyes have now softened into the loving and warm gaze only the pack and I know. His forehead is pressed against my own while his body shakes with quiet sobs. He feels so fragile in my arms.

"I've missed you too." I whisper, my own tears falling from my face.

"It's been a long week looking for you and getting the attack ready." Tate whisper, and I stiffen.

"It's been a week?" I ask shakily with the realization. I had caught snippits of Sam rambling on about me being asleep, but I was too focused on the crippling pain to notice what he was saying.

"Yes, baby, that's how long you were gone. He had you for a week, and I spent every day trying to follow protocol before I was finally able to be let loose. How long did you think it was?" His face is filled with confusion while I clutch his arms, my own tears flowing faster as sobs wrack my body.

"I thought it has only been a day!" I exclaim, my heart wrenching at the fact that I was here for a week and I didn't know it.

"Why would you-" He stops and sniffs my body and frowns as he wraps the blanket tighter around me. I still felt weak and groggy from the drugs that have been used to incapacitate me.

"They used wolfbane on you." He growls out. I can only answer with a nod, seeking comfort in his arms as I continue to sob. I want to go home now.

"It explains why I couldn't reach you and why you wouldn't know it's been a week." He adds as he lifts me up gently. His arms cradle me close to his chest while he stands, turning towards the empty door frame.

"Alpha Tate, we have Samuel in custody." As Mateo comes into view through my tear filled blurry vission. He doesn't seem fazed by the blood covering Tate while he sends a reassuring smile my way before glancing around the blood covered room.

"Glad to see you're safe, Luna Laina." He adds after taking in the damage, bowing his head and moving out of the way to let Tate pass by with me in his arms.

"I would say have a clean-up crew in here, but instead, I want you to burn this place down. I need to get Laina to Rex." Tate orders, his hold on me tightening. I can feel his swirling emotions radiating off of him, and I kiss his mark, trying to calm my mate down. Mateo nods in acknowledgement while Tate carries me down the stairs, where more bodies litter the floor with puddles of blood pooling below them. As we near the front door, the body count increases, with many of them in wolf form.

"They tried to stop me from rescuing you." Tate informs me, and I smile, his eyes catching my curious gaze. I felt no fear knowing the damage my mate has caused. Instead, I kiss his blood-stained cheek and smile lovingly at him.

"You came for me. That is all that matters to me." I reassure Tate and snuggle into his embrace. Walking past the house, he carries me down the street where our pack guards line the pavement until we find ourselves entering a field of wildflowers. Tents and vans scatter the field as make-shift medical tents with a few wolves seeking treatment. It seems like there were no casualties from Bloodsvain and I smile in relief. I hate the thought of pack members dying for my sake.

Rex spots us from his van as he sets up materials for the next patient, his eyes lighting up in happiness and relief before he rushes to our side and giving me a quick once-over before we make our way towards his van. Tate sets me down gently on a metal table, making sure the blanket is wrapped around my body, keeping me warm from the cold fall wind.

"We have all the wolves from Pine Paw in their pack house – pups included." Rex states as he motions for Tate to close the va door.

"Loren is watching over them with a few of our Warriors." He continues, putting on a pair of rubber gloves and readying medicine that is most likely for me.

"Good, we can take care of them soon. Laina has wolfsbane in her system. Do you think you can treat her?" I allow Tate to speak for me, my body becoming heavy with exhaustion as I fight to stay awake. It's been a long day, and the idea of sleeping tucked safely beside Tate is tempting to me. Rex does a quick exam, giving me some medication for the pain and informing Tate that he was lucky he came when he did. I had to whisper out that Sam raped me and that Freelan had stepped in just in time, causing a loud, blood-curdling growl to settle over the field from Tate, his eyes fighting to not turn red.

"Laina will be fine, Tate. The wolfsbane will need a few days to exit her system, but it's nothing that will cause lasting damage." Rex states with an exasperated sigh, sending a small smile my way. I nod in acknowledgement at his words as I reach my hand out from under the blanket to clutch Tate's feeling my mate visibly relax. I see relief in Rex's eyes, probably because I stopped him from going rampant, before nodding for Rex to continue speaking.

"You can take her home after we deal with Pine Paw and Samuel. You have the go-ahead from the Elders to do as you please with him." Rex continues with a smirk, a tinge of bloodthirstiness coming from the Doctor. To think a wolf dedicated to healing would have a similar blood thirstyness like Tate.

"My thoughts exactly! Sam will pay for what he's done." Tate agrees, kissing my forehead. Rex begins packing away his medical materials away before exiting the vehicle followed by yelling and the Doctor ordering people about. Tate scoops me into his arms and carries me to the front passenger seat. I sigh as familiar tingles spread from where his skin touches mine and close my eyes for a moment. The sound of the driver door chimes with the door opening. Rex climbs in and turns the ignition, and in moments the car moves. Leaving behind the Breeder Lane, the car turns onto a familiar road that will take us to the pack house. I watch as houses pass by and the territory I used to run in brings back old memories. But Pine Paw is no longer my home, and the feeling of being here makes my skin crawl with unease. I doze off on the drive to the pack house, only to be gently awoken with a kiss from Tate, a soft smile on his face.

"It's cold out, baby, so put this on. It's one of the shirts you like to steal from me." My heart flutters with the care from my mate as I let the blanket slide off my shoulder, and Tate helps me dress. The long sleeve shirt is comfortably baggy and - as I am helped by Rex to exit the van - the shirt falls almost to my knees. The warmth of the blanket is wrapped around me again by Tate blocking out the cold October wind. Members of our pack line the entrance and perimeter of Pine Paw's pack house, giving off an intimidating aura, but I catch the look of relief in their eyes. Nodding to the wolves we pass, our trio make its way into the pack house, walking side-by-side to the grand ballroom.

The first thing my eyes zero in on is the beaten and battered body of Sam on the center of the stage. He is tied to a sturdy metal chair, slumped over in defeat while blood drips from his wounds and two guards on either side of him—one I recognize as Alex – keep watch in case he tries to end himself prematurly. It is evident that bones are broken as one of Sam's legs is at an odd angle, but I feel nothing for this wolf other than hate and disgust. Part of me had hoped he had died from his fall out of the window. But he will be dead before we leave.

"You monster..."

"He is our Alpha..."

"Why do you always kill packs..."

The crowd of Pine Paw wolves yell in anger and frustration with the heavy scent of fear emanating in the air. I watch as mothers tighten their hold on their pups, keeping them close to their bodies, while guards create a path for us to walk through. Abby's face catches my attention as she stares wide-eyed at me, her mate being detained on stage behind his Alpha, but I ignore the two-faced bitch. As far as I am concerned, she lost the right to be my friend months ago, and her tear-stained face brings no sympathy for her from me. Taking a spot slightly to the left of Sam, I stand as straight as I can, putting on a brave front and waiting for the crowd to settle down. The four remaining Council of Elders members join us, standing to Sam's right, a look of disgust on their faces as Dian sends me a relieved smile. She is definitely my favourite Elder.

"Let me explain what is going on here." Tate starts off with once there is silence in the room.

"Your Alpha here has been creating illegal Breeders for his own gain, and Laina, my mate, was forced to be one about seven months ago." Confused murmurs follow Tate's words with this new revelation. It seems like no one knew the truth about Breeders being illegal. Well, not no one, as Abby's face holds a guilt-stricken look. I know instantly that she knew about this and still allowed me to be turned into one.

"Laina ran away a week after Sam forced himself on her in hopes of creating heirs since he had no mate. About seven weeks ago, she ran into my territory where we learned we are mates, and a week ago Sam kidnapped her, knowing full well she was mated to me. He forced himself on her, nearly killing my mate." Tate continues as gasps of horror fill the air. I see wolves pulling their mate to their sides protectively as their eyes turn to me. I make sure my mate mark is displayed fully for all to see and nod to reaffirm Tate's words. I could see the crowd warming up to my mate and gently reach out to squeeze Tate's hand.

"We also know that Mr. Samuel knew that Breeders were illegal but continued the practice anyways for two years after the law was passed, breaking the laws that we, the Elders, created to protect our kind." Dian states and the crowd breaks out into outraged cries.

"Wait, you're saying that Breeders are illegal now?" A she-wolf asks, pushing to the front of the crowd to search for answers from the Elders.

"They were made illegal over two years ago due to the fact of the trauma the girls went through. Samuel attended the meeting that day with his Beta and Beta Female when we talked to all the North American Alphas and Betas, yet he chose to ignore our laws and continue without informing all of you." Another Elder says, and the crowd grows angry once again, this time at the man they thought was a trustworthy Alpha. I feel a rise in bloodlust emanating from some of the crowd members, catching Alex stiffening. As a child of a Breeder himself, I have a feeling Alex is ready to rip Sam apart.

"It is why we give Tate Randall-Silvermoon permission to kill him in front of you, the pack members of Pine Paw." Dian eplains her cold gaze sending a glare to Sam.

"Samuel and Samuel's close guards attacked Bloodsvain, kidnapped Laina - the Luna of Bloodsvain - and violated her just moments before her rescue. His scentence is death." Dian continues, giving Tate a nod of approval to go ahead with this execution. The crowd roars for the kill, and Tate grins as he kisses my forehead before walking to Sam. Fear radiates once again from the wolf tied down to the chair, with Sam giving pleading looks for his freedom. No amount of pleading will save Sam from his fate.

Tate begins by giving a light kick to Sam's broken leg, causing Sam to groan in pain. The sound of skin ripping away as my mate tears off the broken leg silences the crowd. Blood gushes from the wound where the limb once connected as the dull thud echoes on stage after Tate discards the useless limb. Next came an arm that is torn away quickly, causing the crowd to cheer at the strong scent of blood filling the air. Fingers turn to claws, and Tate reaches out, shredding the now limp penis that Sam used to violate me. The blood-curdling scream from the broken wolf sends waves of satisfaction through me. He deserves this, and I am proud my mate got to be the one to make Sam impotent just before his death.

Finally with Sam getting close to death from blood loss, Tate comes to stand behind Sam, his hands reaching around to slowly tear the head from his shoulder. The screams stop, and silence resumes with the death of Sam. He will no longer be able to hurt another she-wolf again. The crowd cheers the death of Sam, as his Beta is brought in front of the crowd, and Abby is dragged to kneel beside her mate. They were accomplices in creating new Breeders, knowing that they were illegal. Their death will be handled by Pine Paw.

"Laina, please help me!" Abby cries out, pleading towards me. I turn a deaf ear to her pleas while the she-wolf struggles to break free from her captors. Instead, I focus on my mate, who wraps me in a hug. I find myself being lifted into his strong arms once again being carried out of the pack house I plan to never set foot in again. Pine Paw can burn for all I care after today. Entering the van with Rex the driver once again, I settle into Tate's lap, my head resting against his shoulder with a yawn.

"Laina Randall-Silvermoon." I say, testing my soon-to-be last name on my lips and smile a drowsy smile.

"Wolf shield of the silver moon." I translate the last name with a grin, sending a kiss to Tate's mark before another yawn escapes my mouth. Tate chuckles at my sleepy words, kissing my temple and playing with my hair, lulling me to a comfortable sleep now that I am once again safe beside him.

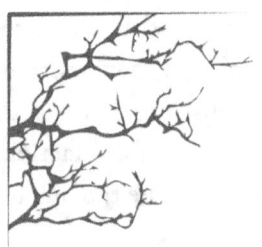

Chapter 31

The vehicle coming to a stop, and the tingles of a gentle kiss on my lips wake me from my slumber. Groggily, I look around, noticing the familiar street and our home still decorated for Halloween. Tears of joy fill my eyes and slowly trickle down my face while strong arms pull me in for a long hug.

Despite Rex driving faster than the speed limit permitted to distance ourselves from Pine Paw, it took our pack two and a half days to return to Bloodsvain. Tate wanted to keep driving all through the night, to get me home as soon as possible, but Rex suggested we stay at a motel the first night because of the wolfsbane coursing through my body. And so with reluctance, Tate agreed to Rex's suggestion. Settling into a comfortable room, I spent the night dozing in and out of sleep, not able to fully find the release of a deep slumber even with my battered and exhausted body. Every time I would fall asleep, I would find myself back in the cottage with Sam above my body that is chained to the familiar wooden bed. Each time that scene repeated itself, I would scream awake from the nightmare, waking Tate who slept beside me and sending him into a panic state as he holds me close until my sobbing ends.

After going through ten nightmares, Tate decided that it would be best to leave the motel and continue to drive home. He refused to let me be alone for a second as I spent the majority of the drive in his lap with his fingers running through my hair. His touch made me feel safe and secure long enough to get some sleep and keep the nightmares at bay for a few brief moments. The only time away from him during our mad drive home would be when we stopped to grab gas and snacks, and I would excuse myself to use the lady's room. Tate's main priority was caring for me, his mate. With the security of being by his side and the closer we were to home, I fell into a deep, dreamless sleep without nightmares interrupting me.

"Good morning, baby girl." Tate whispers, gently brushing my hair out of my face.

"Welcome home." He continues, kissing the top of my head and giving me a reassuring smile. The door opens with Rex greeting us as Tate climbs out of the van still carrying me. The autumn wind breezes by, causing me to shiver from the cold even with the blanket stolen from the motel wrapped around me. Taking in the familiar scents and the decoration that I spent a whole day setting out, I try my best to stifle my relieved sobs. I am home.

Tate rushes us inside, the warm air embracing me as I take in the scent of our home, closing my eyes and opening again to make sure this wasn't a dream. The scent of Tate and I are stale, but Julia's is still fresh in the air as well as Chris and Jack. Right now, the house held no sounds except the two of us breathing. I was happy with having just Tate and I home, not wanting to deal with a crowd of people.

"Can we go for a shower together? I just need to wash the memories away, and it just to be us for the moment." I whisper out, my voice crackling and trembling.

"Please, Tate, help me forget, baby." I plead, wanting my for my mate to take away the horrible experience and love me. I rest my head on Tate's shoulder and kiss his mark. I need his touch and love right now. I need my mate.

"Sure, sounds like a good idea." He answers, carrying me up the stairs and into our bedroom past our comfortable bed and to the bathroom where he sets me down on the marble counter with a chaste kiss. Turning away from me to start the shower, I watch Tate's body move to complete the task. I drop the blanket from around me and carefully remove the long sleeve shirt from my body, watching as Tate also removes his blood-soaked clothing. I will ask him to have everything covered in blood taken away later and burned, not wanting any memories of Pine Paw left in our home. Tate turns to face me, a smile on his face after checking the temperature of the water.

"Come here, baby." He whispers, opening his arms. I hop down from my perch, taking those few steps into those safe, familiar arms and burying my face into his chest—the only part that didn't have blood on him.

"Anything you want to do today, we'll do. Don't worry about our pup. Eeva has Julia for the day to give you some time to relax." He whispers, his face buried in my hair, taking in my scent. I feel each of his muscles relax a little more with each deep breath he takes, his arms pulling me even closer to him. This past week without me must have been hard on Tate, and I could only imagine the worry and anxiety he's gone through with me kidnapped and taken away.

"Okay." I mumble into his warm skin, kissing it gently before I pull away.

"Now, let's get cleaned up." I add with a giggle as I step into the warm spray, Tate following me in soon after. The water turns red immediate from all the blood and I grab a bar of soap, lathering Tate with it. It takes a while to massage the soap into his body, scrubbing away the stress of the past week and rinsing off the blood until finally he stands before me clean and shiny. Even his soft hair is free of blood after a long shampoo. Exhaustion and dark circles hide in his eyes, making my heart throb with slight pain knowing he did not get much sleep. We both need some pampering with each other later.

"My turn to clean you, sweetheart." He announces playfully, taking the soap from my hands and putting it on the built-in shower shelf beside him before spinning me around. At first I am confused until I feel his fingers massage my scalp and realize he is washing my hair. Leaning my head back and closing my eyes as he rinsed the chestnut locks clean, I take in his pampering and know he needs to take care of me just as much as I need to take care of him. He repeats his movements with conditioner, and when I thought he was going to rinse it out, he pulls my hair to the side. Before I know it, he massages soap into my back getting stiff, tensed muscles I didn't know I had until his expert hands find them and releases the pent up tension inside me.

Finally he rinses my hair when he removes the soap suds from my back. I try to turn and face him but he stops me, pulling my clean back flush against him as his soapy hands massage the top of my chest and shoulders. He trails his fingers along my sides over to my stomach before returning to cup my breast, where he massages the skin clean, gently tugging and pinching my nipples, causing a flushed heat of pleasure to shoot through my body as I let out a slow sensual moan. His lips press against my neck where my mate mark is situated, his teeth gently nipping at the sensitive skin, causing my knees to weaken.

"What do you say we go and have some adult fun after our shower, and I show you how much I worship not only you but your body, mind, and soul as well?" He whispers seductively into my ear, nipping my ear lobe gently.

"I say hurry up and get me clean then." I reply back, my voice laced with lust as my arm snakes up and around his neck. The rest of the shower is a soapy blur as Tate moves as fast as he can to get me clean. The water is shut off quickly as soon as the soap and conditioner is gone, and I find myself wrapped a towel held in Tate's arms. He grabs a few dry towels that he throws across the bed before depositing me in the middle, quickly removing the towel from my body before he climbs ontop of the matress. Quickly he finds his place between my legs and massages the tip of his hard cock against me, making me moan again as need built.

He takes his time though, kissing every inch of my body, suckling my breasts as his fingers find a steady rhythm inside me. He kisses his way down my body and swaps his fingers for his tongue, licking and tasting me until I come against his mouth, screaming his name as I grip the wet towels. When I settle back down from the euphoric high, I find him between my legs, smirking as he spreads them wider with his tip against my wet pussy.

"Ready?" He asks playfully, making me giggle and smile.

"For you, always." He chuckles at my sweet reply and slowly pushes inside me, my moan of pleasure mixed with his as he fits perfectly inside. The base of his cock is pressed to my wet lips as he grinds against me for a few minutes, my body tensing from the pleasure he is building. Finally, he starts moving, wrapping my legs around his waist as he starts a slow thrust, building up the speed until he is bent over nipping my neck and amplifying the pleasure as he bites down on my mark while thrusting hard and fast into me. More orgasms rip through my body as I clutch and claw at his back and shoulders, finding my release screaming his name, and hearing him moan mine.

Finally, I feel him tense above me, and the spot he has been favouring on my neck heats up where he bites down once again. The sensation makes me tumble over the edge of ecstasy with him. His seed spills into me as I bite down on the base of his neck where his mate mark already resides, the mate bond strengthening further. We lay there panting, myself curled into his side, the towels now on the ground as the blanket covers us, and I sigh with content. This is where I belong.

"I love you, Tate." I whisper, drawing small circles on his chest.

"And I love you, Laina." He whispers back, pulling me closer to him. Soon his breathing evens out, and I look up to see him fast asleep. Giggling softly, I snuggling into him and join Tate for some much needed rest.

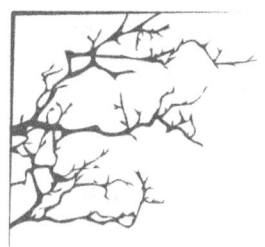

Chapter 32

"Hey, beautiful, are you hungry?" Tate asks, one hand rubbing my back, the other in my hair. I groan as harsh light reaches my eyes. My reaction to bury my face in the warm, solid body next to me is met by chuckling. Sometimes I feel more like a vampire with how much I hate the bright sun when sleeping.

"Yes," I mumble, snuggling closer to him and sighing happily, getting another chuckle.

"Well, we should get up to get food." He says, smoothing my hair away from my face and kissing the top of my head.

"Do we have to?" I ask quietly, blinking my blurry sleep-filled eyes at him before I yawn, my body ready to go back to sleep at a moments notice.

"You're adorable when you're tired, you know that?" He muses, sending another kiss to my forehead and pulling me closer into his arms.

"So I've been told." I mumble and smile at another deep chuckle rumbling from my mate. It feels good seeing Tate relaxed and rested and the dark circles under his eyes less noticeable now.

"C'mon, baby girl. Let's get dressed and make something to eat." He says encouragingly, moving out from under me and causing my body to lie in an uncomfortable position.

"Fine." I groan out reluctantly, stretching out my sore body as I stand and head to the closet where I grab a long fall dress and a warm cardigan and make my way to my vanity where I brush my long hair and tie it in a simple braid. Turning around and coming face-first into Tate's chest, I notice he has dressed as well as he pulls me in for a hug.

"I forgot to give you this." He says, steadying me with one arm around my waist while holding out my phone.

"Thank you, I must have dropped it at some point." I reply, happily taking the device and tucking it into the pocket of my cardigan.

"It was on the ground by the edge of the road." He whispers, his grip tightening on me. I instantly know what he is talking about. My heart aches looking into his pain-filled eyes, and I press closer into his body hoping to ease his anxiety.

"Baby, I'm home safe and sound and in your arms." I whisper, rubbing my hands up and down his arms.

"Everything is fine now, and we have nothing to worry about. I'm here, and I am not leaving." I continue sayinng, hoping to sooth my mate as I move my left hand and press it against his cheek. Standing on my toes, I press my lips against Tate, pouring all my love into this single action and feeling him tighten his hold on me. His lips move against mine, Tate deepening the kiss and taking my breath away until I am left panting and blushing, wanting nothing more than to return to bed and show him that I am never leaving his side again.

"Besides, we have a wedding to plan." I add when my breath returnes to normal, getting his breath-taking smile and a deep chuckle as his free hand lands on the one I have cupping his face.

"I know, baby. Now, let's get you some food." He whispers as my stomach growl to punctuate his words, making me giggle. We make our way down to the kitchen, and I flip the T.V. on, going through the guide to see what we can watch until I find Burlesque about to play and put it on. Tate has ingredients for a late brunch: bacon, eggs, hash browns, and a fruit salad needing to be prepped.

With the movie as background noise, the two of us find ourselves at the kitchen counter and start cooking together. As the movie progresses, I find my mood lifting and end up singing and dancing along, enjoying my return to normalcy and trying to get Tate to dance with me.

"You seem to know the movie pretty well." Tate comments after the third song, Diamonds are a Girl's Best Friend ends.

"I know the dances as well." I retort with a wink, flipping a few pieces of bacon.

"This I have to see." He chuckles, leaning against the counter with his arms crossed over his chest.

"Depends on how sore my muscles are." I retort with coyly, smiling when he moves to wrap his arms around me from behind.

"Well, then they are going to be sore for a while." He whispers, nipping my mark and causing me to moan as his lips leave soft kisses trailing along my neck and shoulder.

"Food first, then we figure out what to do afterwards." I groan out, my breath coming out in pants.

"Okay, baby." He laughs, pulling away from me to place the cooked food onto plates as I plop the last piece of bacon on a paper towel-lined tray. We sit and relax, munching on our brunch-side by-side in the breakfast nook, snuggling and taking our time to enjoy the movie as it gets to the best parts.

"So, what's the story behind this movie?" Tate finally asks, and I giggle.

"It's a musical, basically. Small town girl trying to make it in L.A. in a classy strip club called a Burlesque club. I grew up watching it with Chris because it's a really good movie. I got into dancing because of this, and Chris was more than happy at the time to see me go to the local dance hall in town by the pack." I state, Tate whistling and impressed by my confession.

"So you are an interior designer, an artist, a dancer, and have a killer voice! What can't you do, beautiful? " I blush with Tate's impression of me, taking a sip of the orange juice and thinking of the embarrassing things I cannot do. Deciding on the one thing I know I am horrible at, I look to Tate with a dead-serious look.

"Write. My stories are so horrible, and I give up after a few hours of trying to create anything." I deadpan, blushing slightly from my confession. Tate looks at me shocked before he starts laughing, clutching his stomach and amused by my confession. I want to pout, to say its not funny, but seeing him so happy and carefree cases my protests to die down as I watch bemused by my mate.

"That's okay. You're perfect the way you are." He assures me as he tries to catch his breath, kissing my forehead.

"And so are you." I say quietly, kissing his chin. The stubble tickles my face, making me giggle. He smirks, and I feel his hands on my sides before I start wiggling around, laughing out loud from the tickle attack while I try to squirm out of his grasp.

"B-baby s-stop." I yelp, panting as I manage to slip away from him and rushing to the other side of the table.

"Oh no you don't, missy!" Tate exclaims, getting up and making me squeal in surprise as I jump out of his reach, bolting for the door. I slip on some black flats and race outside while laughing. I could hear my mate laughing behind me as he chases after my fleeing frame, causing me to laugh even louder. I run through the makeshift cemetery and out towards the leaf pile, squeaking when I feel his strong arms wrap around me and lift me over his shoulder then spinning me around.

"I caught you." Tate chuckles spanking my ass, making me jump in surprise while also laughing.

"No fair, I haven't been able to train." I fake whine and pout as I turn to look at his bemused face.

"I know, but don't worry, baby; I don't mind being the protector." He retorts with confidence before biting my ass playfully, making me giggle. Slowly I feel myself being lowered to the ground, my arms wrapping around Tate's neck and his around my waist as we stand there, our foreheads pressed together.

"I love you." He says tenderly, and my heart melts.

"I love you too." I whisper, giggling when he bites my nose playfully. We play in the leaves for a while, acting like children and letting the tension that has built up over the last few days fully melt away. It feels good being carefree with my mate, not having to worry about our pup or the dangers of Pine Paw lurking in the back of our minds. After a well-needed leaf fight, Tate and I lay snuggled together on the leaf-covered ground watching the clouds float by.

"So for the wedding, when do you want to have it?" He asks, playing with my hair.

"Some time in the spring under all the cherry blossom trees we have in the backyard." I answer quietly, loving the feel of his hands in my hair.

"Sounds good. Do you want to wait a few years before we tie the knot?" He asks, smiling down at me. I nod in response, resting my head on his shoulder and closing my eyes to take in the fall scent mixed with my mate's. We are already mated, so we have no need to rush for the wedding—the engagement ring reminding me that Tate and I are already together and meant to be for eternity.

We head back inside a few minutes later, making a quick dinner and snuggling up on the couch to watch another movie on Netflix, barely paying attention to the T.V. as the two of us talk and relax. Eeva arrives at around eight at night with Julia in her pink stroller, a relieved look on my sister-in-law's face as she hands a box filled with cheesecake to Tate and wraps me in a tight hug. I smile with the love she radiates for me while she holds me at arms-length, her eyes scanning my body before she lets out a relived sigh.

"Glad to see you home safe and sound, Laina." She whispers with tears of joy in her eyes.

"So am I." I agree, my eyes also tearing as we pull each other in for another hug.

The three of us head into the kitchen as I hold Julia in my arms, taking in my pup's sweet scent and closely holding her. I've missed my daughter so much, more than I thought I would. With a grin on my face, I take a seat, relishing in as much mommy-daughter time as I can while Eeva cuts the cheesecake and Tate pours us all a cup of hot chocolate.

I get caught up on the things Julia has done in my absence, smiling with the news that she is starting to sleep through the night as well as how Eeva's boys have treated their little cousin. The night ends with Eeva telling us she is pregnant and hoping for a baby girl, before leaving Tate, Julia, and me alone. With my little girl already fast asleep, Tate moves a bassinet to my side of the bed where I lay my baby down and tuck her in before climbing into bed and cuddling with Tate, his warm body and secure embrace as well as the sounds of my pup sleeping beside me helping me fall into another deep sleep.

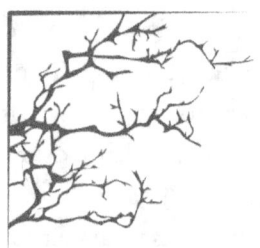

Chapter 33

Staring at myself in the mirror I admire my chestnut hair that falls in loose curls, half of it shaped into a bow at the back upper-half of my head. It's been just over two—almost three—years since I returned home, and news about the fight at Pine Paw has spread all over the world. Due to the incident with Sam and Ross, the Elders visited every single pack for three months making sure everyone knew the new laws of Breeders being illegal.

Many packs were abolished for breaking the laws, Tate being asked to help with punishing those that continued the illigal Breeders even after learning about Pine Paw and Sam's demise while I was left to lead our pack with him and some warriors gone. The last I heard about Pine Paw is that Sam's younger brother Eric and his mate took over, freeing all the Breeders and reuniting them with their pups. All in all, my story is widely known now. I have a strong reputation of being a kind Luna but a brutal fighter when it comes to protecting my pack and family – a reputation that matches my mate's Blood Alpha title perfectly.

"Are you almost ready?" Eeva's voice fills my ears and I turn to stare at my maid of honour, smiling when I notice the look of awe on her face as Julia toddles around us in her lavender flower girl dress.

"Yes, is everyone here?" I ask, smoothing the front of my dress gently. Today is my wedding day, and I am wearing a Pnina Tornai strapless ball gown with a bejewelled, sweetheart neckline. My veil – one that used to belong to my mother and what she wore at her wedding - hangs down just inches above the floor attached to a tiara situated on the top of my head. For the time being, the veil is flipped back away from my face as I wait for the time to come. I really can't wait to see my mate. The night alone in my cousin's house with Julia was excruciating and even though I knew it would only be a few hours, I still missed Tate and yearn to be curled beside him in our bed.

"They are all seated and waiting for the three of us. You look beautiful by the way, sis." She gushes, and my already pink cheeks turn a deeper shade while Eeva picks up my daughter. Eeva had started calling me sis or little sis just a few months after my return home. It made me happy but it irritated Tate to no end. About two years ago, she had given birth to my niece Lora and worked hard to fit into her lavender bridesmaid gown. I couldn't help but chuckle as she twirls around the room with a giggling Julia, who squeals out a "Mommy, help me" before escaping her aunt to hide behind my leg.

"Your Aunty wont hurt you." I chuckle out, looking down at my little girl who has grown so much. Eeva just chuckles, looking at Julia before the door to the guest room opens and Chris walks in, stoping dead in his tracks as he takes in my appearance.

"Wow, Lainy, your parents would be so proud." He whispers, using his childish nickname for me as tears threatening to spill from both our eyes. I sniffle a bit, holding back the tears that threaten to spoil my makeup and walk towards Chris, giving him a tight hug. I take in his lavender suit as he will be walking on my side of the ceremony as my bride's man. I smile at the man who raised me most of my life and thank the Goddess for giving me such a supportive cousin. I don't think I would have made it to today if he hadn't had stepped up to raise me.

"I know they would, but having you here is just as important." I agree sniffling as I try to keep the tears at bay. I see tears slip from Chris's eyes as he dabs a handkerchief at the drops, causing me to laugh at his emotional state. My cousin can be such a cry baby at times.

"Look, both of you need to hurry up before we're late for a very important date." Eeva huffs with a glare, pushing us towards the door with Julia situated on her right hip.

"Really, Alice in Wonderland quotes?" I laugh out, my mood lightening.

"Yes." She answers with a smirk as she continues to push me and Chris towards the door.

"Now move, or else my brother will storm up here and grab you himself if you don't get out there." She adds, and I know she is right. As quickly as I could in three-inch heels, I make my way down the stairs and out the house with my bouquet of fall flowers in hand. Chris sets my veil over my face before I step outside, a look of happiness and pride in his eyes as he gives me one more hug.

Tate and I had decided to marry each other on the day we met instead of the spring wedding I always dreamed of, but I wouldn't change this date for anything else. It was the day my life changed for the better. The day I stopped running as the runaway breeder and became the mate to the scary Blood Alpha. I found my freedom and regained my life that day so it made sense to make this day the day we marry to always remind us to keep moving forward.

Luckily my cousin's house is close to mine and Tate's, helping us decide on a backyard wedding and all I have to do was walk through the forest. The steady march of "Here Comes the Bride" plays as I near the edge of the trees, the guests stand from their chairs while Julia makes her way towards her father in her flower girl outfit. I have a feeling that I am the blushing bride, but as soon as my eyes meets Tate's stare full of love, everything stops and it is just him and I. No one else matters as I stand in front of him. My bouquet is passed to Eeva as we stand on the gazebo, the water lapping slightly in the surprisingly warm early fall weather.

"Today we are here to gather for the joining of Tate and Laina in holy matrimony. If anyone objects, please speak now." The preacher begins the traditional way to any wedding. No one stands to object most likely too terrified of Tate and how he will punish them if they do, and we continue the ceremony happily.

"A wedding is a joyous event in any love, but a wedding between mates is momentous, and I ask that the Goddess bless them and their family and friends." I smile as my eyes focus on Tate, his own orbs never leaving mine as the preacher continues. Soon the rings are passed to us, and we ready ourselve to state our vows with Tate going first.

"Laina, I knew since the moment I saw you that you were my everything. You make me a better man and gave me a chance to be an amazing father. Even though it's been three years since we met, I know that I never want to lose you, and I will cherish you and our children for the rest of my life. I love you, baby girl." Tears of happiness start flowing, and I giggle when he wipes them away while ignoring his own tears to tend to mine. He pulls me close, burying his face into the crook of my neck as he cries. Everyone in the room looks shocked, but I smile warmly, wrapping my arms around my mate and smiling at knowing that he is only this emotional around me. The two of us silently cry in each other's embrace, ignoring the time ticking down until we regain our composure. With me wiping away his tears and him wiping away mine we laugh at each other before the minister motions for us to continue the ceremony.

"Tate, you are my everything, my best friend, my knight in fluffy fur-" That last part has everyone laughing, including Tate, and my smile widens as I take his hands into mine and continue.

"- You are the father of our daughter and my other half. I won't lie and say that I wasn't terrified when I met you because I was. But as I got to know you, I learned you have a softer side, a side only those who are close to you know. I am happy to know I am the one who gets to wake up to you each morning, to smile and laugh and cry with you. I love you, baby, and nothing will ever separate us." By the end of my vows, we are crying again, but this time I am held against his strong chest. I bury my face into his chest, and he buries his into my hair, inhaling each other's scent to calm us down and for once I am glad I went with the waterproof eyeliner and mascara that Jack suggested or else my make-up would have been ruined by now.

"Sorry to interrupt Alpha, Luna, but we really should get the ceremony over with sometime today before the rain hits." The preacher whispers, bowing his head respectfully and causing us to laugh. The ceremony continues, and we say our I Do's to each other then finally hear our names pronounced. Tate wastes no time in pulling me close to kiss me passionately. The crowd is cheering, hooting and yelling out things like "Take it to the bedroom" and "You go, Alpha" before we pull away, making me blush and want to hide my face from their view while Tate chuckles and kisses my forehead.

The party is held inside the pack house. We walk into the ballroom as husband and wife smiling when Tate pulls me close to dance to "I Was Made for Loving You" by Tori Kelly and Ed Sheeran and just enjoying the moment between the two of us. We rarely leave each other side this night, and the pack members as well as our guests from allying packs are drunk and fast asleep by the time midnight rolls around. Chris and Jack took Julia to their house a while ago, wanting to let Tate and I have the night as a married couple to ourselves without needing to worry about our pup.

Slipping away from the drunken guests, Tate and I head home. As soon as we are safe inside our home, we discard our formal wear piece by piece as we make our way to the bedroom. Finally in bed, I find myself pinned under my husband, his thick cock buried deep inside me as he claims my body as his wife. The sounds of our pants and moans fill the house, continuing into the early morning as rays of light shine through the windows. I find myself held in his embrace, my energy fully spent, with Tate drawing lazy circles on my back.

"I noticed you never had anything to drink other than water, juice, and soda. Care to tell me why?" Tate asks lazily, curiosity in his voice as he plays with my hair.

"What would you say to having another pup in the house?" I ask gently, drawing small circles on his chest and feeling him stiffen slightly.

"Do you mean?" Tate asks with hopeful eyes his voice filled with disbelief.

"That Julia will be a big sister, yes." I finish his sentence with a chuckle, squeaking in surprise as I feel Tate roll us over, kissing me happily before moving to pepper kisses on my still flat stomach.

"This is the best wedding gift ever, baby. I love you Laina Randall-Silvermoon." He whispers, tears glistening in his eyes. I smile and grab his face, pulling him towards me and kissing him lovingly.

"And I love you Tate Randall-Silvermoon." I whisper back with my own tears rolling down my face and into my hair as I stare up at the man I love.

My life is finally my own with the man in front of me as my partner forever. I am no longer the runaway Breeder. Now I am a mother, a wife, and a leader. And I have the perfect mate who has helped me more than I ever thought possible. I am Laina Randall-Silvermoon, the Luna of Bloodsvain.

About the Author

Born and raised in Brampton Ontario - also known at "The Flower City"- Alana Dyer started her relationship with books on a "Hate/Hate" relationship as a child that quickly became a passion for reading as she found that novels can bring you places never seen before.

From finding her love of reading, Alana Dyer soon began writing little stories as a child, and in 2015 with the discovery of Wattpad, Alana started writing seriously with the hopes of one day publishing. Five years later after writing for a loyal fanbase, Alana debuted August 30th, 2020, on Amazon with her first full length novel "The Runaway Breeder".

Now in 2023, Alana Dyer has published six novels and two Novelettes under the pen name A. Dyer and spends her days writing, playing with her many pets and planning to expand the distributions of her books.

Rejection Series

THREE SHE-WOLVES LEARN that life can take a turn for the worst and those who are supposed to love you can become your worst enemies. When the Moon Goddess and fate play a cruel card that shatters each of their hearts and a budding war is on the horizon can each one find their true strength that lie within and figure out just who is the mastermind in the war that will change the fate of the werewolf race?

Follow Amberle and her Full Moon Rejection in "Rejection on the Full Moon"

See if Geminie's soul mate regrets "Rejecting the Future Moon Goddess"

Can "Rejection to the Alpha King's Daughter" bring out the true Werewolf Queen in Crystalline

And will these girls be able to piece together the true Soulless Evil that hides behind his War?

Rejection on the Full Moon
Book 1

Soulless - werewolves who have turned rogue with no humanity left, giving in to their beastly urges.

Rejection - an act in which your soulmate rejects the mate bond, causing immense pain to the rejected.

These are the challenges Amberle Crest must overcome after becoming an outcast amongst the wolves her age due to an event outside of her control.

When her mate rejects her on her eighteenth birthday, Amberle realizes that living in a pack where the majority would rather use her as a slave than treat her as an equal is not worth the pain. She becomes the notorious wolf, Fire Foot, vowing that everyone would regret how they treated her, as she leaves her pack in the past.

Now a ghost forgotten by those that tormented her, Amberle does whatever it takes to survive as a lone wolf. A fateful day changes her lonely life to one full of happiness and hope—until ghosts from her own past call for aid in ridding their pack of the Soulless who threatens all wolf kind.

Faced with new friends, old foes, and the threat of a building army, will Amberle be able to fight the ghosts of her past to cherish the pack she has found or will an old mate claim her before a second chance mate can show her what being treasured by someone is all about?

Rejecting the Future Moon Goddess
Book 2

Soulless - werewolves who have turned rogue with no humanity left, giving in to their beastly urges.

Rejection - an act in which your soulmate rejects the mate bond, causing immense pain to the rejected.

Moon Goddess - the deity that created the werewolf race whom her creation worship

Omega - The lowest ranked wolf in the pack sometimes treated as nothing more than a slave or an object

These are the things Geminie Blake learns after being blamed for the tragic Deaths of her Alpha and Luna. With the pack turned against her and failing to shift as a wolf, Geminie faces challenges every day with the hope of one day gaining freedom or her mate saving her. But when her fated soul mate ends up being her ex-best friend and the son to the late Alpha and Luna rejects her, Geminie's life changes drastically.

Learning that she is not Geminie Blake - daughter to the Beta couple - but Geminie Starlite - daughter to the Moon Goddess and Future Moon Goddess herself - Geminie quickly faces the new challenges thrown her way as she navigates her wolf form and Goddess powers, creating a pack that rivals that of Blood Moon and building her life from scratch to one day take up the mantel as Moon Goddess becomes her priority.

Now, thriving and loving herself for who she is, Geminie forces the past behind her as she waits for her second chance at love. When her first mate requests help and aid from a threat created by Soulless and a potential Leader of the wolves that have lost their Humanity, Geminie is forced to face the wounds left unhealed and return to the place she called hell for eleven years of her life.

Will Geminie be able to overcome the scars left by years of abuse and find love once and for all or will the panful wounds of her past and threat from the Leader of the army of Soulless ready to kill at a moments notice take the last bit of happiness this young Goddess has left.

Rejection to the Alpha King's Daughter
Book 3

Soulless - werewolves who have turned rogue with no humanity left, giving in to their beastly urges.

Rejection - an act in which your soulmate rejects the mate bond, causing immense pain to the rejected.

Moon Goddess - the deity that created the werewolf race whom her creation worship

Omega - The lowest ranked wolf in the pack sometimes treated as nothing more than a slave or an object

Alpha King/Queen - The rulers of the werewolf nation

Runt - The smallest of the wolf pack, usually ignored or bullied for being the smallest

Crystalline Thorn grows under the abuse by her father as she trains to take the throne one day and become the Alpha Queen, leader of every wolf in the werewolf nation. She dreams of the day when she meets her mate and be accepted as a strong Queen, especially since she is a runt.

But her dream is soon shattered when on the day of an Alliance her mate discovers her "weak" form and rejects her promptly leading to her father disowning her and her hopes to inherit the throne is dashed. But that is the least of her worries.

Soon, with the help of Geminie and Amberle, Crystalline learns of a war that has been brewing for thousands of years, of a destiny that has been written in the stars by the original Moon Goddess - Luna - and the Goddess of Destiny - Morai - have placed upon her and her connection to the Lost Princess.

Will Crystalline be able to retrieve her throne?

Will she accept the mate that rejected her or chose the second chance mate?

Or will the weight of responsibility handed to her crush her entirely?

The Run

"*The cage doors are released and I open my sapphire coloured eyes, dashing out of the prison and into the forest.*

Seven days for the full moon to be blue.

Seven days from the starting line to the finish

Seven days, that's how long I had to make it to the lodge as an unmated female."

Legends of werewolves have gone back centuries. Always including the Moon Goddess and her blessing of soulmates to the beings she created. But the ugly truth is there is no such thing as soulmates. There is only The Run.

An event created centuries ago held twice a year during a blue moon where she-wolves run from their male counter parts. If they are captured, they are mated and marked, claimed by whoever captures them first.

No one is exempted from this event - not even Grace Harvest.

After being able to avoid attending the event since turning eighteen, Grace finds herself unable to find an excuse not to participate this time. With her last hope of remaining unmated until she can fall in love, she makes a bet with her Alpha. If she wins, he can no longer force wolves of his pack to participate in The Run and allow them to find love. If he wins, Grace will be mated, and her pack mates are forced to go no matter what.

But what will happen when she meets a golden haired wolf by the name Caden Wolfrain, who instantly captures her attention. Will she do all she can to win the bet, will Caden win her heart or will the secrets Caden keeps force her to cut ties with this golden haired wolf without a second thought no matter the heart break.

Books by the Author

CONTACT THE AUTHOR

 alana.dyer.author@
hotmail.com

 author.alana.dyer

 alana.dyer

 Alana Dyer
@alana.dyer.author

E-BOOK | PAPERBACK | HARDCOVERS
available where books are sold

Don't miss out!

Visit the website below and you can sign up to receive emails whenever Alana Dyer publishes a new book. There's no charge and no obligation.

https://books2read.com/r/B-A-LXGX-CHAQC

BOOKS 2 READ

Connecting independent readers to independent writers.

www.ingramcontent.com/pod-product-compliance
Lightning Source LLC
Chambersburg PA
CBHW070926250626
47159CB00009B/3140

* 9 7 8 1 9 9 8 2 6 1 0 2 4 *